A Botanist's Guide to Parties and Poisons

A BOTANIST'S GUIDE TO PARTIES AND POISONS

A NOVEL

Kate Khavari

CROOKED
LANE

NEW YORK

Published in the United States by Crooked Lane Books, an imprint of The Quick Brown Fox & Company LLC.

Crooked Lane Books and its logo are trademarks of The Quick Brown Fox & Company LLC.

Library of Congress Catalog-in-Publication data available upon request.

ISBN (hardcover): 978-1-63910-007-1
ISBN (ebook): 978-1-63910-008-8

Cover design by Nicole Lecht

Printed in the United States.

www.crookedlanebooks.com

Crooked Lane Books
34 West 27th St., 10th Floor
New York, NY 10001

First Edition: June 2022

10 9 8 7 6 5 4 3 2 1

For my very own biologist

CHAPTER 1

L ight poured from the windows of the grand house, illuminating the front steps and graveled drive. The taxi rolled to a stop and Saffron emerged, then was led up the stairs by a liveried footman. A maid took her coat, and for a moment, Saffron stood in the doorway to the lavish sitting room, where about twenty people were gathered. The room was vast and cool despite a fire in the large marble hearth. With tall walls papered with green silk and countless pieces of highly polished heirloom furniture, it reminded her very much of her grandparents' house; it was the sort of place that was heaped with family treasures that were ignored by everyone but the maids.

A ripple of anxiety went through her as she looked at the large group, scanning the faces for the one she wanted to avoid. It was hardly necessary; if Dr. Berking were already here, she would hear his booming voice. Scolding herself for her cowardice, Saffron straightened her shoulders. There was little danger in a dinner party.

Saffron stepped forward and offered her name to the butler. A few curious faces turned to her as he announced her arrival in dignified tones, and an older man moved to greet her. He introduced himself as Sir Edward Leister.

Saffron smiled at her host and said, "I'm pleased to meet you, sir. I understand that you are in large part to thank for making the Amazonian expedition possible."

Sir Edward waved off her comment. His dull eyes barely took her in as he replied, "Of course, I'm happy to share my funds with University College." He spoke a little too loudly to be genuine.

Sir Edward guided her toward several members of the university's staff with whom Saffron was already acquainted. Their inquisitive eyes swept over her. Those that knew her were probably surprised to see her in clothing not marred by soil or dust. Saffron smoothed a hand over the beaded dress. Although the deep cornflower blue, the precise color of her eyes, was understated, the shimmering beading was definitely flashier than anything Saffron would have normally worn. Her limited wardrobe no longer stocked gowns for such occasions, so her flatmate had borrowed the frock from another receptionist in her office. It fell straight from shoulder to below the knees, flattening her figure and leaving her arms bare. She and Elizabeth, her flatmate and oldest friend, had done their best to curl and pin Saffron's brunette hair into a stylish arrangement, and unearthed their best set of silk evening gloves for the occasion.

A tall man with dark hair was looking at her with a serious expression. As their eyes met, he joined her.

"I'm Alexander Ashton," he said. "We're on the same floor in the North Wing. I believe you're Dr. Maxwell's assistant."

The introduction was unnecessary, as it would be nearly impossible for any member of the close-knit biology department of University College London to be unknown to another. Not only that, but Saffron was the only woman currently employed by the department and had been the topic of unpleasant rumors lately.

As for Mr. Ashton, Saffron knew exactly who he was. Saffron remembered him from the beginning of her days as a student, another vaguely intimidating figure in the background as she struggled to settle into her studies and then, in the past year, her work. People spoke of Alexander Ashton with respect, because he had completed his graduate courses in half the time others required, and had crossed the globe to complete studies in exotic locations. She hadn't heard much about his current research, either because the gossips had little interest in his work or because Mr. Ashton didn't bandy about his publications as others did.

Now, towering over her in a well-fitted dinner jacket, with his attention fixed on her, he was just as intimidating. Dark brows framed darker eyes, and his mouth was held firmly beneath a slightly curved nose. Compared to the other men in the room, his complexion stood out against the crisp white of his shirt, as if he'd recently come back from a holiday spent outdoors. The only part of his appearance that was less than tidy was the curl of his hair that his pomade fought against.

"Yes, I am Dr. Maxwell's research assistant," she said. Mr. Ashton took her offered hand, warming her gloved fingers with his. "Saffron Everleigh."

He looked at her blankly. "Your name is Saffron?"

Saffron sighed. Apparently the department gossips did not include her Christian name when they churned the rumor mill. "Yes, of course, how appropriate. A botanist named for a stigma and style of a flower. Very amusing," she said.

A smile threatened in the corners of Mr. Ashton's mouth. "I'm definitely not amused at all."

Unsure of his response, she smoothed a hand over her dress once more. "Yes, well, better than Buttercup or Azalea."

"Perhaps I should change my name to reflect my area of study too. *Brucella melitnesis* might do." He slipped his hands into his pockets and looked down at her thoughtfully. "*Bacillus cereus* sounds a little formal. *Leishmania donovani*, perhaps." Though he said it without inflection, there was a hint of mirth in his voice.

"Leishmania Donovani would be perfect," Saffron said, allowing herself a smile. "We might call you Donovan for short, and no one would be the wiser."

"Considering that strain of *Leishmania* is a parasite that causes anemia and, in some cases, warty eruptions, I don't think I'll choose that one."

Disgust warred with delight at Mr. Ashton's deadpan delivery, and Saffron was almost sorry to see her mentor, Dr. Maxwell, enter the room alongside his friend, Dr. Aster.

Mr. Ashton leaned down to her ear as they drew near and murmured, "Dr. Aster, another aptly named botanist."

She had said the same thing to Dr. Aster as a young girl during a rare visit to the university with her father, and she thought he still remembered her imprudent remark. Saffron stifled a laugh as the professors approached them.

Though the two men were similar in age, both being along the lines of ancient, they looked the opposite of each other. Maxwell's fluff of flyaway hair and overgrown eyebrows made him look warm and grandfatherly, whereas Aster's appearance was so polished and clean as to be severe, rather more like Saffron's actual grandfather.

"Everleigh," Maxwell said warmly, taking her hand.

Saffron smiled at the professor, not missing Mr. Ashton's upticked brow at Maxwell referring to her by her surname. She loved it when he did; it made her feel as if she was just another member of the department rather than a novelty. "How was your trip, Professor?"

"Enjoyable as always, though one always forgets how exhausting it can be, entertaining children," he replied in his breathless voice. "My grandchildren seem to think that I have as much energy as they do!"

Saffron turned to the other professor as Maxwell greeted Mr. Ashton. "Nice to see you, Dr. Aster."

His gray eyes seemed to glint in disapproval, as usual. "Good evening."

Maxwell scoffed lightly at him before saying, "Aster, you remember Alexander Ashton." They shook hands. "Everleigh, you will be working with Mr. Ashton over the next few weeks to ensure he gets whatever materials he needs for the chlorophyll study. He is responsible for making preparations for botany since Chesterfield retired to see to his ailing brother."

The sudden departure had left their small department scrambling, especially considering the expedition had been pulled together on such short notice. Nodding, she asked, "Are you on the expedition team, Mr. Ashton?"

"Not this time," he replied. "Julian Ericson and Martin Gardiner will be collecting the samples for botany."

The professors were absorbed in their own discussion of Dr. Maxwell's fern collection, so Saffron, eager to hear more, said, "But you've gone on other expeditions, I believe. It must be fascinating to travel all over."

"It can be."

"What exactly do you study?"

"Bacteria."

Unsure whether to be amused or annoyed at his sudden reticence, Saffron said, "I did gather that. What in particular?"

She thought she caught a flash of surprise in his expression before he replied, "I was developing a system of rapid identification of new bacteria. Because of my previous work with soil, they gave me botany when they divvied up each of the subdepartments for the expedition preparations."

Now he was speaking in full sentences again, Saffron hoped to keep Mr. Ashton talking. She was here to hobnob with her colleagues and university higher-ups, but she did want to hear more about his experience in the department. "How did you come to work in biology? Or microbiology, rather."

But dinner was announced a moment later. Her question went unanswered, as Dr. Maxwell offered her his arm and guided her into the impressive dining room, where a white-clad table heavily laden with silver and china shimmered in the candlelight.

Half of the table was filled with professors and researchers from the university, some with their wives, and the other half were administrators and benefactors of the university, like Sir Edward. Dr. Lawrence Henry, the man who was to lead the expedition team, sat at the center of the table. Next to him, an auburn-haired woman swatted his arm playfully. From where Saffron sat, it seemed that the woman had a great deal of skin on display, with only a bit of black silk with gold embroidery covering her shoulders and chest. She had a rather adoring look on her heavily made-up face. Saffron could understand the woman's fawning attention. Dr. Henry certainly cut a dashing figure for a history professor. Blue eyes shone from a tanned, rugged face, and his black dinner jacket stretched tight over his broad shoulders. If university rumors were to be believed, he often received such admiration from women young and old.

An elegant woman across the table seemed to be the exception. She was watching Dr. Henry and his dinner companion from the corner of her eye, black hair framing a slightly older face with sharp, dark eyes. The man she was speaking to, a professor of ecology, was talking on and on without noticing his audience was preoccupied. Given the withering look she gave the woman in black and Dr. Henry, Saffron guessed the older woman was Mrs. Henry.

Mr. Ashton was seated at the far end of the table, in conversation with a serious-looking young man. The man he spoke to could have been on the university's staff, though it was hard to be sure. Blond and pleasant-looking, he closely resembled the masses on campus.

Mr. Ashton noticed her looking at him and smiled slightly. Saffron briefly returned his smile and looked away. In her experience, it was best not to encourage her colleagues.

Dr. Berking had, at last, made his appearance, but sat far to the other end of the table, out of Saffron's sight. Saffron sat next to Dr. Maxwell, far down the table near Lady Agatha, Sir Edward's wife. Full of recent discoveries, plans for publications, and university news, the conversation surrounding her distracted her from Berking's odious presence. Saffron mostly listened, hungry for further details about the expedition and what the researchers would do while they were there. The trip had been announced just a month ago, giving the departments hardly any time to prepare.

Harry Snyder, Dr. Henry's assistant, was seated on her other side. With small brown eyes behind wire-rimmed glasses, and thin lips that emphasized his large, impeccable teeth, he looked rather like a rodent. His demeanor, skittish and reticent, matched his mousy appearance.

"Mr. Snyder, will you be joining Dr. Henry on the expedition?" Saffron asked.

"Yes," Snyder replied, his eyes not leaving his plate.

"I understand Dr. Henry visited both India and Spain in the last few years. Have you accompanied him on previous expeditions?"

To this, Snyder only nodded, his black hair slick with pomade bobbing over his plate. Saffron considered her own plate of delicately cut roast beef, wondering if the meal was really that interesting or if Harry Snyder really didn't want to speak with her.

"What do you do for Dr. Henry while abroad?" she asked.

Snyder frowned at her from behind his glasses. "Assist him, of course."

Saffron sighed into her water glass. Dr. Maxwell was occupied in a conversation with another professor on her other side, and so Saffron continued extracting answers from Snyder, like pulling sore teeth.

"For how long will the team be gone? I've heard it's sure to be more than six weeks, but no longer than four months."

Snyder glanced down the table to where Dr. Henry was still entertaining the woman in black. "The plan is to be in Brazil for five months, with two weeks of travel time on either end."

Saffron raised a brow at the cagey way Snyder spoke and, matching his hushed voice, asked, "What sort of work requires the team to be gone for so long?"

He bit his lip, eyes darting down to Dr. Henry once again. "Five departments have representatives going, in addition to those who are going to complete data collection independently."

Saffron was coming to enjoy taunting Snyder with her questions. He seemed to think it all a big secret, and Saffron loved uncovering secrets. She added, "Where, precisely, are you going in Brazil?"

Snyder looked torn. He patted his mouth with his napkin, then examined his wineglass as he said, "I don't think I can . . . er, well, I shouldn't say . . ." When it became clear Saffron would continue to look at him expectantly, her eyes wide and inviting, he cleared his throat. "We'll be focused mostly on the mouth of the river and Marajó Island. Keeping close to civilization, that is."

"Why is that, Mr. Snyder? Certainly a lot of exploration has already been done in that part of the world. Alexander Van Humbodt sent back nearly fifteen thousand species from his travels. And he was hardly the first nor the last to explore there."

He looked mildly affronted, his hesitation to speak on the subject evaporating. "Not everything about an area can be learned in one go. Besides, if you've had the benefit of examining a map, you will find that Venezuela is quite a distance from Brazil."

With patience she didn't feel, Saffron replied, "What I mean is that the Amazon, which extends far beyond the limits of Brazil, has been a focal point of exploration for hundreds of years. Has Dr. Henry been in contact with Percy Fawcett? His descriptions of the lost city of Z are fascinating. It sounds like a terrestrial Atlantis."

Snyder snorted. "Fawcett isn't a true academic. The things he claims to have seen are hardly worth contemplating. A dog with two noses? A snake the length of an autobus? I think not. Dr. Henry believes there is quite a bit about the *real* history and culture of the indigenous people in the area that has yet to be discovered." With a sneer, he added, "The animal and plant people can always find more to look at."

Snyder clearly didn't recognize her as one of the "plant people."

Dr. Maxwell turned toward their conversation and smiled wryly. "Yes, indeed. Thousands and thousands of organisms in every square meter of land over there. A most intriguing place. I'm sure Dr. Henry will find more than what he is looking for there."

These last words looked to taste a little sour to Maxwell, Saffron noted. His eyes lacked their usual softness, and he quickly turned back to his supper.

Snyder seemed to think this was the end of the conversation, which was fine with Saffron. As she ate bites of Waldorf salad, her eyes fell again on the woman she suspected to be Mrs. Henry. She was now looking down the table to the man Mr. Ashton had spoken to earlier. The man seemed to smirk back at her. Though no doubt a decade older than him, her returning look was sly, almost smiling.

Saffron realized Mr. Snyder was speaking to her again.

"I'm always so shocked by who wants to come on these grueling trips. Dr. Henry has to reject most applications just based on lack of experience in the field alone." He leaned closer to her, near enough that Saffron could see the fingerprint marring the shine of his eyeglasses. "Although there are other considerations. Take Dr. Maxwell, next to you. Dr. Henry rejected his offer to join the expedition outright."

Snyder shot a glance to her left at Dr. Maxwell, deep in conversation with a professor of mineralogy.

"Dr. *Maxwell*?" Saffron repeated, trying not to sound surprised. Dr. Maxwell surely hadn't applied to go on the expedition. He was far too old to be traveling down a great river in the heat of the equator! She'd thought his comment about his wife declaring he couldn't go was a joke.

"Oh yes," Snyder said, stabbing his salad with his fork. "Dr. Henry was surprised when he said he intended to come along, and he tried to let him down easy. Poor man seemed fairly cut up, though." Obviously, he didn't know that she worked for the professor he was gossiping about. Nor did he seem to mind talking about the expedition now he wasn't revealing their plans. Before she could say anything, he pressed on. "They had a rather dreadful row, I'm afraid. Dr. Maxwell told Dr. Henry that we'd be lucky to return from the expedition with all our men alive, with so many dangerous things lurking in the jungle. Animals and natives everywhere! Just waiting to creep up on you . . ." His enthusiasm seemed to fade slightly. Then he perked back up, saying, "But that's why Dr. Henry insisted on leading the crew. His experience and skills will no doubt ensure our safety."

Luckily, Snyder had little else to say to her the rest of the meal. Irritation and confusion dampened her appetite, and Saffron spent the rest of the meal wondering if she'd regret venturing out of her little corner of university life.

⚘

At dinner's end, Saffron stood carefully to ensure that none of the embellishments on her borrowed dress were caught on the chair, and followed the ladies to the drawing room. Electric lights glowed around the rose-red room, and a large fire had been constructed in the monolithic hearth to take the edge off the spring evening. Saffron chose a seat near the fire, not anticipating participating in the kind of conversation the other women were likely to share. Her grandmother had ruled such gatherings, always with a subtle but sharp barb ready to remind her that, given Saffron's interests, her conversation was not welcome. Considering she was among ladies of similar class now, she wasn't likely to be a great conversational partner. It had been years since she'd kept up with London gossip. She'd been far too willing to leave it behind when she'd began working in earnest toward her goal of becoming a botanist.

To her surprise, the hostess, Lady Agatha, brought her a cup of coffee. Her peach dress fluttered as she settled next to her. "My dear, I'm told you are Thomas Everleigh's daughter. How wonderful to meet you." She looked exactly like her grandmother's compatriots: women of taste and means who had preserved their beauty to the best of their ability, but in the end looked like wilted flowers in silk and pearls. "Your father used to join us quite often when he was a professor, you know. What a charming man."

"Oh, how nice," Saffron replied with a noncommittal smile. Though she heard such comments often enough, it was usually from fellow scholars who were familiar with his work. She doubted Lady Agatha knew much about plant pathology.

"And such a gentleman! A great pity that we lost him well before his time. Dr. Everleigh put his colleagues to shame, those that were not brought up quite the same." Lady Agatha gave Saffron a meaningful look. "I cannot imagine what it's come to, when the halls of a prestigious institution such as University College are open to just anyone."

To have her father's death commented on so casually, to hear her father's memory used to put others down, made Saffron's insides roil. With saccharine sweetness, Saffron asked, "You mean those not brought up to have the same appreciation of academia?"

Lady Agatha's frown was brief, covered by a brittle smile. "Of course, my dear."

The hostess made a few more polite comments before joining a cluster of ladies on the other side of the room. Saffron watched her go with satisfaction.

Though he'd been raised in the upper class, thanks to her grandparents, Thomas Everleigh had all but rejected his status as heir to a viscountcy and taken up botany. His parents had indulged his studies, never thinking that he would make science into a profession. A life among the peerage hadn't appealed to her father in the slightest, and that view had rubbed off on Saffron. She had been raised with a dual future in mind: her grandparents' vision of a good marriage, and her parents' hope that she would find her own way. So far, her way looked much like her father's. She'd given up a lot to reach her goal, including the financial support of her grandparents, but she was reminded now of why she'd been so willing to turn her back on high society.

The woman who'd paid such attention to Dr. Henry during dinner sunk onto the couch next to Saffron. Black silk lavished with gold beading was held up by scant straps at her shoulders and gathered at her hips in a draping knot, mirroring the gold headband circling the crown of her meticulous russet waves. She was far more adorned than any of the other women and, despite heavily kohl around her hazel eyes and dark lipstick, was very young now that Saffron saw her up close. Her long red nails were wrapped about a cup of black coffee, and she wore an expression of practiced ennui. "Well, this is rather dull."

Saffron waited for an introduction or some hint as to why this woman had chosen her to complain to, but none was forthcoming. Saffron took a sip of her coffee and tried to be objective in her reply. "Yes, I suppose it is. I never saw the point in sending the men and women off separate ways after dinner. It's not as though we digest differently."

The woman gave her a curious look. "No, I don't think that is the issue . . ." She set her untouched coffee on a table next to the couch and withdrew a cigarette and a lighter from within the recesses of her matching gold handbag. Her dark lipstick coated the end of the cigarette as she lit it. "Daddy was absolutely gutted that he couldn't come, considering this dinner was meant to celebrate his contribution," the woman drawled, "so he sent me to tend to his friends."

That enigmatic statement wasn't followed by further explanation. Saffron still had no idea who this woman was, though she was clearly wealthy if her father had contributed enough to warrant a dinner being thrown in his honor. Had Saffron not been included in the invitation so last minute, she might have known who she, and her father, were.

"What did Lady Agatha have to say? She's a bit of a busybody." Fingering her string of jet beads, the woman asked innocently, "Anything good?"

"No, I'm afraid not," Saffron said, wishing the half hour or so requisite time was up.

"Too bad. I hear even in small ponds like a university there can be interesting things going on." She blew out a puff of smoke and looked meaningfully at Saffron. "You know, who does what and with whom."

Saffron withheld a sigh. This was precisely why she hadn't missed society. "I think most of us are more interested in our fields of study, actually."

"Oh, you work at the university, do you?"

Saffron nodded, deciding it was time to figure out who this noxious woman was. "I'm Saffron Everleigh. I'm a research assistant."

A slow smile spread over the woman's face. "Miss Everleigh? Well, then."

Saffron's spine straightened at the odd look the woman was giving her. "I'm afraid I didn't catch your name."

The woman tapped ash from her cigarette into the crystal dish on the side table. "Eris Ermine. My father is Cedric Ermine."

Saffron vaguely recalled the name Ermine from her earlier days in London but couldn't remember anything specific. She gave Eris Ermine a polite smile and took another sip of coffee. To her relief, the gentlemen filed back in, carrying glasses of scotch or port, several puffing on cigars.

Miss Ermine sighed. "Never was one for the books, myself. But there are some values to working in academia." Her eyes followed Dr. Henry as he entered, drink in hand.

"Er, yes," Saffron agreed. "You know Dr. Henry? I believe he's heading up the expedition."

"Of course—he's a favorite of my father's." She spoke in a low voice, eyes still on the man in question. "I might have to change my tune, though, if what I've heard about the university is true. Seems like some of you academic lot tend to spend a lot of time *researching* each other." With that, she shot Saffron a sly smile and walked off toward Dr. Henry.

Saffron stared after her. What did that mean? Was that a reference to Dr. Berking? He'd said something nearly identical to her the last time she had spoken to him.

Saffron stood, deciding that it had been a mistake come to the dinner at all. Making connections simply wasn't worth it.

In a moment, Mr. Ashton was before her. "May I get you a drink, Miss Everleigh?"

She blinked at him, surprised by his offer. "No, thank you. Excuse me."

She'd just turned away to search out the lavatory when lumbering footsteps approached her. Her entire body tensed like it was preparing to flee, as if running away was the answer for dealing with the man she knew was behind her. His voice cut through the clinking of glasses and loud conversation surrounding her.

"Ashton, glad to see you abandoned your pretty petri dishes and joined us!"

Dr. Berking's voice was the equivalent of a series of bombs dropping across her evening. Mr. Ashton turned toward the professor, and Saffron, gritting her teeth, did the same. The department head was a head shorter than Mr. Ashton and round as a barrel. Dr. Berking had a robust head of graying red hair and small blue eyes, with a mouth that was almost always curled into a grin. Now, that grin was as slimy as one of Dr. Maxwell's butterwort leaves and just as benignly predatory. Saffron looked away, hoping he'd ignore her.

"I bet you're regretting your choice not to apply to join us on this adventure, aren't you, Ashton?" Berking nodded, chuckling. His eyes slid to Saffron. "Why, you are looking delectable this evening, Miss Everleigh!"

Her face heating, Saffron kept her gaze on the floor. He wanted to see her squirm under his lascivious glare. If she ignored him—

Berking lowered his booming voice slightly. "But then again, you always look good enough to eat. And the right flavor too."

Saffron's eyes snapped to Berking's jeering face, and she swallowed her gasp of rage. He wasn't looking at her, but to Mr. Ashton, looking to share a laugh.

Before she could muster up words to defend herself, Mr. Ashton said sharply, "That's quite enough, Dr. Berking."

Humiliation burned her face, that Mr. Ashton had to not only hear Berking's comments but defend her against them. If the floor could open up and swallow her, she'd have been eternally grateful. Rather than sink into the carpet, Saffron stood stock-still as Berking put a large hand on her shoulder and chuckled. "Miss Everleigh knows I am the consummate joker, of course."

He winked at Alexander and disappeared into the crowd.

Saffron managed to mumble, "Excuse me," before slipping away.

CHAPTER 2

She should really leave soon, Saffron decided, staring into the mirror of the lavatory. She'd told herself she'd been waiting until the pink faded from her skin after scrubbing her shoulder with a dampened hand towel, but it was more than that. It had been years since she'd hidden out of mortification. She'd thought she'd outgrown the childish propensity, yet here she was. And all because of wretched Dr. Berking.

She'd managed to avoid him for weeks now, not just so he could forget their encounter, but so she could forget it too. But feeling his hand on her skin tonight took her right back to that horrible meeting. She shuddered.

It was silly—stupid really—to be so upset over it. From what Elizabeth had told her, what Berking had done wasn't unusual, or even so bad. She'd gone to the department head's office to discuss her latest idea for research. If she wanted to stand out from her peers and be selected to carry on with graduate work, she needed the support of the department head. Saffron had had no illusions about Dr. Berking, who'd been brash and insulting from the beginning. She had braced herself for an unpleasant interaction but had hoped that somehow he would hear her out and maybe even say yes to her proposal. She was very wrong. The results of that meeting lingered in the stirrings of fear she experienced whenever she heard the bark of Berking's voice, the ominous thunder of his laugh. But he would be gone to Brazil for six whole months. She could cope for two more weeks.

Saffron stepped back into the hallway but took her time returning to the din of the drawing room. She slowly made her way down the hall paneled with dark, polished wood and paintings that likely individually cost her annual salary. She rounded a corner and gasped, the sound turning to a laugh when she realized the man she'd nearly run into was Mr. Ashton, who seemed to be about to drain his glass into the bedraggled potted palm next to him.

"No, no, it's clearly seen a lot of parties with bad sherry," Saffron said with a smile. She removed the drink from his hand, placing it on the sideboard tucked behind the rescued palm. "Much better! No plants harmed."

Mr. Ashton, who'd looked just as startled as she had when she'd rounded the corner, smiled. Before he could reply, a doorway beyond opened, and the high voice of a woman began speaking. Saffron had no desire to churn up more rumors about herself by being caught in a lonely stretch of dim hallway with someone, but the woman's voice was drawing closer. She stepped further into the corner. Without a word, Mr. Ashton moved next to her, their backs to the paneled wall. She looked up at him, ready to make it clear that this was not an opportunity to make advances, even if he had acted gallantly earlier, but he looked just as uncomfortable as she felt.

The rustling of a gown told Saffron the woman had stopped just beyond where she and Mr. Ashton stood.

"What about him?" a cool voice asked.

The high voice whispered, "How do you put up with it! He's gone off with Cedric's daughter on the balcony. I saw them from the window."

Mr. Ashton glanced down at her, his eyes questioning. *"Should we go?"* he seemed to ask.

"Has he now? Charming selection," drawled another woman.

Saffron shook her head. Leaving now would only cause more problems, however much she didn't want to be overhearing this conversation. This was clearly in reference to Dr. Henry and Miss Ermine. The cold voice must belong to Dr. Henry's wife. Saffron eased herself deeper into the corner, where she'd be obscured by the potted palm. Mr. Ashton followed suit, the silk of her glove brushing against his hand as he drew closer.

"Why don't you talk to him again, Cynthia, dear?" A sympathetic tone colored the high voice.

"What's the point? Everyone knows what sort of man he is, and he'll be gone soon anyway."

"Yes, dear, but they know that you *let* him carry on. Surely it stings, even if—"

"Stings? Maybe before the first dozen women were paraded past me. I've little cause for concern."

A few muffled footsteps, and a dark-haired head emerged from the hallway. Luckily, she faced away from their hiding place. Mr. Ashton did his best to shrink, but it only brought him closer to Saffron. She glanced up at him in question. He grimaced apologetically.

"Perhaps they're just discussing the funding. You know, my husband said Mr. Ermine—"

"Yes, dear Lawrence made sure the funding came through." The voice was as cold as ice.

The high voice came tentatively from around the corner. "Have you spoken to your solicitor? You mentioned something a few months ago . . ."

Saffron's eyes widened in surprise, but then she recalled that this was a private conversation. She hoped Mr. Ashton hadn't noticed her interest. That was certainly not the way to make a good impression. But then, they were shoulder to shoulder, both hiding. He wasn't doing any better than she was.

There was a quiet, humorless laugh. "I haven't decided if I will. The man will be out of the way quite soon. And I'm not exactly suffering in solitude."

With that, the two women came fully into view as they cross the wide hallway. Lady Agatha hurried after Mrs. Henry. The dark-haired woman's gown swished languidly as she went. For all her biting words, she seemed unruffled. The two women disappeared down the hallway without a backward glance.

Saffron released a relieved breath.

Mr. Ashton cleared his throat, and began, "I apologize. That was—"

A cheer from the drawing room made them both jump. Saffron gave him an uncertain smile. "We'd better return."

He nodded and followed her down the hallway and back into the party. The drawing room was too bright for her eyes, and she squinted as a glass of champagne was pressed into her hands.

Mrs. Henry made her way to where her husband stood next to Sir Edward and Lady Agatha, looking dutifully pleased. Dr. Henry had eyes only for the champagne. Slightly behind Dr. Henry stood the man whom Mr. Ashton had spoken to at dinner, who looked drolly on at the proceedings.

Sir Edward raised his glass and called, "To our extraordinary team of adventurers, we wish you the best of luck on your voyage. May you achieve greatness!"

Dr. Henry tipped his glass to Sir Edward.

"Here, here!" chorused the crowd, lifting their glasses. Everyone sipped.

Saffron took a small sip of the bubbly wine and eyed the man behind Dr. Henry, who was now in close conversation with Mrs. Henry. "Who is that man talking to Mrs. Henry? The one you spoke to at dinner."

Mr. Ashton was looking at something beyond her as he replied, "Richard Blake. He coordinated the funding for the expedition, reaching out to donors."

Saffron was about to ask if she needed to protect another plant from the contents of his champagne glass, but when she turned to him, he'd already disappeared into the crowd. Slightly put out, she resolved to thank her hosts, retrieve her coat, and leave.

The noise level had significantly increased with the good cheer provided by the toast and the champagne. Saffron began to make her way toward Sir Edward and his wife at the far end of the room. She squared her shoulders when she saw Dr. Berking was among the group they were conversing with. Surely he wouldn't make untoward comments to her when they were among important donors. Saying them before Mr. Ashton had been bad enough.

"Once we're done on the ship, we'll be in the clear," Dr. Henry was saying, his voice rough and slurring. "Once that's done, we'll be gone and it'll be fine." He took another gulp of champagne.

"Yes, sir, the voyage across is always the most dicey," said Harry Snyder, keeping a hold of Henry's considerably taller shoulder, as if to hold his employer steady. "So many unpredictable factors. The expedition itself is far more flexible."

Dr. Berking smirked into his glass. Saffron, paused behind the Leisters, had gone unnoticed. She opened her mouth to speak.

Sir Edward shook his head to an offer of more champagne from Henry, who'd snatched up a bottle from the table before them. "Can't trust large ships much these days—any little thing can throw their schedule off course. I was approached about investing in a shipping company, and not two days after I declined, a ship in their fleet faced waves so large that the thing nearly capsized. They were nearly stranded near—"

Lady Agatha cut him off, saying, "Dear, no one wants to hear about things going wrong on voyages just as they're setting out on one." She laughed awkwardly.

Mrs. Henry looked at her husband for a long moment and set her nearly empty glass down. "Indeed, I shudder to think what might happen. Whatever would we do if something were to happen to you, Lawrence?"

Saffron wasn't the only one surprised by the coolness in her tone. Henry's unfocused glare swung around to his wife. With a snort, he reached for her lipstick-stained glass. Berking nudged Henry with his own glass for a refill. Henry blinked at him as if he couldn't believe his impudence. Had this not been the middle of a party, Saffron might have liked to see the two men square off.

Mrs. Henry watched her husband and Berking and rolled her eyes. Saffron edged nearer to the Leisters, intending to say goodnight while Berking was distracted.

She'd barely gotten a word out when Berking turned toward her and the Leisters, his malicious grin stretching across his face, having won his wordless duel with Henry. Mrs. Henry murmured, "Thank you," to Mr. Blake. Saffron wondered if anyone else noticed how her fingers lingered on his as she took the refilled glass from him with a smile.

Mr. Blake gave her a hint of a smile in return.

Dr. Henry glared at Blake and snatched the champagne glass from her hand. "I can pour my wife's drink well enough, Blake." He sloshed a dollop of liquid into her glass, refilling what he had just caused to splash out. He smiled obnoxiously at Mrs. Henry as she accepted the glass from him and took a drink.

With a cold smile to her husband, she said, "Thank you, darling."

Then Mrs. Henry crumpled to the floor and lay quite still.

For a long moment, nothing happened. All eyes were on Mrs. Henry, as if waiting for her to get back up. Then Lady Agatha shrieked, the shrill sound rousing the rest of the group. Sir Edward and Mr. Blake dropped to their knees. Her view of Mrs. Henry now unobstructed, Saffron could see the woman's mouth working. The chokes she emitted cut off abruptly after a moment. Without her dark eyes to animate her face, Mrs. Henry looked like a corpse.

Saffron stood frozen. Beside her, Dr. Henry, too, stared without a reaction. Sir Edward and Mr. Blake attempted to revive Mrs. Henry. Mr. Blake looked up and said to no one in particular, "She's not breathing."

Sir Edward got to his feet and called for someone to summon a doctor, his voice hoarse.

By that point the entire room was aware of something having gone wrong. There were many doctors present, but only one medical doctor came forward to offer aid. Saffron was shouldered out of the way, waking her out of her shock with a jolt.

The doctor murmured, seemingly to himself, as he checked over Mrs. Henry. After a moment, he looked around for Dr. Henry. "Is your wife allergic to anything?"

Dr. Henry gazed down blankly at his wife, not responding to the doctor.

The doctor ordered an ambulance be called, and Saffron looked around to see who was moving to summon it. Lady Agatha was being helped into an armchair by Mr. Snyder. Dr. Berking was standing off to the side, speaking to a few other guests, with his eyes rapt on the action.

Sir Edward stood stiffly next to Dr. Henry, his eyes darting to the doctor and the door. Dr. Henry blinked dazedly, then swore. He began to pace, running his hands through his hair again and again, and asking for a drink despite several bottles being within his reach. Mr. Snyder finally slapped him smartly, which seemed to help.

Saffron and the other guests were soon ushered into another parlor. Saffron's hands hadn't stopped trembling. She wished she could do something useful. Anything was better than standing in the midst of all these people droning on in hushed voices, expressing the usual sentiments of well wishes for the ill woman, amid speculation. The general consensus, spread by those who were close enough to hear the doctor, was a sudden and severe food allergy. Saffron looked about for Dr. Maxwell but couldn't find him.

Before long, Sir Edward announced that Mrs. Henry had been attended to. The crowd seemed relieved, but Saffron didn't feel it. The guests quickly disassembled, wanting to forget the unpleasant ending to an otherwise pleasant evening.

CHAPTER 3

As Saffron arrived at the university Monday morning, she wondered for the hundredth time what had become of Mrs. Henry. She'd spent the weekend recounting the story for her flatmate, Elizabeth, and trying not to consider just how ghastly the whole affair had been. A fair few of the inhabitants of the North Wing had attended the party, and no doubt information and rumors would be circulating in equal measure.

The long stretch of campus buildings stood tall against the cloudy sky. The north and south halls bracketing the dominating Wilkins Building formed the Quad, where, in addition to the greenhouses a street away, Saffron's entire world had been contained during her time as a student. The simple gray facades of the buildings had once been imposing, unfriendly to her eyes— a reminder of all she had to live up to as Thomas Everleigh's daughter. But now the campus of University College London felt familiar, comfortable. She did belong there, which she proved by being hired by the botany department as a research assistant. Soon she would make herself a more permanent fixture at the university.

Saffron entered the North Wing through the unadorned black door off the Quad and walked up the stairs to the second floor. Murky sunlight came through the windows, not quite illuminating all the corners of the clean and quiet hall. She paused outside the door to Dr. Maxwell's office. The glazed glass panel was dark. The professor wasn't yet inside, not surprising considering it was barely eight o'clock. Saffron sighed. She really did need her own key to his office, as this was not the first time she had been locked out.

Rocking on her heels, Saffron looked up and down the empty hallway. Maybe she could see if Mr. Ashton had arrived yet, to get a head start on whatever work she needed to do to help him prepare for Maxwell's study.

Her low heels clicked on the polished white and black tile, the sound especially sharp in the quiet building. Mr. Ashton was on this floor, as he'd said, but she didn't know which office was his. Conveniently, she turned the corner to find the man in question balancing a stack of books with one arm and attempting to unlock his office door with the other.

"Here, let me," Saffron said, moving to open the door for him.

Mr. Ashton shifted his grip on the books. "Thank you." He stepped back from the doorway to allow her to open the door. "I didn't think anyone else would be here this early."

He left the door open as he crossed to the desk and carefully deposited the stack of books on top, straightening the spines precisely.

"I usually come in early," Saffron said, leaving it unspoken that it was to ensure she didn't stay at the university late any more. She didn't want to be alone in the building when certain lecherous department heads might linger.

Mr. Ashton's office was the same design as Dr. Maxwell's, rectangular with a window overlooking the Quad. His desk, the same warm oak as lined the walls, was gleaming and bare but for his spotless blotter and an articulating lamp without a speck of dust on its bronze shade. The books along the shelf next to it were perfectly aligned. A small couch with faded gray uphol-stery had been backed up to the unadorned white wall opposite the desk.

"You have a rather spartan sense of style, Mr. Ashton," she remarked.

"I find it makes it easier to find what I need." He straight-ened his blotter and the stack of books again before settling into his chair and looking at her expectantly. He was tidy in a gray suit and sober blue tie. Only his dark hair continued to defy his perfect order, with a wave that pomade couldn't seem to control.

"I came to see how I might assist you with the expedition preparations," Saffron said.

"Unfortunately, I haven't had the opportunity to take a look at the materials from Dr. Maxwell yet. I was kept busy with the police yesterday."

"The police?" Saffron repeated in surprise.

"I assume that means you haven't spoken to them yet. They're looking into what happened to Mrs. Henry," Mr. Ashton said.

"But why would the police be interested in an allergic reac-tion?" Saffron asked.

"It wasn't an allergic reaction." Mr. Ashton hesitated, then added, "Mrs. Henry is in a comatose state. They said it was poison."

Saffron gasped. "Poison?"

"They think it was something in her drink. You know, the champagne. It was being passed all around, and someone could have easily put something in."

Shocked, Saffron sunk into the chair opposite Mr. Ashton. Mrs. Henry seemed like a normal person. Perhaps a bit unpleas-ant, considering the conversation she'd overheard in the hallway, but not so bad as to warrant being poisoned. "But why would someone poison Mrs. Henry?"

Mr. Ashton spoke slowly, as if weighing each word. "The police asked me an hour's worth of questions, mostly about Dr. Henry."

"Do they think he poisoned his wife?"

At this, he looked back to his desk. "I couldn't say."

He didn't seem inclined to say more about it, and assured her that he would let her know what he needed for the preparations.

Saffron walked slowly down the hall, which was beginning to buzz with scholars, hoping Dr. Maxwell had arrived and had more information about Mrs. Henry. She found the white-haired professor scribbling on a piece of paper at his desk. Putting her bag on her chair on the far side of the cluttered room, she smiled at him when he looked up.

"Good morning, Everleigh," he murmured, his voice gruffer than usual.

"Good morning, Professor," she replied and began removing her gloves and hat. "Have you had a chance to look over the notes I left?"

"No, just wrote a few things before I forget them. I don't suppose"—he raised his bushy eyebrows at her—"you've seen the police poking about?"

"No, I haven't," Saffron replied. "Though I suppose they would come here to question the guests from the party."

"I gather you've heard about Dr. Henry's wife."

"I heard it wasn't an allergy after all. Alexander Ashton told me."

Dr. Maxwell frowned. "Everleigh—"

A sharp knock at the door interrupted him. Maxwell stood up with a grunt, but Saffron was there quicker.

There were two men at the door, a middle-aged man of perhaps forty and a younger man in a navy policeman's uniform, who couldn't be much older than Saffron. The older man was as bland and somber as his dark Hamburg hat. The uniformed officer, with wide blue eyes and blond hair peeking out from under his domed custodian helmet, looked as though he were play-acting at being a police officer.

"Detective Inspector Green, Criminal Investigation Department," the older man said. "This is Sergeant Simpson." He gestured back to the young man. "Is Dr. Alan Maxwell available?"

From behind his desk, Maxwell's face went slightly pale beneath his snowy beard. Saffron stepped aside for the policemen to enter. Maxwell's hand trembled as he offered it to Inspector Green. "Inspector, this is Miss Saffron Everleigh, my assistant."

The inspector nodded to Saffron. Sergeant Simpson remained by the door and took out a notebook and pencil.

Inspector Green turned to the professor. "Dr. Maxwell, we are here to follow up on our questions from yesterday regarding the poisoning of Mrs. Cynthia Henry."

Maxwell glanced at her. "Perhaps we should excuse Miss Everleigh?"

The inspector's impassive brown eyes flicked to her. "Miss Everleigh, were you also in attendance at the party at the Leister residence?"

"Yes, I was," she said, determined not to be intimidated by the inspector's cool manner.

"If you wouldn't mind stepping out for a few minutes while we speak with Dr. Maxwell, Simpson will retrieve you when we are ready to speak with you."

Unsettled, Saffron went into the hall.

She paced the cool tiled steps of the stairwell, paying no mind the students passing by. Her mind was occupied once more with Mrs. Henry and the fact that Saffron had also drunk the champagne passed around at the party. It could have been her on the floor, rather than Mrs. Henry, if the poisoner had mixed up the glasses or bottles. She shuddered. She'd possibly spoken with the person responsible, sat next to them at the dinner table—a table that had been full of her colleagues. Did that mean the poisoner was at the university now?

She flinched when the voice of the younger police officer calling her name interrupted her morbid train of thought. She hastened back to the office, where Dr. Maxwell stood anxiously at the door. As Saffron approached, he offered to stay with her.

"Thank you, Professor, but I'll be all right." She patted his arm and smiled reassuringly.

The inspector took Dr. Maxwell's desk, Saffron sat in the chair before him, and Simpson did his best to be unobtrusive by the door. His hands were shaking slightly, which Saffron diagnosed as either a lack of breakfast or an abundance of nerves.

After recording her full name and address, the inspector began. "Miss Everleigh, what is your role here at the university?"

Saffron drew herself up and said, "I assist the professor in his research. I am also a botanist."

"You were at the party Saturday evening, but your name was not on the guest list Sir Edward provided."

"The invitation was extended to the whole botany department at the last minute, on Thursday," Saffron said. That was the reason why Dr. Maxwell had cut his family visit short, so he could attend. She'd have expected him to grumble more about it, actually.

Inspector Green asked, "When did you arrive?"

Saffron described the various events of the evening, the inspector pausing here and there to ask a clarifying question. "You say you excused yourself from the party just after the men entered the drawing room, and remained out of the room until the toast. That would have been about twenty minutes. What were you doing?"

Resenting the embarrassment she felt at admitting it, she said, "I was seeing to my personal needs. And then I ran into Alexander Ashton, and we had a conversation in the hallway."

"I see. What were you talking about?"

"Well, we . . ." There was no point in dancing around the fact that she'd eavesdropped, especially since it was probably important to the investigation. Not to mention he'd likely already heard of it from Mr. Ashton. "We accidentally overheard Mrs. Henry and Lady Agatha, actually."

Saffron briefly described the conversation between Lady Agatha and Mrs. Henry. She finished by explaining how she had been quite close to Mrs. Henry when she fell. The inspector didn't respond immediately. Saffron glanced over at Simpson, who was watching Inspector Green avidly as the inspector wrote his own notes.

"I was so shocked to hear that it was in fact poison, and not an allergic reaction as the doctor said," Saffron said, wondering how much information the inspector would reveal. "I accidentally consumed a poisonous plant when I was a child and had a very different reaction. Still, every toxin has its effects, I suppose."

"Yes, they can have diverse effects on the body."

"What sort of poison was it?"

The inspector didn't look up from his notes. "I'm afraid I can't say."

"Do you think that Mrs. Henry was the intended victim of the poisoning?"

Inspector Green shot her a sharp look. "Why do you ask?"

Her off-handed question must have touched on something relevant. "It's just that the champagne, which might have contained the poison, was passed around left and right. The intended victim would have simply passed it on and never known the glass was meant for them."

Standing, Inspector Green said, "Could be, Miss Everleigh. We have several other guests we need to question. We'll be nearby if you think of anything else."

He and Simpson left. Dr. Maxwell returned a moment later.

"What did they say? What did the inspector want to know?" he demanded, brow furrowed.

Having never been questioned by the police before, Saffron couldn't say if his questions had been out of the ordinary, though they'd seemed basic enough. But Dr. Maxwell looked so on edge, she gave him a bracing smile. "Nothing of great importance, Professor."

CHAPTER 4

They attended to business until lunch. Dr. Maxwell, who continued to be agitated, didn't notice how often Saffron was distracted from her work. The events of the past days circled in her mind, stirring up unanswered questions. Who would poison a woman in the midst of a party? Was Mrs. Henry the intended victim? Why her?

Saffron wanted to ask Dr. Maxwell for his thoughts and maybe hear some reassurances too. Her list of people she could confide in was short, and he was near the top. But she also wanted to ask about his rejection from the expedition crew. It hurt that he hadn't mentioned his interest in going to the Amazon, and had even gone so far as to apply to join the expedition without telling her, as if her future wouldn't be affected.

But she held her tongue, and after lunch, Maxwell sent her off to the library to do some research, with the expectation that she would be there for the rest of the day.

In the main floor of the Wilkins Building, at the center of campus, was the library. The long hall was filled with soaring stacks standing sentinel over students hunched over rows of scarred tables. The librarians didn't dare expose the books to the elements, so there was no chance of a cool spring breeze from the tall windows lining either side of the hall to blow away the scent of old tomes and anxious young men. The air was not still, however, but rife with the fluttering of turning pages and the coming and goings of scholars as they mined the stacks for knowledge.

Saffron didn't bother approaching the botanical section, but instead ventured off through the lofty stacks into the medical section, looking for texts on poisons. It would be impossible to concentrate on work when the inspector's questions and her own buzzed in her head like flies to a blooming *Amorphophallus titanium*. She picked a promising looking book off the shelf. Flipping through its tightly written pages, however, she found it was arranged by a list of toxins by name rather than by symptom. She replaced it and pulled down several others, no doubt sullying her white blouse and gray skirt with dust.

Saffron sat at one of the long center tables, dredging through unfamiliar medical terms for five minutes before returning for a book of medical terminology. After looking at list upon list of poisons, Saffron began to wonder if Mrs. Henry had been given a manmade toxin, something readily available. Saffron was sure that, somewhere, the minions of Inspector Green would be scouring the shops near the homes of all the partygoers, looking to see who had bought rat poison recently.

The inspector said he couldn't say, but something in how he'd spoken of the poison and glanced at his sergeant made Saffron think they didn't know what the poison was. Surely he'd spoken with the doctors. If it was a common poison, then the doctors would recognize its symptoms and possibly identify it through a blood test of some kind. It was probably something obscure, then. Unfortunately, the faculty at the university had access to all kinds of toxic chemicals and plants. Had Inspector Green considered that? Yet another question.

Saffron contemplated all the plants in the university greenhouses. She knew all the plants growing there by heart, including which were currently flowering and producing fruit. She wrote the list out, then crossed off the ones that would not have any seriously toxic effects if consumed, and put a question mark next to the ones she was unsure of. Inspector Green would have his hands full narrowing down the possibilities. If, indeed, the inspector thought that a plant was responsible.

Her eyes fell on the name of a plant from south-central Mexico, brought back decades ago by Dr. Maxwell. The vine was a sickly yellow color and zigzagged around trees as it grew, clinging tightly to its host. Maxwell had named it the xolotl vine, after the Aztec god of death and lightning, since the growth pattern resembled a fork of lightning and the toxin in its leaves struck as quickly. Saffron had the feeling that Maxwell enjoyed the notorious reputation of his plant, occasionally still telling secondhand stories of people dropping to the ground immediately upon consumption. He'd warned everyone to treat the *Solandra xolotum* with the greatest caution and always wear gloves when tending to it. As a result, most people avoided it in the greenhouse, allowing it to take over a large section of a relatively empty greenhouse. Mr. Winters, the caretaker of the greenhouses, generally ignored it except for giving it water.

Saffron had a creeping feeling of discomfort. Everyone knew that xolotl was brought here and championed by Dr. Maxwell. From what she'd heard of it from others, they seemed to think it was wildly dangerous. And Mrs. Henry had dropped to the floor nearly the moment the champagne had touched her lips. Dr. Maxwell had been very nervous this morning . . .

No, Maxwell couldn't have anything to do with the poisoning. What would he have against Mrs. Henry? Lurking within that question was a truth she didn't want to acknowledge, making her heart pound as it formed in her mind. Dr. Henry could have been the target, and Dr. Maxwell certainly had something against him.

"Miss Everleigh."

The voice made her jump, and its tone suggested this was not the first time her name had been spoken. She looked up into the dark eyes of Mr. Ashton, who was eying her curiously. His jacket was slung over his arm, the other holding a stack of books. His close-fitting charcoal-gray waistcoat and subdued blue tie were still perfectly tidy, though his white shirtsleeves were rolled to his elbows.

"Do you have a moment to discuss Dr. Maxwell's samples?" When she gave him a blank look, he added, "For the expedition."

"Yes, of course," she said, nodding absently. She shuffled her papers together and tucked them under her notebook in an attempt to straighten out her thoughts along with them. Clearing her throat, she asked, "What exactly did you need to know?"

"I heard from my department head this morning that Ericson has dropped out of the trip. His wife apparently took issue with him being absent when their child is to be born," he said with a small smile. "So I was asked to replace him."

A hint of envy threatened to dampen Saffron's smile, but she said brightly, "Congratulations! How very exciting!"

"Thank you. I've been combing through Ericson's papers and saw I have only a vague outline of Dr. Maxwell's experimental design and a specimen list that looks only partially complete." He set down a stack of books and put his jacket over the back of a chair, then withdrew a paper that he handed her. A large scar ran the length of his right arm, which had been obscured by his jacket. His tanned skin brought the scar into sharp relief. A few flecks of white marked his hand and his wrist, and beyond was a maze of mottled and puckered skin in shades of white, pink, and tan. Saffron wondered at him rolling his sleeves up in public. Most would attempt to hide such a flaw.

Hoping he didn't notice her staring, Saffron quickly dropped her gaze to the paper. It was indeed a half-completed specimen list in Dr. Maxwell's scrawling handwriting. Irritation clipping her words, she said, "Dr. Maxwell has been rather dragging his feet about completing his design."

Mr. Ashton's dark brows shot upward. "We leave in two weeks. The project designs were due a week ago."

She knew the deadlines all too well. They were the source of some of the only disagreements she and Maxwell had ever had in nearly five years of mentorship. Her heart ached a little to think of how he'd told her she couldn't understand the pressure he was under, the stakes. Why he simply hadn't asked for her help, she didn't know. Withholding a sigh, Saffron said, "I understand, Mr. Ashton. Let's start with the specimen list."

They worked until the light faded from the tall arched windows. The green banker lamps atop the tables were soon the only sources of light. Silence, usually broken by the shuffle of pages turning and the murmur of voices, lay thick and heavy around them. When a librarian pushing a rattling cart of books cleared his throat pointedly at them, Alexander looked about, then glanced at his wristwatch. Six o'clock. How had two hours already passed?

"I didn't realize the time," he said, frowning at the windows showing gloomy, dark skies. Thunder rumbled faintly beyond. His nerves pricked at the sound, but he ignored them.

"And we're not even halfway through," Miss Everleigh said, though she didn't appear put out by the long list of specimens they hadn't yet covered.

Indeed, she hadn't objected to the slow and thorough way Alexander required his research to be put together, though it was clear from the haphazard notes in her notebook and her frequent jumps between texts that she wasn't used to a more disciplined approach. It made Alexander cringe internally, but she was eager to help and certainly knew the list well, barely needing to reference any of the guides that were stacked on the table between them.

Alexander stood. He needed to get moving before the storm brewing outside set in. He could never trust himself entirely when thunder and lightning were involved. He unrolled his shirtsleeves, forcing himself to do it at a normal pace. Miss Everleigh had stared, as everyone always did the first time they saw his scarred arm, but that was no reason to rush and make it obvious that it bothered him. He didn't do up his cufflinks—he didn't care to struggle with them in front of her—and pulled on his jacket.

Miss Everleigh stood and gathered her things, and arms loaded with books, gave him a pretty smile. He felt his lips lifting to return it, and let himself smile back.

They set off through the stacks, their footsteps loud in the hushed space. He preferred the library when it was quiet like this. The hush was familiar and soothing.

They turned through another arch to the gently curving atrium lined with light blue silk paper and adorned with classical reliefs. The Flaxman Gallery had only just reopened after a lengthy redecoration, and now the small, octagonal space shone with refreshed beauty. Even for someone who cared little for art, there was nothing to compare to the bright light of a clear morning illuminating the gallery and making the ivory casts along the walls glow. Now the domed room was faintly blue and dim but for small electric lights casting a yellow glare on the reliefs from below. The dramatic statue in the middle of the room, St. Michael bearing down on an ophidian Satan, stood frozen in shadow as they passed.

Miss Everleigh paused at the edge of the portico. Past the classical columns, the white steps were darkened with fat drops of rain. A gust of wind caught leaves and discarded papers, scattering them across the Quadrangle's large oval of pavement. The breeze was heavy with the scent of rain. The back of Alexander's neck tingled unpleasantly.

They'd barely managed a step toward the stairs when a flash of lightning seared the sky, followed by an enormous crash of thunder that shook the ground beneath their feet. The sound froze the air in Alexander's lungs, but his vision didn't dim, nor did his heart stutter. He forced his fingers to loosen around the books in his hands.

In the moment it had taken him to breathe deeply and collect himself, the electric lights of the Wilkins Building and the others surrounding the Quad had gone out. The sky opened up and a torrent of rain began.

Moisture dusted his face as the rain fell heavily beyond the cover of the portico. He stepped back from the edge of the stairs and back toward the door.

Rather than shy away from the sheets of rain and rolls of thunder, Miss Everleigh's face was upturned, her eyes closed, a soft smile on her lips. With the meager light of the twin gas lanterns at the doors to the gallery, her fair skin almost glowed.

She breathed deeply. "It's lovely, isn't it?"

Alexander couldn't help but arch a brow at that. More often than not, rain took him back to a dark, muddy trench.

She peered at him, smile lingering as she added, "You know, fresh rain, wet grass, flowers, the scent of Earth's renewal?"

Alexander forced a light tone. "I can't say I've ever noticed."

Miss Everleigh's blue eyes opened wide, and she took another step back under the ledge, toward him, saving her books from further damage. With incredulity in her voice, she said, "But it's one of the best things about spring! It keeps me awake at night!"

He blinked, entirely unsure how to respond to such a comment.

Miss Everleigh blushed deeply, but she continued on in a less whimsical voice, saying, "You know, spring insomnia. My father had it too, every spring. He said he'd lie awake for hours every April and May, with the windows open, just enjoying the scent of rain and earth and listening to the insects and frogs."

Mention of Miss Everleigh's father brought memories floating back through Alexander's mind of another Everleigh, a professor he'd had before the war. It was vague, perhaps dimmed by all he'd faced in the years between, but he was quite sure it was the same man. "I had a professor called Everleigh when I first began my studies. He taught an introductory course to botany, I believe. A relation of yours?"

A surprised smile lit up her face. "Yes, that must have been my father. He was a professor here for a short time."

"He must be very proud of you." Lord knew, his own father would have been proud had he stuck to the plan and become a solicitor too.

Her bright smile faltered, and she said quickly, "How did you come into the field of biology? I believe you escaped the question at the party the other night."

Alexander turned to the invisible rain. He'd rather not speak about why he'd chosen biology over law, but she'd been so artlessly open about her love of spring and rain, he felt an earnest reply was owed. "When I entered university, I planned to study the law," he began. "I wasn't convinced, but my father was determined so I went along with it. Then the war . . ." His words, never abundant to begin with, dried up. What was there to say about it that wouldn't weigh down the humid air between them? "It was no worse for me than anyone else. I . . . was lucky. But I came back, as many did, done with war, death, and loss. When I returned to the university, I took one look into a microscope and was hooked. Biology is the study of life, after all."

He risked a glance at her, surprised at how much he hoped she wasn't looking at him with pity.

Her large blue eyes were full of pain rather than unwanted compassion. "My father left his position here to fight. He died," she said quietly. "I've always wanted to follow in his footsteps. I want to make him proud, doing what he loved."

Alexander couldn't think of anything to say in response to so starkly stated a sentiment.

Flashes of lightning illuminated the sky and the grounds, silhouetting the trees in the Quad. Rain and wind slashed through the darkness. They might have gone back into the foyer or the gallery to wait it out, but Miss Everleigh didn't seem to have any inclination to return inside, and Alexander realized he didn't either. Usually, he'd be holed up in his flat or his office, pointedly ignoring the flashes of light and cracks of thunder, but he found he could take it all in without his anxiety roaring to life. Miss Everleigh had very effectively distracted him. The storm was secondary to their strangely intimate conversation.

Before long, the electric lights of the buildings around the Quad buzzed back to life.

"Ah! I suppose I'll see you tomorrow, Mr. Ashton," Miss Everleigh said, turning back to the door.

Her easy return to the formality of the past few hours made him feel like his necktie was too tight. "Alexander." He opened the door for her, his eyes on the hallway beyond. "Please, call me Alexander."

CHAPTER 5

The raucous storm the previous evening had cleared the way for brilliant blue skies, and the day promised to be pleasant. Saffron had dressed accordingly in a copen blue blouse and matching skirt. Saffron made her way down the narrow hall of the Chelsea flat she shared with Elizabeth.

At the doorway of the kitchen, Saffron looked with affection at the woman sipping coffee at their little kitchen table in a dramatic dressing gown of crimson, a pleasant breakfast laid out before her. She and Elizabeth had always been the best of friends, growing up together in the heart of Bedford as neighbors. Saffron had thought that they would spend their lives together, entwined by youthful hopes of a match with Wesley, Elizabeth's brother.

Along with robbing the Hale family, and Saffron, of Wesley, the war had decimated the Hale family's fortunes. When Elizabeth had been expected to do her part to refill their coffers with a convenient marriage to a ghastly old man, she had escaped to London with Saffron.

At first, it was a grand adventure, exploring the city together when Saffron wasn't busy with lessons. Saffron's grandparents soon realized that her commitment to her studies was just as serious as their son's had been, and they cut her off. Even with the meager funds Saffron's mother managed to give to Saffron, she and Elizabeth found themselves suddenly and desperately short on money. In addition to finding employment, Elizabeth had taken to domestic responsibility with more than just the enthusiasm stoked by the need to prove to their families they didn't need their support. She seemed to have a real talent for cooking and household organization. She had made it possible for Saffron to complete her degree without having to find employment that would distract her from her studies, and had staunchly supported her friend at every turn.

Glancing up from her morning paper, Elizabeth smiled. Her makeup was done, though her sandy bob was still held in place by pins. "Saff, dear, do you have anything important going on today?"

"No, just going on with Dr. Maxwell's tasks." Saffron snatched up a piece of toast—perfectly crunchy and slathered in butter—as she went about fixing herself a cup of coffee. "Why do you ask?"

"You're wearing earrings."

She was wearing little pearl earrings, a birthday gift from her mother. "So?"

Elizabeth scoffed. "Darling, you never mind what you wear unless there is a grandparent to defend against or a man to intrigue!" She gasped, red varnished nails glinting as she pressed a hand to her throat dramatically. "Don't tell me we're expecting your grandparents!"

Saffron shuddered. "I would never spring that on you without at least a week's notice. We'd need time to gird our loins." They may have cut her off financially, but they'd come around to making an effort to be a part of Saffron's life. A strict, overwhelming part.

"Right then, who is the man?"

Saffron laughed and brushed her fingers off over the sink. "I never said there was a man."

Elizabeth followed her out of the kitchen and down the hall, her dressing gown swishing around her generous curves. "Surely not that fellow you told me about! He studies bacteria, darling. What sort of job is that?"

"I must be going." Saffron smiled her most winning smile as she snatched up her coat and hat, ducking out the door before Elizabeth could press her further.

She pinned her hat over her coiled bun as she hopped down the stairs to the sidewalk below. With spring emerging fully now that it was mid-April, she decided to enjoy the lengthy walk from the tiny flat in Chelsea, rather than immediately hop on the bus.

She amused herself by contemplating the poetry of the emerging blooms, pear trees swollen with lacy white blooms and tulips parting their red mouths, but decided in the end to leave that field of endeavor to Elizabeth. In addition to working as a receptionist for a minor government minister whom they referred to as "the lord," Elizabeth published poetry under a pseudonym, which, given her rather racy subject matter, Saffron agreed was wise. Elizabeth loved hearing Saffron's indulgent descriptions of plants. Saffron once had a professor tell her off for using too many adjectives in a paper, and took it to heart that she was first a scientist, then an enthusiast.

After cutting through Hyde Park, she stepped onto a two-tiered red bus that took her through the tangled streets of Mayfair and into Fitzrovia. When she reached the Euston Square stop, she stepped off the bus and paused, as she always did, before the obelisk in the center of the square. She gazed at the bronze figures that guarded the four corners of the tall stone monument. She said a silent prayer for the lost souls from the war, for her father; her fallen sweetheart, Wesley; and for countless others, before finishing the brief walk to the university.

Saffron dodged the onslaught of students in the Quad and made her way to the second floor of the North Wing. Her momentum slipped when she saw Detective Inspector Green standing outside Dr. Maxwell's door.

Gripping her handbag tightly, she asked, "May I help you, Inspector?"

The inspector looked at her steadily. "I'd like to speak to Dr. Maxwell. Do you know when he will be available?"

"I believe he will be attending a syllabus meeting in twenty minutes, in Dr. Berking's office."

"When will the meeting conclude?"

"They usually take forty minutes, perhaps an hour if the other professors are feeling chatty." Saffron paused, eying the inspector. "May I pass along a message for you?"

"I have a few additional questions for him. I'll return later."

Curiously unnerved, Saffron watched the inspector disappear down the hall. She entered the office and took in the mess. In the few hours she'd spent in the library yesterday, Dr. Maxwell had managed to undo all the tidying she'd done while he was away. The small, wood-paneled room held a large desk centered with its back to the window. Saffron knew it was there, somewhere, beneath the haphazard stacks of books and sheaves of papers. The bookshelves flanking the desk were full to bursting with thick volumes. The filing cabinet was crowned with an enormous fern whose fronds obscured the out-of-date labels on the first two drawers. The only clear space in the room was the wall opposite the desk, where a framed painting caught the morning light.

Saffron had painted *Houlletia tigrina*, the professor's favorite species of orchid with bright watercolors and given it to him on the occasion of her graduation from University College last year. It was an insufficient token of appreciation for each kind smile and each shared celebration or commiseration over the years. How many times had she felt ready to give up and return to the stuffy society affairs she'd fled? Maxwell would share a seemingly off-the-cuff reminiscence of his own student days, and she'd recover her nerve. How many tears had fallen in this office, stemmed by Maxwell's gentle reminders of Thomas Everleigh's own struggles and triumphs? A mere painting could never approach compensation for his guidance and support. She still remembered the way Maxwell had worked to speak, his voice hoarse with feeling as he thanked her for the gift. She'd burst into tears on her first day as his assistant when she saw he'd hung the painting in his office.

Sighing at the memory, she put her things down at her table and moved to the teetering pile of papers on Dr. Maxwell's desk. Her nose wrinkled as she found two cups of cold tea hidden by a series of files stacked precariously near the edge of the desk. She narrowly avoided sloshing it over a report from 1863 on the "Cultivation of Chinchona in India."

Nearly an hour passed before the room looked less like a windstorm had passed through and more like a place of study. Saffron sat down at her little desk to begin her work. It wasn't just secretarial nonsense, but actual research and legwork for his current study. The professor was increasingly fascinated by chlorophyll. Recent work by Richard Willstätter, a German scientist, had inspired him to investigate the subject further. Saffron was to find any and all references available regarding plant pigmentation and sunlight, and so had been thumbing through all kinds of texts for months. She had designed her own study based on what she'd found, something that would complement Dr. Maxwell's research and enable her to continue working with him throughout her graduate studies.

The shine of her new position had rubbed off a bit recently. Working with Dr. Maxwell was perfectly fine, though researching plant pigmentation didn't particularly inspire her. But she had never planned on being his assistant forever, and had wanted to earn a place in the department so she could do her own research as well as teach, like her father had. The reception she'd received upon being hired was less than warm, and Berking's actions the past few months had made her question her plans more than once. He was a relatively young department head and had decades to torment her. He would be inescapable, and she would require his approval for all her work. Could she really bear to have her career in Berking's hands?

Another sigh escaped Saffron's lips. All this business with the police and the poisoning was making her morose.

Resolving to be in a better mood, Saffron set aside her concerns and cracked open *Annals of Botany*, Volume 34, to resume her note taking.

⚘

Several hours later, Saffron was ready for a break, both from examining texts and from wondering where the professor had gotten to. He and Dr. Aster had likely gotten caught up in a debate again and were holed up in Dr. Aster's office. She'd half hoped to see Mr. Ashton—Alexander—again, but he hadn't turned up either.

Eager for a change of scenery, Saffron put on her coat and hat and made her way out of the North Wing. The conservatory at her grandfather's estate, where she grew up, filled with her father's impressive private collection, was nothing compared to the university's multitude. The five greenhouses contained an extensive collection of plants from all over the globe, and though she had no official business to take her there, that was where she went.

Situated in a small park one street away from the Quad, the long glass buildings stood out from the squat brick buildings bordering the green. Condensation fogged the panels of glass and obscured the trees, ferns, and vines inside. Saffron pushed the door to the first building open and the humid air, heavy with the scents of loam and the fragrance of a hundred exotic blooms, wrapped around her, as familiar and comfortable as a favorite jumper.

At the old worktable across from the door, Saffron slipped on thick pair of leather gloves and tied on an apron. She didn't require her short, mud-caked boots, lined up next to the others.

A wizened man stumped toward her through the greenery. His steel-gray hair was scraped over his ruddy forehead, his clothes worn and smudged with dirt beneath his leather apron. "Everleigh," Mr. Winters said by way of greeting.

"Hello, sir. How is the ziziphus?" Saffron asked, noting a few jagged cuts crisscrossing his perpetually dirty hands.

"Just has more thorns by the day. Don't know why they care about the ruddy thing! Waste of space and fertilizer if yer ask me," he muttered.

Saffron looked fondly at the old man. Mr. Winters was a groundskeeper turned greenhouse minder in his old age. He expertly cared for every plant that could be reasonably found in Europe, but took audible offense to caring for the exotic plants that filled in the greenhouses. Privately, Saffron thought he wouldn't mind them so much if he would wear gloves. Despite the thriving biology department, which encompassed botany and a handful of other disciplines, the greenhouses were not a popular place, perhaps because of their curmudgeonly caretaker.

Saffron made her way through the other greenhouses. She observed a few new aerial roots descending like thick ropes from the largest philodendron. One of the larger cacti had a black spot on one arm, another seemed to be nearly ready to flower. Her wandering steps brought her to the back of the largely unoccupied greenhouse, the last in the row. The entire back wall was covered with vines spreading like a yellow stain. She stepped closer to examine the heart-shaped leaves, pointing down at the floor with sharp tips. At their widest point, the leaves of the xolotl vine were the size of her palm, though she was sure she'd read in Maxwell's research that they grew to the size of a man's entire hand in their natural habitat. Her stomach dropped as she examined one of the lower vines. Above one of the scaly brown nodes, a clean cut had sliced off a portion of the vine. It was recent, given how the pale flesh hadn't yet scarred over.

Mr. Winters was still in the first greenhouse when Saffron returned her gloves and apron. He was elbow deep in a trough of dirt, grunting as he turned it over to prepare to transfer the tray of sprouts next to him.

"Have you seen Dr. Maxwell today, Mr. Winters?" she asked.

He shook his head. "I haven't. Came in the other day, but he comes and goes every few days." He tugged his arms out of the dirt and tenderly picked up a sprout.

"Did you . . ." she began, wondering how to phrase the question so as not to enrage the greenhouse keeper. "I saw that someone had taken cuttings from a few of the plants. The xolotl vine, of all things!"

Mr. Winters looked up, scowling. "No damned respect for the property of the university. And no damned respect for themselves! Everyone knows that infernal thing is a ticket to the afterlife."

Saffron gave him a weak smile and departed. The sun had crossed to the western part of the sky, casting short shadows onto the pavement. Saffron walked swiftly back to the North Wing, suddenly anxious to see Dr. Maxwell. No matter how angry Maxwell was, there was no possibility of him being a poisoner, but the inspector didn't know that.

Once Saffron reached the hall, she was shocked to find several uniformed men, who seemed to be duplicates of Sergeant Simpson, with boxes lined up in the hallway. Dr. Maxwell's door was open, but Simpson was inside, not the professor. Two more men stood at the professor's desk, shoving documents into boxes.

"Excuse me," Saffron said from the doorway. "What are you doing?"

Simpson's mouth thinned slightly as he took her in. "Collecting evidence."

"Evidence of what?" Saffron asked, moving out of the way of one of the men carrying a large box. The other policeman moved to the bookcase, and she said, "Be careful with those!"

Simpson didn't reply.

"Do you know where I can find Dr. Maxwell?" She opened her mouth to repeat her question, but the other policeman began tossing books off the shelf and into a box, and she darted over. "You can't throw those—some of those are hand painted!" Huffing, she marched back to Simpson. "You can't just take Dr. Maxwell's materials, Sergeant. We have an expedition to prepare for! Where is Dr. Maxwell?"

Simpson didn't look up from his notes, though his eyes were still and not moving over the words any longer. "He's at the police station for questioning."

Saffron sucked in a breath. "But why? Didn't the inspector speak to him here earlier?"

"He's under suspicion." With a stony expression quite at odds with his boyish face, Simpson turned and walked into the hall. He ruined this air of authority by tripping over one of the boxes, sending his tall helmet crooked on his head.

"Wait!" Saffron hurried after him. "What do you mean he's under suspicion?"

A handful of young men paused in their conversation to watch. Saffron's face heated.

Simpson shoved his helmet back into place and told her firmly, "With regards to the poisoning of Mrs. Cynthia Henry. And the suspected attempted murder of Dr. Lawrence Henry."

He signaled to the group of men, and they went off down the stairs, arms loaded with boxes. Saffron was left in the middle of the hall, sputtering as she searched for words. The eyes of the curious bystanders burned into her, and she retreated to the office, snatching the keys left hanging in the door before closing herself in. She sat heavily on the well-worn leather couch, staring at Dr. Maxwell's desk.

The room was in a state of disarray not unfamiliar to her, but far emptier than before. Inspector Green must have come to the same conclusion she had—why else would the police have taken Dr. Maxwell's things? Anyone on the staff of the North Wing might have suggested Dr. Maxwell and the infamous xolotl vine as suspects, and others must know of Dr. Maxwell's disagreement with Dr. Henry.

She stood and searched for any remaining notes or papers mentioning xolotl. She looked in every nook and cranny, in every drawer and through every book that hadn't been taken by the police. Nothing. Her throat and eyes stung with the building pressure of frustrated tears. How on earth was she going to prove Maxwell wasn't responsible if she had no information?

Saffron dashed to her little desk, snatching up her handbag and stuffing her arms into her jacket. Her mind was racing to match her heart. How quickly could she get to the police station?

CHAPTER 6

The taxi stopped outside the police station, and Saffron, despite her nerves, paused when she stepped onto the bustling pavement. Would she even be allowed to see Dr. Maxwell? As she wasn't his relation or his solicitor, she wasn't sure. Maybe she could at least leave him a message.

She squared her shoulders and stepped into the police station. Inside it was dim and depressing. The walls were gray and smudged with dirt, the tile beneath her heels discolored and cracked. A portly man with a florid complexion sat at the front desk. She inquired if she could see Dr. Maxwell. The man gave her a beady look and, in a jovial West Country accent, asked, "Are you family?"

"Er, yes," she said, accepting the premise immediately. Maxwell certainly felt like family anyway. "I'm his niece. Could I please see him? You see, he has a rather weak heart, and I'm terribly concerned for him." She didn't have to try to look anxious.

He called to another sergeant, who led her through a set of doors and into a large room full of desks. The air was faintly musty and heavy, despite constant activity. Echoing voices, shouts, telephones ringing, and the sound of shuffling of papers thickened the atmosphere. Saffron followed the sergeant past the cluttered clusters of desks and down a short corridor. Everywhere she looked was gray and crowded. The sergeant opened a door into a little room, and she blinked hard at the image of her mentor inside.

Dr. Maxwell sat at a small, scuffed table, his white hair less fluffy than usual. His face was grim and pale. He looked up as they entered and jumped to his feet as fast as his arthritis would allow.

"Uncle!" She stepped forward and gave him a wide-eyed look of warning.

"My dear," he croaked, glancing worriedly between her and the sergeant. "Whatever are you doing here?"

"I had to see you! Mother has been so worried since you haven't telephoned her." She sat across from him as he sank back into his chair, wondering how she could possibly communicate all she needed to. "It seems your little . . . ah, *bird*, has been causing mischief."

Maxwell blinked at her and tapped his ear as if worried he hadn't heard her correctly. "My bird?"

"Er, yes," Saffron said slowly, leaning over the table. "Your bird, you know, the one you brought back from Mexico. With such lovely bright *yellow* feathers. He loves to *climb* things."

"Y-yes," Maxwell said with a furrowed brow. His eyes opened wide and he nodded quickly. "Yes, yes, of course! My bird!"

Relieved, Saffron nodded. "Your bird is being blamed for all kinds of trouble, unfortunately. But, you see, I can't do anything about it because your research . . . ah, your ornithology reference books are gone."

Maxwell held her gaze for a long moment as he thought. "Yes, you're right," he said slowly. "Someone did take my reference books, didn't they?"

"I'm afraid your neighbor"—Saffron hesitated, looking to see how attentive the sergeant at the door was—"er, Mr. Green, has all the rest of your guidebooks. Clearly word has spread about what a unique bird he is."

The sergeant sneezed and they jumped. Maxwell rubbed a hand over his brow and shook his head. "They say my bird is dangerous, Saffron, and there is no evidence to the contrary. I never saw the effects of the . . . bird firsthand. Even with my books and reports, there would be no way to prove my bird isn't responsible."

Saffron drew herself up slightly at the defeated tone in his voice. "I also came to tell you that although Mother doesn't think she can cope with the bird if he returns, I said that I would try to track him down myself." Saffron wasn't sure that the professor would understand her bizarre stretch of the metaphor, but she gave him a determined smile that would let him know that she wasn't convinced of his guilt and would work to free him.

The sergeant had wandered back into the hall a few steps, obviously very bored by their bird conversation. Saffron inched closer to Maxwell and whispered, "What on earth happened, Professor? Why are you here?"

Maxwell's voice shook as he replied, "This arrest is all a misunderstanding."

All the blood drained from Saffron's head, making her woozy. "You've actually been arrested?" she choked out.

Maxwell gripped her hand. "It will all get cleared up soon. Just a misunderstanding between Dr. Henry and me. He must have taken my words to heart. Please, Saffron, you must stay out of this. For heaven's sake"—his voice dropped even lower—"your father wouldn't have wanted you in the middle of a police investigation."

Trying to keep desperation out of her voice, she whispered quickly, "Professor, where are your notes from your paper on the xolotl vine? The police can't have found all of them. If I could just look them over, I could prove—"

He cut her off at the sight of the sergeant walking back to them. "Please, please let it be. I will be all right—it'll all get sorted. But please," he spoke in a hoarse whisper as the sergeant wandered back into earshot, "leave that wretched bird alone!"

The university was bustling with students knocking off from classes by the time Saffron returned. She moved swiftly past the crowds, her fingers clutching the frayed notebook she'd retrieved from Dr. Maxwell's house. Mrs. Maxwell had been equal parts relieved and distressed by her visit. Once Saffron explained what she needed, however, her distracted chattering gave way to determination. They scoured what was left on the endless dusty shelves of books, files, and notebooks of Dr. Maxwell's cramped study. The police had already torn the place apart but hadn't managed to find everything. If she knew anything about Maxwell, it was that he always had more papers squirreled away somewhere, and she'd been right. Within the hour, Saffron had emerged with exactly what she was hoping to find.

Instead of entering the North Wing, Saffron continued past it. Dr. Henry must have told the police that Maxwell was responsible and that in addition to the common knowledge that they had argued, as well as xolotl's reputation, must have led to his arrest. The evidence against Maxwell was mounting higher and higher, and Saffron had to do something.

Saffron stole into the greenhouses and took a knife from the table. Gloves on, she carefully took a cutting and wrapped it in her handkerchief. She walked back out, casually waving at Mr. Winters as she passed him. She then headed to the staff room in the basement of the North Wing. A few minutes later, she walked cautiously into Maxwell's office, carrying a glass of steaming water. She wrote a few words on a paper, then moved to prepare the infusion.

Though her hands shook as she placed the venomously yellow leaves into the water, Saffron was confident this would work. All she had to do was drink, then write down faithfully what happened. She already knew, sort of, what to expect. It would be a small inconvenience, she assured herself as she lifted the cup to her lips. Worth it when compared to the strong possibility of Dr. Maxwell being stuck in jail for years.

Saffron had just drained the glass of hot bitter water when a knock rapped on the frosted glass of the door. Alexander Ashton strode into the office a moment later with an armload of books.

Saffron had just a moment to wonder why he'd just barged into the office before his gaze swept over the supplies on the desk. His eyes widened as he took in the yellow leaves in the glass in her hand.

"What are you doing?" he demanded.

But it was already done.

He took a step toward her. "Saffron—"

She didn't hear anything else. A huge, shuddering jolt like a bolt of electricity hit the top of her spine. Her back arched backward and the glass slipped from her hands. Then it was all black.

"Are you mad?"

Alexander had waited for five minutes to ask this question of Saffron. Despite the immense relief he felt at seeing her eyes blink open, he was furious.

He had her by the shoulders as she slumped onto the couch he'd moved her to when she'd first collapsed. His eyes roved over her pale face. She struggled to speak, finally emitting a feeble, "Bin." He frowned in confusion briefly before he sprung up, bolted to the desk, and snatched up the rubbish bin before returning to her side. Gingerly, he straightened her up and leaned her toward it. She was sick for a good while before slumping back onto the cushions, her eyes closed and strands of dark hair plastered to her forehead.

Alexander was at a loss of what to do.

The notebook on the desk was of small comfort. In the minute he'd spent searching for answers before Saffron woke, he'd found the partially illegible account scribbled on age-worn pages. He'd scanned the tattered book with a shaking hand. That his hand trembled only made him angrier, even if the words were hopeful.

It indicated that the symptoms would pass quickly, but Alexander wasn't inclined to trust stories from strangers, although Saffron apparently did. The paper he'd found next to it with her name, the date, and the dosage of xolotl infusion was proof enough of that. How she thought drinking down a tea made with the same leaves the police believed poisoned Mrs. Henry, if the stories going 'round the North Wing were to be believed, would help her professor, Alexander didn't know. He had a hard time believing she would be so foolish.

He lingered on his knees next to the couch, ready to prop her up again if needed.

Saffron breathed hard through her nose and kept her lips pressed together as if to prevent anything else coming up. She looked miserably ill. Alexander contemplated for the twentieth time his line of reasoning for not taking her to hospital immediately upon finding her. The university's hospital was just across the street.

The pile of papers and books he'd shoved off the couch to make room for her wasn't helping his anxiety. The broken glass taunted him from across the room. His fingers itched to clean it up. In fact, this room made his whole body vibrate with the need to fix the enormous mess that was everywhere. But he didn't have to clean it now. He didn't.

After a few long minutes, Saffron spoke in a soft, croaking voice, "What's the time?"

Alexander shook himself from his calming fantasy of sweeping the mess out of the window. "I won't be party to this absurd experiment, Saffron."

Saffron grimaced, her eyes still closed. "Just write it down on the paper."

That placid order nearly undid all the work he'd done to keep calm. He was out of his mind with worry, and she was acting like nothing was wrong. His words came out harshly. "You can't be serious. You can't experiment on yourself. It isn't safe."

"You don't need to rage at me," Saffron mumbled, stirring a bit from her stupor. She opened her eyes and glanced around. "Did you take down the time? If not, give me the paper, and I can."

"I should tear that blasted paper up."

"Alexander—"

Temper getting the better of him, Alexander glared down at her. "What is it? To save Dr. Maxwell? It's being handled by the police. To prove yourself? I understand that it's hard to be a woman in academia—one that has ambitions—but this seems a stupidly dangerous way to go about it. Why didn't you just take the bloody journal to the police?"

Saffron fixed him with a weary look of disdain that he wouldn't have thought her capable of. "The police suspect that Cynthia Henry was poisoned by the xolotl vine. They've taken all of Dr. Maxwell's research, but I'm absolutely sure there was nothing in it depicting actual accounts of poisoning. That journal provides a decades old secondhand account recorded by the very man they believe is responsible. The police would never actually test it out on someone. I dosed myself with xolotl so I didn't have to see Dr. Maxwell imprisoned because of insufficient evidence." This speech seemed to tire her out, as she breathed heavily and somehow went even paler. She didn't relent, however, and with a tremulous voice, added, "I can't lose him. I won't let it happen."

Alexander stood up, pushing his hair through his hands. She was right about the police not trusting the contents of the journal, and right that they wouldn't test xolotl on someone to find out if the symptoms listed were accurate. But it was still absurdly dangerous that she'd taken it herself.

"I should really summon a doctor," Alexander muttered, half to himself.

Saffron blinked up at him, the brilliant blue of her eyes stark in the whiteness of her face. "Please, Alexander. The journal says exactly what is going to happen, and it's been right so far. Intense pain followed by a brief loss of consciousness, vomiting, coldness and numbness in extremities—"

"*What?*" Alexander stared at her. "Numbness in your extremities?"

She nodded. "I suppose you didn't get that far in the journal, then. I can't move my hands, feet, or ankles. I assume it'll be my legs, next."

The admission was made with shocking detachment, as if she really did think this was just an experiment. He stared down at her, noticing for the first time that she wasn't wearing stockings. Why, he couldn't fathom. He'd absently noted her shoes were on the floor next to the glass.

"Damn it all, Saffron, you could be in serious danger. I'm calling for a doctor." He moved toward the door.

"And what exactly will you say?"

Alexander stopped and matched her glare. "You're not at all concerned that you can't move?"

"Of course I'm concerned!"

His blood pressure spiking, Alexander pinched the bridge of his nose and breathed deeply before responding. "Then why are you arguing about retrieving a doctor?"

"Would you be kind enough to examine my feet and ankles, please?" Saffron asked politely, her expression infuriatingly calm.

Gritting his teeth, Alexander jerked his chair to the end of the couch, where Saffron's slender limbs rested against the cushions and sat.

"What . . . what are these lines?" His eyes traced the blue lines streaking her pale toes. They were faint, no more than the press of veins against fair skin, so much so that Alexander thought for a moment that was what they were. But the pattern didn't seem correct. The lines zigzagged like lightning bolts.

"The journal describes them as marks like branches of a tree. Is that what they look like?" Saffron sat up further. Her skirt, the same shade of blue as the lines, slid up her knee an inch more. "Oh my, they really do look like that, don't they?"

The fascination in her voice was off-putting. He stood and retrieved the journal, eyes rushing over the page, trying to make sense of the indecipherable words.

"Here, let me," Saffron offered. "Dr. Maxwell's handwriting would make anyone lose their mind."

He handed her the dilapidated journal, and she made no movement to take it from him. She smiled slightly and looked to where her hand lay at her side. Blue tinged her fingers. "You'll have to hold it for me."

Alexander moved his chair a few inches and sat, propping the book up in his hands so she could see it. He was close enough to see her individual eyelashes, like when they were cloistered together in the hall during the dinner party.

Saffron cleared her throat, those dark eyelashes fluttering. "It says, 'The blue lines mark the progression of the paralysis, receding when movement returns.' So, you see, the marks show exactly how severe the paralysis is, and will fade when I regain movement. Which should be soon."

The bright enthusiasm in her words didn't quite disguise the tension in her eyes. She was afraid, just as Alexander was. Just the word "paralysis" might prove to be too much for him.

She must have seen he was unconvinced, because she added a touch sardonically, "I don't think either of us particularly wants to explain to a doctor or the police why I'm suffering from poisoning while we're both involved in a poisoning investigation."

As if that would stop him from getting her assistance. When he opened his mouth to object, she added, "And I'll remind you that I didn't ask you—"

Her words were stymied at the fierce glare he gave her. "Give me one good reason not to retrieve a doctor right now."

Saffron frowned up at him. "If the lines reach my neck, I'll agree to you calling for a doctor."

"If they reach your neck," Alexander bit out, "that means the entirety of your body would be paralyzed. I'm not waiting until then to get help."

He attempted to pace around the room, but it was impossible with the clutter.

"Look at the lines now," Saffron said. They'd reached her calves and wrists, staining her fair skin with blue. "They've progressed, as has the sensation of coolness and paralysis. It's going exactly how it said it would. Given how little xolotl I consumed, and that I, er, got rid of it immediately after—"

"You're basing your hypothesis on incredibly unreliable information."

"That has thus far proven to be exactly accurate," Saffron said. Her shoulders shrugged, and Alexander realized she must have been attempting to throw her hands in the air with exasperation. "How long has it been—ten minutes? Fifteen? Give me half an hour more. If it's still progressing and not receding, then I will agree to call for a doctor."

CHAPTER 7

The incessant hum of anxiety Alexander hadn't felt in months had returned with full force when he watched Saffron collapse, and it had barely eased when she woke up and croaked for the bin. Arguing with her had only goaded it further. So, under the guise of considering her suggestion to wait for the doctor, he gave in to his urges and began to tidy. Careful, methodical movements while he brushed the glass from the floor onto a piece of paper with a makeshift paper brush; the press of his hand against cotton as his handkerchief soaked in the yellow drops of xolotl infusion dotting the surface of the desk; crisp papers shuffling into piles; the steady slide and thunk of books on and off the shelf as he put them into order.

All the while, Saffron sat silently, occasionally checking on the progress of the blue lines. His eyes flicked to her bare legs often, watching the vine-like blue markings travel higher and higher.

When he could no longer put off his need of the lavatory, Alexander murmured something about needing to step out, and Saffron suggested he lock her in the office with the keys from her handbag. "That way no one will come upon me lounging on the couch barefoot," she said with a tight smile.

He didn't know whether or not to be amused by the carefully folded pair of stockings he had to push past to find the keys.

The halls had quieted in the half hour they'd spent locked up in Dr. Maxwell's office, so it was impossible to miss the guffawing of Dr. Berking. He was thundering up the stairs Alexander had just passed on his way back to Dr. Maxwell's office, his voice carrying through the tiled passage.

". . . Absolutely not, totally out of the question!" Berking's tone was mocking.

Another male voice murmured something unintelligible over the stomping footsteps and huffing breath of Berking climbing the stairs. Alexander swore under his breath. An encounter with Berking was the last thing he needed right now. He sped his steps.

"And *I've* said, it is not a concern! Everyone knows he got his funding through less than savory means, so it's no surprise at all!"

The large man rumbled to the top of the stairs and paused, whipping out a handkerchief and blotting his shining face. Another man, thin and reedy, with pale hair that might have been blond or white, frowned at Berking. Berking caught sight of Alexander standing in the hall, causing Alexander's insides to lurch unpleasantly as he grinned and started toward him.

"Ashton, my boy! What are you still doing here! Should be out strutting around with some beautiful bird!" His booming voice set Alexander's teeth on edge.

Alexander wondered if he should pretend he was on his way back to his office. He was in the middle of the hall, no doubt looking suspicious. "Bird, sir?" he repeated absently.

"Yes, Ashton, a bird! A woman!" Berking's face was red with exertion.

"I have to prepare for the expedition. Plenty of birds and fresh air in Brazil," Alexander said with a half-hearted smile. He forced his eyes to stay on Berking rather than on the light shining through Maxwell's office door, lest he give Berking the idea to drop in on Saffron.

"Of course, Ashton, of course! But I've heard that Brazil is full of many kinds of birds with voluminous, colorful plumage." Berking winked a bloodshot eye at him and wiggled his eyebrows, clearly not referring to birds at all.

Alexander opened his mouth to reply, but Berking laughed suddenly.

"Or is it that you have a bird in the cage, Ashton?" Berking nearly managed a normal speaking voice, clearly his idea of a whisper. He nodded his head toward the office door they stood before, saying "Don't want to be disturbed, eh, Ashton? Is that Miss Everleigh you've got in there?"

Alexander cleared his throat, hating how his eyes darted to the door. "That's not—"

"No need, no need!" Berking winked. "I would take advantage while you can; that particular bird is a rare one to capture. You might pass on your technique to us!"

His jaw clenched, but Alexander tried to look just embarrassed. It wouldn't do to bring even more attention to him or Saffron by arguing with Berking's implications.

"Let's go, Glass, let's leave the young to be young. We have work to do!" Berking barked at the man, Glass, and clapped a heavy hand on his back again, making the pallid face wince. He nodded to Alexander, clearly not as approving of his supposed exploits as Berking, and they made their way down the hall and out of sight.

Alexander slipped into the office. He crossed to Saffron, who was craning her neck back to look at the door.

"Is he gone?" she whispered. The pallor of her face had deepened, rendering her deathly pale.

"It looked like he was going up to his office," Alexander said. "Are you all right?"

Saffron turned back, but not before Alexander caught her expression. It was not unlike the bleak expressions of relief he'd seen on his fellow soldiers when silence fell after a merciless volley. Grateful for the reprieve, but weary of the constant onslaught.

On a face he was most used to seeing smiling, the look worried him. "I doubt he'll try to come in here."

She looked at him in question.

"He seemed to think we were . . . spending time together," he said.

From the way she looked away, he probably shouldn't have said that. He'd heard the gossip making the rounds through the building, the same as everyone else. Unlike most, he'd written off the story of her failed attempt to seduce the head of her department as vicious talk, especially considering Berking was a pig. But perhaps there was something to it.

"Of course that's what he thinks is happening in here," Saffron muttered. She shook her head slightly. "Would you mind looking at my arms? I can't see how they're progressing anymore."

Alexander nodded and sat in the chair. Her eyes followed his hand as he reached for hers. The streaked skin was smooth and cool to the touch.

His eyes lifted to hers. "Can you feel that?"

She shook her head, eyes wide. "I can't . . . I can't feel it at all."

Swallowing some of the tension this pronouncement inspired, Alexander frowned down at her sleeve. "Should I . . .?"

Saffron nodded firmly. "Yes."

As gently as possible, Alexander undid the small pearl button at her elbow. He hoped she didn't notice how his hands shook—his right hand, especially—and wouldn't mistake it for something more puerile. Under the thin blue fabric, more lines were revealed. Above her elbow, a patchwork of lines fragmented the white of her skin.

He glanced up, finding Saffron frowning, with her teeth sunk into her bottom lip. He dropped his hands from her arm immediately. "I didn't mean to make you uncomfortable."

"No," Saffron said quickly. "You didn't make me uncomfortable. I know—that is, this is science, not . . ." Her eyes searched his. "I trust you."

The way she said it made it seem like this was a surprising realization. To cover the strange feeling it brought on, he smiled wryly. "I'm afraid I didn't give you much of a choice."

He was rewarded with a slight smile. "I suppose you didn't."

She did a little wriggle, as if trying to sit up straighter. The result was her sliding farther down, causing her skirt to climb yet another few inches above her knees. Both were covered in blue. To avoid the skin on display and address the issue at hand, Alexander tapped Saffron's shoulder. "Can you feel that?"

"Yes."

He tapped down her arm, an inch at a time, until he thought he found the threshold. It was just a few inches above her elbow.

"Roll up my sleeve," Saffron instructed. "There's a pen on the desk—you can mark where the lines stop, and then you'll be able to better tell when they start receding. The journal said it was hours, but it's already been almost an hour now. I don't think my dose will take that long to subside, as it was only an infusion rather than the actual leaf."

Alexander quickly rolled up her sleeve and stretched her arm out to examine it. Every inch of skin was cold to the touch. Saffron frowned as she caught sight of the lines on her inner arms, reaching upward like tree branches toward the sky. Alexander marked where the furthest line ended in a faded point in the middle of her inner arm.

Neither of them mentioned doing the same on her legs. It occurred to Alexander, however, that she might be cold given how frigid her arm was. He shucked his jacket and draped it over her legs.

"Oh, thank you." Her cheeks tinged pink.

When Alexander settled Saffron's arm gently with her hand in her lap over the edge of his jacket, she asked, "Would you mind writing down some notes?"

Grateful for something to do, Alexander wrote all he could recall of the timing and progression of Saffron's symptoms, then took down her notes too. When he looked up from the papers, the mellow half-light the shadows of the domed Wilkins Building cast over the Quad had faded into deeper, cooler dusk. Saffron's offer of half an hour was long since up.

When the notes were completed, Alexander asked to see her arm again.

"Good idea," Saffron replied, her face brightening. He wondered if it was because she wanted to regain use of her limbs or because she was interested in the progress of the symptoms. Her enthusiasm for the scientific aspect of her experiment hadn't wavered.

The black notch on her soft inner arm was officially above where the blue lines lay.

Saffron grinned at him. "At least we know we won't be here all night!" Her smile fell, replaced by a look of wide-eyed dismay. "I mean, I don't—" She looked like she would have liked to bury her face in her hands.

"I know you didn't mean anything by it." Alexander looked back to the notes, jotting down the update. "I don't put much store in rumors, Saffron. Or what Berking says. Or implies."

Saffron was quiet for a long moment. "I met with him about my research proposal for the expedition in March. He said some things to me—terrible, disgusting things." She looked down at her hands. Alexander opened his mouth to assure her she didn't need to share more, but she continued, her words rushed. "He pulled me toward him and grabbed at me and kissed me, if you can call it that." Saffron shuddered. "I got away before he could . . . do anything else, and he tripped on the carpet and fell over, and then his assistant came in . . ." She sighed, dejected. "So, you see that rumor isn't quite all rumor."

His insides, already boiling at the images in his mind, burned still hotter at the shame engrained in her last words. "I'm sorry," he said gruffly.

She let out a shaky laugh, still looking down. "Don't be ridiculous—you didn't do anything wrong. By some standards, Berking didn't either. And I shouldn't have gone to his office when I knew his reputation for—"

"It was not your fault," Alexander ground out. Her eyes flew to his. Alexander moderated his tone and added, "You can't blame yourself for his behavior. I'm sorry that it happened."

"Oh." Saffron paused, looking nonplussed. "I . . . I appreciate that, Alexander."

An awkward silence fell. There were a lot of things Alexander wanted to say, but none felt right. Nodding toward her arm, he said, "That's regressed a bit more. Can I get you a glass of water or perhaps tea?"

She nodded, and by the time he returned, the blue marks were down to her elbows. With a bright smile, Saffron reported she could move both her arms and her legs, demonstrating inelegantly before insisting he write it all down. They agreed that the lines were fading faster than they'd developed. Alexander didn't admit it aloud, but he found that fascinating.

Alexander helped her sip from the glass of water he'd retrieved, and then went to finish arranging the bookshelf. When the lines had vanished from her hands, Saffron flexed and rubbed them together before she carefully took up the glass of water and finished drinking it with a grin. "Just a bit stiff."

Unsure what to do now, Alexander simply wrote down the information.

"I should go."

He looked up from the notes, surprised, and jumped to his feet to steady her as she rose from the couch, her hand braced on the arm. "But you just regained feeling—"

"I can walk, I think. I should go home." Her voice was patient and tired.

Another protest was on the tip of his tongue, when Saffron straightened up, surprising him with her closeness. Her face was inches from his chest. Saffron took an uncertain step backward, and he took her by the shoulders to steady her. She looked up at him, a little frown wrinkling her brow, and said softly, "Thank you, Alexander. Would you excuse me for a moment?"

Alexander didn't bother arguing as he stepped into the hall so she could adjust her clothing. He certainly could not insist that she stay locked in the office with him. She seemed, shockingly, well enough, and according to Dr. Maxwell's journal, no other effects should develop.

Alexander walked with Saffron, arm in arm to keep her steady, into the chill night air. He hailed her a taxi home, where she assured him her flatmate would keep an eye on her.

The taxi disappeared into the steady stream of evening traffic. It was a damned foolish thing to do, Alexander reflected as he slowly made his way back to the North Wing and his own office, but Saffron's experiment seemed to have achieved her goal. The blue lines on Saffron's skin, the fact that she wasn't in a coma—they all pointed to the xolotl vine not being responsible for Mrs. Henry's poisoning. But he wasn't sure it would matter. If the police wouldn't believe the written account, he didn't see why they would believe the report of a woman who felt strongly enough about Dr. Maxwell to administer poison to herself to prove his innocence.

CHAPTER 8

Saffron wasn't aware of the time when she awoke. Her curtains were closed, and her body was senseless as to how long she had slept. She sat up, rubbing her stiff neck. She looked about for her notebook and jotted down her observations of her condition, sore and feeling rather like she'd been hollowed out. Looking over the notes from yesterday, written in Alexander's surprisingly messy hand, she realized for the first time just how hastily she'd made the decision to poison herself. But she wasn't sorry she'd done it. After all, she'd achieved her goal of proving xolotl wasn't responsible. But it wasn't well done of her to have conducted the experiment so haphazardly.

She pulled on her dressing gown and padded into the bathroom, where she ran a bath. The warm water soothed her twinging muscles. She stared at the bubbles, wondering if her lethargy was a result of the lasting side effects of xolotl or from sleeping through breakfast.

She was mindlessly gazing into the water when a voice in the hall caught her attention.

A man's voice.

She hastened from the water and, clutching her dressing gown around her, cracked the door open and peered into the hall. She just caught sight of a tall man passing through the door of the sitting room and heard Elizabeth's low voice. Had she slept so long that Elizabeth had returned home from work?

The tiny bathroom window revealed it was dusk, the dove gray sky leaning toward pink. She blinked, shocked. She truly had slept an entire day. She would have to add that to her notes.

She tiptoed down the hall to her room, luckily on the opposite end from the sitting room. Unfortunately, that meant that her ability to hear any conversation was nil. She quickly dressed in a simple dress and pulled a jumper on, not even considering powder or hairpins. She braided her damp hair into a long tail. Hoping she could creep past the sitting room and avoid Elizabeth's visitor, she opened her door silently and tiptoed down the hallway.

Quiet voices floated down the hall. Elizabeth sounded worried. ". . . but perhaps I ought to see if she's all right . . ."

Her guest didn't respond, so Saffron was surprised when footsteps approached her with such speed that she couldn't retreat. Elizabeth turned the corner, her usually healthy complexion lessened by a pallor Saffron recognized in an instant was caused by concern.

Elizabeth's eyes opened wide as she noticed Saffron lurking in the hall. She was dressed in a green housedress patterned with flowers, rather than the typical suits she wore to work, though her face was artfully made up as usual. Saffron dragged her into the small kitchen and closed the door.

Elizabeth began loudly making tea to cover her hushed words. "That would be your Mr. Ashton in the sitting room. He telephoned last night, you know, just after you walked in like a ghost and went to bed," she said, eying Saffron as she filled the kettle. "He explained, or rather barely explained, that you had accidentally eaten something while in his office and refused to tell me anything else about what it was or what I should be watching for. You are truly an idiot, darling." She slammed the kettle onto the stove. "What kind of scientist would eat something in the office of a man who studies bacteria?"

Saffron couldn't decide if she was flattered by Alexander's concern or annoyed that he had told her flatmate enough to worry her. "Why is he here now?"

"I told him I'd telephone him when you woke up so he could be sure nothing dreadful had happened. He was most insistent"—Elizabeth raised her thinly penciled eyebrows—"on coming to see you."

Saffron didn't meet her eye and instead loaded the tea tray with cups, plates, sugar, and milk. Elizabeth arranged some ginger biscuits on a tray. They made their way into the sitting room, where Alexander stood at the small window. He looked out of place in the feminine space, his charcoal-gray suit looking harsh against the creams and whites of the walls and furniture. He turned, expression solemn, as they walked in the room.

"Alexander, you didn't need to come all the way here," Saffron said.

"It was no trouble. I see that you're much better than yesterday." He glanced at Elizabeth, clearly not sure how much he should say in front of her.

Saffron wasn't sure how angry Elizabeth would get if they said much else, and she didn't feel up to being shouted at. "Yes, luckily. Would you like some tea?"

They sipped their tea and worked through stilted conversation for ten minutes. The topic of Saffron's unusual habit of not putting milk into her tea lasted awhile, then about Alexander's departure to Brazil in a few weeks. Elizabeth was mostly interested in hearing about the nonscientific parts of the journey, which Alexander admitted he knew little about at present.

"But surely you'll get to see Rio de Janeiro or São Paulo?" she asked.

Alexander replaced his teacup on its saucer and said, "We'll be meeting to discuss the particulars next week, but I don't think so."

After a long pause, Saffron said to Alexander, "I forgot what time I left your office yesterday. Did you happen to notice?"

"It was just before seven," he said, glancing at Elizabeth again. "Right."

An awkward silence fell. In the absence of conversation, she realized that Elizabeth was waiting for Alexander to leave, and Alexander must be waiting for Elizabeth to leave. Saffron shot a meaningful look at Elizabeth, who gave her a hard look, then rolled her eyes as she stood with the tea tray.

"Won't be a moment, I'll just make a spot more." She left the room, hips swaying in her usual exaggerated way.

Alexander broke into speech the moment she cleared the door. "I don't mean to intrude."

"It's quite all right, I appreciate you checking in on me." After a deep breath, she continued, "I appreciate all you did for me yesterday. I know it was not the safest way to go about it, but I still think it brought valuable information to my, er, investigation."

He stood, a frown creasing his brow. "Investigation? Saffron, if anything had gone wrong yesterday, you could still be paralyzed. Worse, you could have died. The information in that journal could have been completely wrong. You won't do yourself or Dr. Maxwell any good—"

Though she knew he was absolutely right, Saffron stood too, crossing her arms over her chest. "I'm not trying to do myself any good. If I was, I wouldn't have poisoned myself!"

"What?" Elizabeth was frozen in the doorway, her face a mask of shock.

Saffron put her hand to her temple. Now she had done it. She sank back into her seat and braced herself.

Elizabeth stomped into the room and slammed the tea tray on the table. Hands on her hips and color already high, she stalked toward Saffron. "Saffron Everleigh, have you lost your senses? You let me think this was an accident! *You* poisoned yourself? Intentionally? On purpose! By your own hand!" She was ramping up into a full blown, one-sided row, her voice climbing to a shriek. "You know they have people to help people like you, darling—psychiatrists! Find a Freud man next time! Honestly, I sometimes wonder if you've spent too long in hot greenhouses." Elizabeth rounded on Alexander now, glaring at him. "What did you do? Egg her on? Did you need a test subject or something?"

Alexander looked at her stonily. "Of course not."

"Eliza!" Saffron snapped, shocked by her friend's rudeness. It was one thing to shout at her, another to yell at Alexander when all he'd done was help. She got to her feet and crossed to Elizabeth, her voice low, though it would be impossible for Alexander to miss her words. "He had nothing to do with it. Besides, if he had put me up to it, he hardly would have called you up to tell you that I was ill." Elizabeth's eyes narrowed. "I took the toxin that the police think Mrs. Henry was given at the party." Elizabeth gasped, but Saffron pressed on. "I was doing an experiment to see if it would cause the same side effects. I took a very small dose and wrote everything down so I could show the police. They think it was Dr. Maxwell, Eliza. I can't let him go to prison!"

Elizabeth scowled at her. "Do you really think that Dr. Maxwell would want you to put yourself at such risk for him? The man who has been like a father to you wants you lying on the floor, poisoned?" She took a few angry paces, then turned sharply back to Saffron, her anger and volume flaring again. "And what would have happened if you had given yourself even a bit too much? You could have gone into a coma yourself! Or died! What precautions did you have in place? Who did you tell before you took the stuff? And what about Mr. Ashton? You could have died right there, and then what would have happened to him?" Saffron bit her lip. She hadn't thought about that. "He would have a dead woman that he wouldn't be able to explain away to a doctor or police. He would have been arrested too." Elizabeth shook her head, one hand on her temple. "It was a stupid thing to do." With that, she left the room.

Saffron stood frozen, looking after Elizabeth as her words reverberated in her head. The full depth of her recklessness finally occurred to her. She'd thought it was enough to have the journal, but that felt like a paltry assurance of her safety now. She'd been paralyzed and *refused a doctor*. How could she have been so stupid? Tears welled and fell without her interference.

Behind her, the clink of china sounded as Alexander busied himself with tea. He pushed a hot cup into her hands without commenting.

Saffron patted her eyes dry with the sleeve of her jumper and took a sip of tea. She hesitated to look at Alexander. If he did look at her with censure, she would deserve it. She hadn't thought for a minute of the consequences for his tangential involvement in her experiment if something had gone wrong.

"I'm sorry." She cleared her throat. "Knowing what I did about the xolotl vine, I thought it would be all right. I was thinking only of my own ideas. It never occurred to me that it would have put you into a terrible position should I have needed a doctor or . . . or if something worse had happened."

Alexander nodded stiffly. "Let's not make it a habit." He stood up. "I should be going."

Saffron was caught off guard by this abrupt departure. "Please, I . . ." She swallowed the lump in her throat that wouldn't go away. "Dr. Maxwell has always been the only one at the university who supported me." Maxwell's face came into her mind, enraged as she cried to him about what Dr. Berking had done, the very events she'd described to Alexander a day ago. Shame washed over her again. Her voice broke. "I can't let him be blamed for something he didn't do."

"And if you had died in his office, after consuming the very plant you were trying to prove didn't harm Mrs. Henry, Dr. Maxwell would have been blamed. He'd have been even worse off." Saffron flinched at the cold words and the even colder look Alexander gave her. "I'm glad you're all right. I'll see myself out."

Elizabeth had very little sympathy for Saffron and her woes. She slammed around the kettle and frying pan early the next morning, awakening Saffron from fitful sleep.

Elizabeth, as was her wont, went to elaborate lengths to ignore Saffron, turning her whole body this way and that as Saffron walked around the kitchen, avoiding her face entirely. Saffron was used to this tactic, although her friend hadn't deployed it since the time Saffron had ruined a beautiful silk scarf Elizabeth had lent her six months ago. Elizabeth would forgive her. They had been friends far too long for this recent episode to end their friendship.

From there she progressed through glaring while frying eggs, muttering while eating them, and finally to huffing as they did the washing up. Elizabeth always cracked after huffing.

"Elizabeth," Saffron began after a particularly loud sigh, "look, I know I did a very stupid thing—"

To her amazement, Elizabeth let out a great sob, letting a soapy plate sink back into the dishwater and splashing water over their dressing gowns.

"Eliza, what on earth—!" Saffron set the dish she was drying down and swept her arms around Elizabeth.

"Y-you are so stupid, Saff!" she choked out, wiping her eyes. "You are! How could you poison yourself? Not after those dreadful berries you ate. You were sick for days. Your parents thought you were going to *die*!"

Saffron was overcome again with guilt. Of course Elizabeth would remember the time she'd eaten berries of one of her father's specimens as a young girl. She had indeed been sick for a week, and the doctor had been uncertain of her fate for the first day or two. Saffron barely remembered the incident, apart from resolving to avoid eating things off her father's plants in the future.

Saffron squeezed her friend's waist. "I'm sorry. You're absolutely right. It was terrifically idiotic."

"I just don't want to see anything happen to you. You're practically my sister. We've been through life and death together! How could I explain to your mother how I let it happen? Can you imagine how I felt when Mr. Ashton called?"

Saffron sighed and rested her forehead against Elizabeth's heaving shoulder. What would her mother have said when she heard her only child had died of a self-administered poison? After the ordeal of her father's death, Saffron didn't know if her mother could handle another. Losing her husband had nearly killed her. The thought filled her own eyes with tears. "I really am terribly sorry, Eliza."

Elizabeth wiped her tears forcefully away, wriggling out of Saffron's embrace.

"I'm feeling much better, pretty much back to normal really," Saffron said with a watery smile.

"Lovely." After a long interval of sulky glances at Saffron, the table, and the stove, she said, "What did *Alexander* say when I stormed out? Did I scare him off?"

Saffron made a face at her and sat down to the table. "No, I think I did that myself. I apologized, then he just left."

"Skittish, is he?" Elizabeth brought the kettle to the table. Her tone turned businesslike. "Dear, have you had any sort of conversation with him? Set anything up yet? Stepping out?"

"Certainly not! I've known him a week, Elizabeth."
Granted, he'd examined her bare arms and legs at length yesterday, but she certainly wasn't going to tell Elizabeth that. She
might faint from excitement. Excitement over nothing more
than a passing interest. It would be hard *not* to be interested in
Alexander Ashton. His intelligence and academic accomplish-
ments were attractive, yes, but he'd been kind. He hadn't shied
away from her when she'd described Dr. Berking's actions, but
in fact had defended her on more than one occasion. And, apart
from his reaction to the obvious misstep in her planning with
the xolotl experiment, he seemed to be a level-headed sort of
man. That his dark eyes were rather captivating was an added
bonus.

Elizabeth gave her an arch look.

Saffron slumped back in her chair, stabbing a spoon into the
bowl of sugar with a sigh. "Even if I did want to know him better, what would be the point? He's off to explore a jungle in a
few weeks."

"Oh, you have a problem with a strapping young man fighting through the jungle while pining for you?" Elizabeth's hazel
eyes gleamed.

Saffron shook her head at her friend. Of course her anger
had dissolved at the mention of a potential romance. "Don't you
think six months is rather a long time to string along a man
you've known for a few weeks? What if he meets someone and
cables me, 'Never mind about all that. I've found a beautiful
Amazonian to fall over.' I would be quite crushed."

"Bosh," Elizabeth said with a snort. She poured the tea.
"You would cry your heart out for a day and feel better the next.
That's precisely what you did after that nonsense with Archie
Davis last year. Saff, you work at a university. It's practically
crawling with men who'd love to listen to you discuss the intri-
cacies of pollination in tropical environs!"

Saffron couldn't manage a laugh. All scientists were not created equally as romantic interests, as she'd discovered thanks to Archie. She'd thought she might have found a partner in more than just the romantic sense when the zoologist had done his very best to sweep her off her feet. That impression was short-lived. She could still hear his nasally voice encouraging her to "recant on this university business" and "take up her proper place with her family," preferably with him in tow.

Alexander, though he was older and better qualified, had shown respect and even deference for her expertise in the short hours they'd worked together. Even when she'd acted a fool, blabbering about rain of all things, he'd taken it in stride. He'd reminded her of Wesley, who'd listened patiently to her describe every flower and leaf as a girl. But now she'd made what was likely to be too big of a mistake for Alexander to overlook.

Looking down at her cup of tea, Saffron sighed heavily. "I might have completely ruined it. It might not matter whether I like Alexander or not."

Elizabeth looked at her friend thoughtfully. "Darling, if you had heard him on the telephone or seen his face when he walked into the flat, you wouldn't be so worried."

CHAPTER 9

Saffron decided not to go to the university that morning, not because she didn't feel fully recovered yet, but because she was sure she'd go to pieces again on seeing Dr. Maxwell's ransacked office. Avoiding Alexander was another benefit.

While the radio cranked out ballads and important-sounding voices recited important-sounding news, Saffron sat at the desk in the sitting room and wrote letters to her mother, grandmother, and cousin John. Her mother heard all about the dramatic poisoning at the party and Saffron's speaking to the police. Her grandmother heard all about the party, the importance of which was exaggerated for her grandmother's benefit. Neither of her grandparents were the least concerned about her work, apart from disapproving that she was working. Their relationship was, at times, precarious, communications having only just reopened in the last year, when Saffron graduated. They would perhaps be gratified to hear she'd dined with the Leisters. To her cousin John, whom she'd always been close to, as she had no siblings, she wrote about it all: the party, the police, the poisoning—though not the self-administered kind—and Alexander Ashton. John would appreciate her showing an interest in something other than plants for once.

A knock on the door right after lunch interrupted her just as she was affixing postage to the envelopes.

Saffron peered through the viewer. Her stomach twisted at the sight of Detective Inspector Green.

She let the inspector and Sergeant Simpson inside. They declined the tea and stood awkwardly in the sitting room until Saffron requested they make themselves comfortable. Watery afternoon light illuminated the space filled with books and magazines, all neatly in place after Elizabeth's most recent cleaning. Inspector Green, sitting in an armchair, looked just as bland as she remembered, with his plain, dark brown suit and his unremarkable brown hair and eyes. The sergeant took up his usual position by the door, his rosy cheeks and fair hair almost comical beneath his domed helmet.

Saffron settled onto the couch opposite the inspector. She attempted to leave her unease out of her voice as she said, "How can I help you, Inspector?"

"I'm sorry to bother you when you're feeling unwell, Miss Everleigh," the inspector began, "but I had an interesting conversation this morning that I wanted to hear your opinion on. One of my sergeants came to me with news that Dr. Maxwell's niece came to see him, and they had discussed, among other things, a bird with a foreign-sounding name." His eyebrows lifted slightly. Saffron's heart began to pound, but she arranged her face to look politely interested. "This niece was described as young, dark haired, and slim. Dressed in blue. I believe you wore a blue dress when I saw you at the university yesterday morning."

"It is a common enough color, Inspector. I would think your wife owns several blue dresses herself." Saffron held his gaze while waiting for him to pass judgment. She was quite sure she'd done nothing illegal, even if definitely dishonest.

After a long time, Inspector Green frowned and said, "I believe you took up the guise of a concerned niece. Seems to me that either you are trying to cover up your crime or assist someone in the completion of the business."

Her eyes opened wide. "The completion of the business? Would that be finishing off the Henrys?"

The inspector shrugged. "As you say."

She glared at him. Finishing off a woman she hadn't even spoken to! "Inspector Green, I don't know Mrs. Henry. I don't work with Dr. Henry or know either of them personally. What motive would I have to harm his wife?"

"That is what I am trying to discover."

Saffron opened her mouth and then closed it. She thought furiously, but nothing helpful came to mind. He'd hardly believe she was trying to discover the truth. She could give him the xolotl notes now, but the tone of the conversation was distinctly hostile, and she didn't think it would be at all well received. Her suspicion was confirmed a moment later when the inspector spoke again.

"I'm given to understand that Dr. Henry has a fondness for young ladies." The inspector stood from the armchair and walked a few paces, his steps muffled on the cream-colored carpet. From the mantle, he said, "Perhaps he caught your eye, and Mrs. Henry was in the way."

Saffron nearly laughed but caught herself. No man, however handsome or charming, was worth that much trouble. Dr. Henry, a renowned flirt and philanderer, would be at the bottom of Saffron's list, right next to Dr. Berking and his like.

"I can see you're amused by my theory. Let me try another one." The inspector's eyes bore into hers. "A research assistant, hard-working and intelligent, goes to work in a department where her value is boiled down to her good looks, and her acceptance is predicated on her father's reputation." Saffron bridled at those words but kept her mouth shut. "A professor takes her under his wing, a man she grew up knowing and admiring, and gives her opportunities that others won't. Another professor, a bit of a brute, puts her down and harasses her. Rumors are spread, the kind that would end her young career." Saffron's stomach lurched. The inspector's voice droned on smoothly, weaving his sordid tale. "The assistant goes to her champion. The professor has just been dealt a blow to his ego—he isn't to go on the impending international expedition, the opportunity he needed to make his research relevant again. They are angry. They hatch a plan to eliminate both offending men in one blow, using a toxin they have on hand that is unidentifiable to anyone but them."

In the silence that followed, Saffron struggled to analyze the theory as justly as she could, having just been accused of plotting murders. "That's very good, Inspector, right up until the end. Am I correct in assuming that you're suggesting Dr. Maxwell and I attempted to poison Dr. Henry?"

"Are you refuting it?"

Saffron's brow pinched together at the careful tone. Her eyes wandered to the stack of letters on the desk. What would Inspector Green do if she telephoned her mother or grandfather and asked for them to send one of their solicitors? Her grandfather would likely make it impossible for her to stay in London, as he'd threatened to do countless times. This time, when faced with his granddaughter being accused of attempted murder, he would almost certainly follow through. She'd better find a way out of this herself.

She drew herself up and said calmly, "I don't think I need to, but I shall now. A simple evaluation of facts will prove your theory incorrect."

Simpson shifted behind her, and Inspector Green lifted an eyebrow. "Indeed?"

Saffron saw the same idle doubt on the inspector's face as she'd contended with a hundred times. She could handle it again. "When did I place poison in the glass? I was far across the table from both of the Henrys during dinner. During the first go-round of champagne glasses, I was in the hall with Mr. Ashton, accidentally overhearing the conversation between Mrs. Henry and Lady Agatha, which I reported to you. I had no opportunity to touch either of their glasses, as when we returned the toast was already being made. Later, I came to say goodnight to the Leisters after they had already poured their champagne and the glasses were in their hands, apart from Mrs. Henry, who was handed her glass as I attempted to speak to Lady Agatha. Others can vouch for my being far from Mrs. Henry and the champagne. Dr. Maxwell was nowhere near Mrs. Henry for the entire evening either, nor did he interact with Dr. Henry, to my knowledge. Furthermore, I have never been in Dr. Henry's office or his home. I daresay you and your colleagues have taken up using fingerprints. I'm happy to provide you a set of mine, and you may check it against those found on Mrs. Henry's glass. Finally, I fail to see how the professor who you say harassed me plays into it at all."

Inspector Green sidestepped her. "You claim that you were in the hallway with Mr. Ashton while the first round of champagne glasses were passed around."

"Mr. Ashton can confirm it," Saffron replied confidently.

"The trouble is, Miss Everleigh, that your relationship with Mr. Ashton is such that he could say whatever suited the situation to ensure your alibi."

"My relationship with him? We're colleagues. We work in the same building."

"You were seen with him at the party."

"We were *introduced* at the party. And as I've said, we're colleagues. It is natural to converse with one's coworkers," Saffron said, working hard to conceal the anger she felt. Gossip seemed to follow her everywhere she went!

The inspector cocked an eyebrow. "In a dark hallway, for example? Seems an odd place to converse with a man you met that evening. You must have become very fast friends, to have been seen around campus and each other's offices so often."

From behind her, Simpson made a noise like a stifled laugh. Inspector Green shot a quelling look over her shoulder.

Saffron tried to restrain her indignation, her hands clutching together in her lap. "As I said, we work together. We just began collaborating on the work for the expedition. Mr. Ashton is my department's representative, as botany sits under biology. Dr. Maxwell's tasks for the expedition have been assigned to Mr. Ashton, and they require preparation, research. As you have detained Dr. Maxwell," she added with a glare, "I have to do more to assist Mr. Ashton."

"As you say," Inspector Green demurred.

Unsatisfied, Saffron continued. "I still fail to see the relevance of my unfortunate experience with the professor."

Without blinking, Inspector Green said, "Dr. Maxwell threatened Dr. Berking when he heard of Dr. Berking's behavior toward you on the sixteenth of March."

Shock rolled through her, followed by a warm glow of gratitude. Saffron doubted Dr. Maxwell would seriously threaten anything apart from an insect eating his exotic specimens, but that he would pit himself against Berking on her behalf was enough to make her willing to drink down xolotl for him all over again.

"According to who?" she asked, determined to bolster Maxwell's defense. "Dr. Berking? He can hardly be trusted to report accurately."

"That may be true, but we have alternate sources to confirm it," said the inspector as he stood. "I must ask you to stay in London for the duration of the investigation. Thank you for your time, Miss Everleigh."

Closing the door after the policemen, her anxiety rose. Why did the inspector think her capable of murder? What did he know about her—or rather, what had people said about her?

It seemed as if she'd only managed to get herself in more trouble. Now, it looked like she was under just as much suspicion as Dr. Maxwell.

CHAPTER 10

A lexander arrived at the office determined to cross a few things off his to-do list. Staying busy would keep his mind where it belonged—on the expedition and ensuring he was ready for it.

The prospect of the expedition left Alexander feeling restless, as if he needed to immediately be in motion. Six months in the jungle would break up the monotony of lab work nicely. His last expedition had been more than a year ago. It was time for another. He'd managed to convince himself—or rather, his mother had convinced him—that staying in London was a sound decision. The guilt of her worry and heartbreak over him, during and after his service, meant he found it next to impossible to deny her. In the end, he was relieved that he'd been asked to step in. He enjoyed the single-mindedness of an expedition; one was there to do the job, and that's all there was to it.

First among his tasks was ordering equipment. Dr. Henry's assistant, Snyder, had provided him with instructions for gear and the dates of the voyages and a rough itinerary, being sure to point out on multiple occasions that it was likely to be dangerous and uncomfortable. Between his previous travels and his experience in the army, Alexander was used to both, so he didn't find Snyder's wide-eyed warnings disconcerting.

Alexander spent an hour going over the study designs from various professors and jotting down notes on what he'd need to order. He followed this up by going to each professor and double-checking everything before turning in the equipment forms to Richard Blake's office.

Of course, all this took longer than it should have because Saffron Everleigh and her determination to save Dr. Maxwell would not leave his mind. Even though she'd seemed fine yesterday, apart from when her flatmate had thoroughly scolded her, the urge to make sure she was all right hovered in the periphery in his mind all morning.

Rather than climb the stone steps into the library as he'd planned, Alexander crossed the Quad, deciding it was time for a break. Clouds skittered across the sky as a stiff breeze swept through the city. Alexander cut through the Wilkins Building and down the street beyond, toward the greenhouses. He entered, not wanting to admit that he was curious about the vine that had caused so much trouble.

Distracted by the rush of color and humidity upon entering the glass structure, Alexander walked into an elderly man with dirty trouser knees leaving the greenhouse. A terracotta pot shattered on the ground, and the dark earth scattered, exposing white, spidery roots. Apologizing, Alexander knelt down and helped him scoop the dirt back up.

"And why are you bustin' into my greenhouse, mister?" the man growled. He was old and wrinkled, his red face weathered by years spent outdoors.

"I came in to take a look," Alexander said, a little taken aback by his tone and a lot taken aback by the filth layered under the man's fingernails. He must be the caretaker. "Miss Everleigh suggested examining some of the species found here."

Eyes narrowed, he asked, "You with University College?"

"Yes, sir, biology."

"Everleigh sent you, you said?"

Alexander nodded.

The caretaker studied him another moment before huffing and muttering, "Fine," before slouching off.

Alexander carefully picked up the little plant with his handkerchief. It was a vine, with heart-shaped leaves. He recognized the noxious shade of yellow. He examined it until the man returned, wondering which part was the most dangerous. He had barely been able to look at the xolotl leaves when he found Saffron in the office, and had quickly disposed of them without any observation.

The caretaker returned and knelt next to him with a muffled groan. He dropped the vine into the man's hands, which Alexander was grateful to see were now covered with gloves. With a brush and dustpan hanging from a nearby hook, Alexander swept up the rest of the spilled dirt.

The older man set the plant on the top of a worktable, then began shuffling things about beneath.

Eying the plant as he dumped the fallen dirt into a garden bed, Alexander said, "I've heard that plant is particularly poisonous."

"Hm!" the caretaker grunted again. He straightened with a groan and set another pot on the table. "The blasted police want a sample of it. Then they've gone and asked me all about it. Who can get at it, if anyone's been around askin' *questions* about it . . . not my job to know. I just have to keep 'em alive."

"Of course," agreed Alexander, suddenly wanting to know the answers to those questions, too. Summoning the appropriate manner for a chat, he added, "They can't expect you to keep up with what isn't your responsibility."

"Humph! Too right!" the caretaker said, huffing as he patted dirt into the pot. "Who bloody cares about those pointy, poisonous things? Plenty of nice green outside, things that actually flower or give fruit you can eat."

"Indeed. But still, this place is full of odd people with odd interests. I have a colleague who studies the insides of horses. He goes on and on about what different kinds of grass do to their digestion," Alexander said, feigning disgust. He didn't enjoy hearing about horse excrement, but it was a sound way to get information about their intestinal flora. "I'm sure you've seen all sorts of bizarre things in here."

The caretaker took the bait, giving Alexander a dark look. "Don't get me started! Between Maxwell and Berking and the lot bringin' back strange foreign cuttin's and tellin' me the dreadful things that happen to people who look at 'em funny, and random characters walkin' in askin' about this or that—enough to drive me to drink!"

The caretaker apparently didn't consider him a random character. "This one, for example." Alexander gestured to the little yellow vine in the caretaker's gloved hands. "I'm sure it's more trouble than it's worth."

"This thing . . ." The caretaker scoffed as he glared down at it. "Been very popular these days. Don't know why. It'd been growin' in the corner of Greenhouse Five for years, nobody payin' it no mind. Then the past few weeks everyone suddenly wants it."

That was very interesting. "Those botanists are mad for all plants, of course."

"Aye, they're an odd bunch, that. But they know not to mess about with it." Alexander opened his mouth to ask who exactly had been asking about the plant, then, but the caretaker snapped his gloves onto the table and growled. "Now, I have to give the blasted thing to the blasted police. Don't touch nothin' in there, young man, unless you want to get pricked or cut or poisoned." He made a long-suffering face and stumped off.

Mindful of the caretaker's words, Alexander moved deeper into the humid greenhouse. Giant sheaves of green swayed in the warm, moist air as he passed by. The xolotl vine had been a popular plant recently. That wasn't very helpful. Anyone could suggest a member of the botany department had sent them in, as Alexander had. It didn't seem like the caretaker kept track of the members of the botany department visiting.

He paused next to an array of massive leaves segmented by many holes. Why exactly was he cataloguing helpful information about the poisoning investigation?

Shaking his head at himself because he knew exactly why he was thinking about it, Alexander took out his lengthy list of specimens the botany department wanted from the Amazon. Because he was in the greenhouse, he could practice identifying plant features.

Alexander searched among the endless green for anything matching the insufficient descriptors until his head grew fuzzy and frustrated. How could he find these plants in the vast, chaotic jungle if a mere roomful of unorganized potted ones flustered him? He closed his eyes for a moment and took a deep breath. Then another. He forced himself to focus on nothing but taking deep pulls of the stifling, warm air.

"Alexander?"

He spun around, embarrassed to be caught deep breathing in the greenhouse. It was Saffron, looking timid in a lavender coat, with a matching hat covering her dark hair. She stood beneath a tree so tall it brushed the glass ceiling.

"Hello," he said, attempting to sound nonchalant. He was still a bit unsure of their nascent friendship, especially after so abruptly leaving her flat the previous day. Was he angry with her? Was she with him? He didn't feel angry on seeing her, not like he had when he'd had half a chance to consider the full short-sightedness of her experiment and his own foolishness in allowing it to move forward. "I was just practicing."

"Practicing breathing?" She smiled at him, still a little uncertain.

He held up his notebook. "No, identifying plants. Apparently I'm no good as a botanist."

She smiled more fully now and crossed the crowded, leafy room. "I happen to know a few things about plants. Perhaps I can help?"

"By all means," Alexander said. "But if you came to work—"

"Oh no," she said quickly. "I was going to speak with Mr. Winters, the caretaker. You haven't seen him, have you?"

"You just missed him." Alexander paused, wondering if it'd be churlish to keep back his whereabouts. "He was taking a sample of xolotl to the police."

Saffron's mouth formed an "O," her eyes widening to match.

"He mentioned that it's been rather popular recently," he found himself adding.

"I thought the same thing. I noticed that the plant had been trimmed, which suggests that someone had taken some of it. Other than me, of course." Her words rushed out, but the sudden glimmer of excitement faded as her face flushed. "But you had plants to examine, you said. What exactly did you need to find?"

Alexander accepted her subject change, even if he didn't understand it. She was clearly eager for more information for her so-called investigation. "I was just looking to see if I spotted any bipinnate leaves, as Dr. Miller has requested several specimens with such leaves. I'd like to be able to differentiate features easily."

Saffron nodded. "Well, there are some around. Which do you think meet the definition?"

Alexander examined some plants in the section nearest to where they stood, pointing out the ones he could clearly tell were palmate, as their leaves radiated from a central point. Once he reached a brilliant green fern, however, he looked back to Saffron. "These leaves have developed along a central structure . . . But the leaves don't seem to be individually attached to the stem. So . . . not pinnate?"

Saffron nodded with approval. "Yes, depending on the fern, it can be tricky." She scrutinized its long leaves. "*Polypodium chionolepis*, from Ecuador, I believe. One of Dr. Maxwell's. Do you see how the lobes don't quite touch the rachis? That's the word for the stem, since this is a frond. You're quite right. The word for this is 'pinnatifid.'"

Saffron enthusiastically took him through each unfamiliar term and showed him an example of each in the plants present. They zigzagged back and forth between the greenhouses, Saffron sketching little drawings of leaf shapes and diagrams of flowers in Alexander's notebook. Sweat dotted his brow, and both he and Saffron shed their jackets as they explored. Saffron insisted he find an example each time she taught him a new term, so the half hour he'd intended in the greenhouses stretched into an hour.

Alexander mused that his experience in Dr. Thomas Everleigh's class was poor preparation for class with his daughter. Though it was frustrating, and a little embarrassing, to be so thoroughly made aware of his ineptitude in botany, it was nice to know that it would only matter for a brief time and then perhaps never again. He could remember an extra fifty terms for a few months. He said as much to Saffron, who laughed.

"Oh, woe betide the man who improves his vocabulary!" Saffron's eyes gleamed in the fading light. "This is information you can use the rest of your life, Alexander. Wouldn't you like to know what sort of plants are growing around you? Their structures tell a story just as those of an animal or bacteria does."

They paused at a connecting door with a faded "Five" nearly obscured by a tangle of leaves and tiny purple flowers.

"Anything interesting in there?" Alexander asked.

Saffron's smile tightened. "Not really. Not much is planted in that greenhouse."

"The infamous xolotl doesn't rate?" Alexander gave her a sidelong glance.

"Well, I didn't . . ."

The way her eyes avoided his suggested she was either afraid of the plant now, or she was afraid he would treat her as he did yesterday. He doubted it was the plant, considering she'd not shied away from any plant she'd described as poisonous during their tour.

"I'd like to see it," Alexander said, offering an olive branch.

Saffron opened the door. The air was still heavy with moisture, but without the thick, floral scents of the other greenhouses. Here, it smelled more of dirt than anything else. A handful of sad-looking palms in decorative pots were clustered in one corner, as if the caretakers of other campus buildings had simply dumped unhappy plants there. The garden beds were dark with unused soil, and dirt and humidity clouded the glass panes of the walls and roof. Along the back wall, however, towered a lattice of yellow. That venomous color sprawled across the wall, reaching up to the ceiling. The leaves looked razor-sharp.

"What can you tell me about it?" Alexander asked, more out of curiosity than politeness.

Saffron spent a few minutes describing Dr. Maxwell's travels into the jungles of Lacandón in southern Mexico. When she mentioned the Mayan god of lightning, Alexander couldn't help but smile.

"Named for the blue lines, I suppose?" he asked.

Saffron frowned, her hand straying to her neck. "I would guess more for the sensation it causes. I've never been electrocuted, but the feeling . . ." She smiled slightly and shook her head. "Have you heard anything about Mrs. Henry's condition?"

"I haven't," Alexander replied. "I haven't seen the police around campus either."

Saffron gazed at the xolotl, biting her lip. "I suppose if you haven't heard anything, the expedition is to go forward after all."

"What do you mean?"

Saffron turned to walk back to the doorway into greenhouse four. "Without Dr. Henry. He certainly can't go to Brazil when his wife is lying in hospital. Even if she wasn't still in a coma, he must be one of the main suspects. Surely, Inspector Green wouldn't let him leave for six months!" She let out a gasp, stopping him with a hand on his arm. Her wide eyes met his. "But of course! This is the ideal opportunity to get away, isn't it? I'd bet you anything that the poisoner is a member of the expedition team. They frame Dr. Maxwell so the expedition is allowed to move forward, they lay low until the team arrives in Brazil, then they disappear."

"It would be a good way to disappear," Alexander said slowly, "but they've left rather a long time before the ship sails. Two weeks is a long time to linger with the police investigating."

Saffron tapped a finger on her chin. "The party was two weeks out, and there were so many people there. The poisoner likely hopes he'll be lost in the crowd of suspects. As we've seen with Dr. Maxwell, it would be very easy to frame someone else and then just wait it out before slipping away."

Unable to argue with Saffron's logic, Alexander merely nodded. She was probably right. He tried to ignore the sinking feeling in his stomach. After all, he would be traveling with team. But by then, no doubt this would all be over, and the poisoner would be on the way to prison. He was surprised he hadn't considered that sooner. But his mind had been on other things, like the woman next to him.

They made their way back to the steaming air of greenhouse one. The light had faded from the sky, leaving the air cooler but still heavy with moisture and scent. By the time they returned to the worktable by the door, Alexander had made up his mind.

"It's a bit late," Alexander said, glancing at his wristwatch as if the time was of interest. "I actually managed to get some work done today, so I was just going to go have some dinner. Would you like to join me?"

"For dinner? Yes, thank you."

He didn't miss the flush on her cheeks, nor the smile on her face.

CHAPTER 11

The cool evening air was bracing after the overwhelming warmth of the greenhouse. Saffron was glad she had kept her coat on rather than leaving it in the office when she had arrived earlier.

She'd gone to the university after Inspector Green's visit, not to work, but to get some answers. She had proof, at least proof enough for her, that the xolotl vine was not the cause of the poisoning. Her first task was to speak to Mr. Winters to get support in her theory that someone was using xolotl to frame Maxwell before going to Inspector Green, but had instead found Alexander. She hoped they could be friendly again. Working together meant they'd see each other every day. A good working relationship was important. And if something more came about . . . Well, Saffron wouldn't mind at all.

Dusk faded into evening as they walked, quiet but for the automobiles and buses trundling by and snatches of overheard conversations from open doorways and windows.

They settled into a casual place for students Saffron had visited a number of times. Alexander and Saffron ordered pasta, and the waiter inquired whether they wanted wine.

"None for me," Alexander said.

Saffron shook her head. "Nor me, thank you."

The waiter vanished. Remembering the party and the full glass of scotch Alexander had tried to get rid of, Saffron said lightly, "I thought all hearty explorers scoffed at temperance."

He shifted in his seat, eyes on his glass of water. "I avoid alcohol altogether whenever possible."

Saffron's mind jumped to her uncle, who had died after a night of heavy drinking when he returned from his deployment. Curiosity getting the better of her propriety, she asked, "After the War?"

His dark eyes stayed on his water glass. "People have different ways of coping with whatever burdens they came back with. Alcohol is common enough."

Saffron was glad he wasn't looking at her, as he surely would have seen the surprise on her face. She had never heard anyone speak about lingering effects apart from in very general and impersonal terms, not even her family when her uncle died. Most found it too embarrassing or too risky. It was difficult to maintain employment and relationships if people thought one was shell-shocked.

At once, she was terribly curious about the man across from her. What burdens had he borne, or might he still bear? It was clear he must have been injured, given the extensive scarring on his arm. Mindful of not wanting to come off as either pitying or nosy, she asked, "What would be your method of coping? If you don't mind me asking."

Alexander's lips lifted into an enigmatic smile. "A few years ago I learned how to meditate from a professor who studied in Tibet. He taught me a breathing technique I find effective. It's about controlling your breathing, your thoughts. Alcohol does the opposite."

His expression was neutral, and Saffron couldn't tell if he was serious. It all sounded rather outlandish. He began on another topic before she could confirm it.

The meal was spent in conversation about work. Saffron knew relatively little about bacteria, and when Alexander protested that it was not considered polite dinner conversation, she reminded him that he'd already brought up warty eruptions. The surprise of his full, deep laugh made her feel filled with electricity again.

Night had fully fallen when they departed the restaurant. The orange-tinted street lights illuminating white blossoms on trees created the impression of tangerine clouds hovering near the lampposts. As they walked in the direction of Hyde Park, their conversation returned to Mrs. Henry's poisoning.

"The problem is that Dr. Maxwell does seem to have a credible motive," Saffron explained. "According to Harry Snyder, he was very upset about not being allowed to go on the expedition."

"This expedition seems to be getting less and less popular the more I hear of it," Alexander said with a sigh.

"What do you mean?" Saffron asked.

"Dr. Henry was very . . . forthcoming, about some issues regarding the expedition. He tends to speak freely when imbibing, and at the party, he told me quite a bit about his debates with Dr. Berking about his inclusion on the team. Apparently, Henry has a problem when he's the victim of strong-arming rather than the perpetrator."

"Berking forced his way onto the team?" Saffron was surprised. If anything, she'd expect the head of the department to want to stay in the comfort of his office, where he could prop up his feet and terrorize his staff members. Or just her. But it was very glamorous to be on a scientific expedition, and would bring more prestige to Berking's reputation as a botanist, what with all the opportunities to discover new plants and especially determine their taxonomy. Getting the chance to discover a new species was all some people in the biology department thought about, it seemed. Regardless of his reasons, Saffron was glad Berking was going to Brazil.

"That's what Henry said. Richard Blake is going too, though I'm not sure why he'd want to, considering he and Henry have a dispute over the funding."

"Richard Blake? The funding coordinator?" Saffron asked, remembering his blandly handsome face.

"I overhead Berking talking about it the other day." They paused beneath a streetlamp, Alexander frowning. "I thought he'd been talking about Dr. Henry securing the rest of the funding for the expedition. He said something about the money being ill-gotten. That's the source of Henry and Blake's argument. Blake is supposed to contact the donors and solicit pledges, but apparently Henry went straight to Cedric Ermine himself. Blake mentioned, rather bitterly, that they had finally secured the last bit thanks to Dr. Henry's, er, ingenuity."

Saffron laughed at Alexander's serious tones. "I can't imagine a man like Dr. Henry having much ingenuity beyond building a jaguar trap using sticks and leaves."

"I got the impression it wasn't that sort of ingenuity," Alexander said.

Saffron thought again of Miss Ermine and her fawning over Dr. Henry. She could guess what he meant. She sighed, continuing on down the sidewalk. "I'm afraid I'm as confused as ever."

"The police will sort it out, no doubt. Once they figure out what poison it was, Dr. Maxwell will hopefully be in the clear."

It was still early when they reached her building, though their walk was quite a long one. Saffron invited Alexander up to continue their conversation about the function of color variegation. Or at least, that was the reason she gave. She wasn't going to waste a moment of Alexander Ashton being talkative and perhaps even a little flirtatious.

"Eliza!" Saffron couldn't help but smile too. "All right—you are very nearly correct. You did rather interrupt, though." Saffron was actually glad of her interruption. It didn't feel right to be so happy sitting on the couch with Alexander after discussing her father and Wesley. It had gotten easier, but that guilt was never far from her mind, even after five years.

"Shall I recall a sudden appointment?" Elizabeth offered.

"At eight in the evening? That might be a little obvious," Saffron replied with a sigh. "Come along, then."

Elizabeth followed Saffron back into the sitting room.

"So, how goes the preparation for your expedition, Alexander? Have you gotten your itinerary?" Elizabeth asked smoothly, busying her hands with preparing tea.

Alexander accepted a cup. "We're to sail on the seventh of next month, arriving the twenty-first."

Elizabeth continued peppering him with questions as they sipped their tea. Saffron was pleased Alexander didn't balk at her friend's polite interrogation, though he responded without embellishment to each question.

Finally, he said, "We'll land in Brazil at São Luís, but our base will be Macapá, at the mouth of the river. Several groups will go much farther up the river. Dr. Henry seems—or rather, seemed—very sure most of our time would be spent camping out along the river."

Elizabeth asked, "Do you think Dr. Henry did it? Poisoned his wife?"

Unperturbed by the shift in conversation, Alexander said, "More likely him than Dr. Maxwell, no doubt."

Elizabeth nodded as though this was the correct answer, her penciled brows arched.

Caught by a sudden thought, Saffron set down her teacup and said, "But Dr. Henry would be more likely to go at her in a rage, don't you think? Plus, he was completely drunk by the

Saffron stepped in first to see if Elizabeth was home, and she wasn't. She flicked the radiator and the lamps on in the sitting room, checking for any stray embarrassing articles, and invited Alexander in.

They sat in the sitting room for a while, Saffron chattering about the various examples of variegation and whether they were of benefit to the plants. Alexander's theories become more and more outlandish, concluding that the cause for the darker green lines on the swordlike sansevieria plant in the corner of the sitting room was because there was a draft in the room and it was alternating too hot and too cold. Laughing, Saffron went to get a reference book with more information on the sansevieria, which was more of an excuse to powder her nose.

When she returned, she found Alexander examining the photographs on the mantle. Perched in a small silver frame was a photograph of Saffron and her parents. In the photograph, Saffron had been fifteen, a gangly girl with big eyes. Her mother had a smile very similar to Saffron's, though in the black and white photograph it wasn't clear that Saffron shared her coloring with her father. Thomas Everleigh stood proudly with his family, bright eyes framed by glasses and his graying brown hair smoothed back.

Next to Saffron's family portrait was Elizabeth's family, a group of light-haired, tall people. The Hale family all looked as strong and robust as their name suggested, like they'd spent their days hiking through the hills and fields of Bedford, where Elizabeth and Saffron grew up. Elizabeth sat in the middle of her mother and father, and two older brothers stood behind, both wearing uniforms. The oldest looked steadily into the camera. The younger brother glowed with pride. The familiar pang of heartache touched Saffron when she looked into Wesley's eyes.

"Elizabeth's family?" Alexander asked.

"Yes. This was just before her brothers were sent out." Saffron indicated the older brother. "Nicholas is still in the military, off doing something important, Elizabeth says. But Wesley died at Flanders."

Alexander's eyes lingered on the brothers for a long moment, a strange expression on his face. "You and Elizabeth grew up together?"

She nodded and turned to the couch, where she sat with the book in her lap.

"You must have known her brothers quite well," Alexander said, sitting down next to her.

"Yes, our families spent a lot of time together," Saffron replied. "Wesley was just two years older than Elizabeth and me. Usually he was chasing me around or throwing things at me. Just before he left, we became quite close."

"It must have been a shock to hear of his passing."

"It was soon after my father died. It was a hard year." Saffron busied herself with the book in her lap. Pages slipped past without her taking them in; she was too focused on the sting of grief and the contrasting guilt and appreciation of Alexander's warmth at her side.

They sat together in silence for some time. Saffron continued thumbing through the pages. "I was home for the Easter holiday when we heard. My father was stationed at Ypres. He was among the first attacked with mustard gas."

Glancing up, she saw Alexander's eyes had widened in understanding. He swallowed hard. "I'm sorry."

"Thank you. It was quick, at least." She remembered the strangeness of that sentiment, so often repeated, that it was better her father had died right away rather than linger with some of the horrifying effects that only became apparent months later. Her eyes seemed to drift to Alexander's scarred arm of their own accord. "Where were you stationed?"

"In France, Fromelles."

She nodded. She didn't know what to say. Coming of ag during the Great War and immediately after, the false hope an positivity that came with the end of the War left a bitter taste i her mouth. There was nothing hopeful about her father bein gone or her first love dying.

Alexander reached for the book. "We don't have to tal about it. It was all anyone talked about for years. It's probabl time to find something else to discuss." He turned to a ran dom page. "For example, this terrifying creation." He pointe to a flowering *Dracula simia*, whose jeering face peeked out omi nously from within its pointed petals.

The click of the lock and the squeak of the door, followed b a long-suffering sigh, announced Elizabeth's arrival. Her voice carried through the flat, complaining that the lord requested he to work on Saturday to prepare for a special event. She turne into the sitting room and stopped with a delighted smile whe she noticed Saffron sitting with Alexander on the couch, obvi ously not spotting the open book in their laps.

In a dramatic swirl of magenta and with a brief, "Oh, beg pardon!" Elizabeth noisily retreated to the kitchen.

"You'll have to excuse me a moment," Saffron told Alexander with a grimace.

In the kitchen, Saffron found Elizabeth fighting a smile as she filled the kettle.

"Saff, you bad girl, you haven't offered your guest a refresh ment! You must have been distracted by something to so neglect your hostess duties," she scolded.

"I know what you're thinking, Elizabeth," Saffron said in a dignified voice, "but you're entirely wrong."

"I'm wrong to think that you've made up with your biologist and you were in here studying . . . biology?" Elizabeth didn't try to hide her grin.

time the poisoning happened. I should think that most murderers would want to keep their senses about them. It's hard to think on your feet and come up with alibis and all that if you're stewed."

Elizabeth nodded and said sagely, "I don't think it was Dr. Henry. I've seen his type many times, definitely not the sort for poison. I believe they say that poison is a woman's weapon. Any ladies on the scene who make good suspects?"

Saffron shook her head. "There weren't that many women there—mostly the wives of the professors and researchers. Lady Agatha wouldn't have poisoned her. What would be her motivation? They talked as if they were friends, anyway, when she suggested that Mrs. Henry try to reason with Dr. Henry about his dalliances. Unless Lady Agatha was secretly having an affair with Dr. Henry . . ." Saffron tried to imagine the muscular Dr. Henry sweeping the wispy, graying Lady Agatha off her feet and shook her head. "That is highly unlikely."

"I didn't see Dr. Henry speaking with any women." Alexander frowned. "Apart from the young woman, Miss . . .?" He looked to Saffron. "Dr. Henry followed her out onto the terrace."

"Miss Ermine?" Saffron recalled Lady Agatha mentioning something about a terrace. "Eris Ermine was very interested in Dr. Henry."

"*Eris* Ermine?" Elizabeth turned to Saffron with a scowl. "Saff, you didn't tell me Eris Ermine was at the party! Well!" She picked up her teacup again.

Alexander and Saffron exchanged a confused glance. Elizabeth huffed impatiently at their clueless expressions.

"Eris Ermine, the heiress of the Ermine fortune? They're nouveau riche, made their money in watches during the war. Their familial drama lined the pockets of the scandal sheet publishers for weeks a few years ago when Mrs. Ermine ran off with a foreign count or something. A bit cliché, of course, but the man apparently made it out of Bulgaria with heaps of jewels, and they now reside in Switzerland, of all places."

She finished her recital to their blank stares. Elizabeth shrugged. "Well, it might not have been quite so melodramatic. Scandal sheets aren't exactly known for getting all the facts right. The point is, when the wife ran off, Cedric Ermine threw himself into all kinds of charitable activities in an effort to pull his family's name from the gutter. Or just to distract himself. Eris was left to herself, more or less."

"How old was Eris when her mother left?" Saffron asked.

"I'm not sure, but part of the scandal was her coming out not too long after. She had no one but her father to take her around. As he was often too busy, he made a sordid deal with the Kentfields. Lord Tyrell—the earl, you know—he was in terrible debt because his son, James—" Her waving hand paused as she noticed she was losing her audience. "Anyway, Cedric Ermine essentially paid Lady Tyrell to take Eris around, and the gossips made a point of bringing it up whenever possible."

Saffron frowned. It would be too easy for a flashy man like Dr. Henry to charm a lonely young woman like Eris. The thought made Saffron's skin crawl.

"Perhaps Eris Ermine was going after Dr. Henry, Mrs. Henry caught wind, then Miss Ermine poisoned her?" Elizabeth suggested.

"I didn't see her in the room during the poisoning." She considered it for a moment before letting out a frustrated breath. "But we don't even know if the poison was in the champagne! It could have been mixed in with her food or something. Or she could have ingested it hours before, and the effect wasn't apparent until she fainted."

"The poison could easily not have been intended for her. Plenty of other motivations for getting rid of Dr. Henry," Alexander said.

Saffron stepped in first to see if Elizabeth was home, and she wasn't. She flicked the radiator and the lamps on in the sitting room, checking for any stray embarrassing articles, and invited Alexander in.

They sat in the sitting room for a while, Saffron chattering about the various examples of variegation and whether they were of benefit to the plants. Alexander's theories become more and more outlandish, concluding that the cause for the darker green lines on the swordlike sansevieria plant in the corner of the sitting room was because there was a draft in the room and it was alternating too hot and too cold. Laughing, Saffron went to get a reference book with more information on the sansevieria, which was more of an excuse to powder her nose.

When she returned, she found Alexander examining the photographs on the mantle. Perched in a small silver frame was a photograph of Saffron and her parents. In the photograph, Saffron had been fifteen, a gangly girl with big eyes. Her mother had a smile very similar to Saffron's, though in the black and white photograph it wasn't clear that Saffron shared her coloring with her father. Thomas Everleigh stood proudly with his family, bright eyes framed by glasses and his graying brown hair smoothed back.

Next to Saffron's family portrait was Elizabeth's family, a group of light-haired, tall people. The Hale family all looked as strong and robust as their name suggested, like they'd spent their days hiking through the hills and fields of Bedford, where Elizabeth and Saffron grew up. Elizabeth sat in the middle of her mother and father, and two older brothers stood behind, both wearing uniforms. The oldest looked steadily into the camera. The younger brother glowed with pride. The familiar pang of heartache touched Saffron when she looked into Wesley's eyes.

"Elizabeth's family?" Alexander asked.

"Yes. This was just before her brothers were sent out." Saffron indicated the older brother. "Nicholas is still in the military, off doing something important, Elizabeth says. But Wesley died at Flanders."

Alexander's eyes lingered on the brothers for a long moment, a strange expression on his face. "You and Elizabeth grew up together?"

She nodded and turned to the couch, where she sat with the book in her lap.

"You must have known her brothers quite well," Alexander said, sitting down next to her.

"Yes, our families spent a lot of time together," Saffron replied. "Wesley was just two years older than Elizabeth and me. Usually he was chasing me around or throwing things at me. Just before he left, we became quite close."

"It must have been a shock to hear of his passing."

"It was soon after my father died. It was a hard year." Saffron busied herself with the book in her lap. Pages slipped past without her taking them in; she was too focused on the sting of grief and the contrasting guilt and appreciation of Alexander's warmth at her side.

They sat together in silence for some time. Saffron continued thumbing through the pages. "I was home for the Easter holiday when we heard. My father was stationed at Ypres. He was among the first attacked with mustard gas."

Glancing up, she saw Alexander's eyes had widened in understanding. He swallowed hard. "I'm sorry."

"Thank you. It was quick, at least." She remembered the strangeness of that sentiment, so often repeated, that it was better her father had died right away rather than linger with some of the horrifying effects that only became apparent months later. Her eyes seemed to drift to Alexander's scarred arm of their own accord. "Where were you stationed?"

"In France, Fromelles."

She nodded. She didn't know what to say. Coming of age during the Great War and immediately after, the false hope and positivity that came with the end of the War left a bitter taste in her mouth. There was nothing hopeful about her father being gone or her first love dying.

Alexander reached for the book. "We don't have to talk about it. It was all anyone talked about for years. It's probably time to find something else to discuss." He turned to a random page. "For example, this terrifying creation." He pointed to a flowering *Dracula simia*, whose jeering face peeked out ominously from within its pointed petals.

The click of the lock and the squeak of the door, followed by a long-suffering sigh, announced Elizabeth's arrival. Her voiced carried through the flat, complaining that the lord requested her to work on Saturday to prepare for a special event. She turned into the sitting room and stopped with a delighted smile when she noticed Saffron sitting with Alexander on the couch, obviously not spotting the open book in their laps.

In a dramatic swirl of magenta and with a brief, "Oh, beg pardon!" Elizabeth noisily retreated to the kitchen.

"You'll have to excuse me a moment," Saffron told Alexander with a grimace.

In the kitchen, Saffron found Elizabeth fighting a smile as she filled the kettle.

"Saff, you bad girl, you haven't offered your guest a refreshment! You must have been distracted by something to so neglect your hostess duties," she scolded.

"I know what you're thinking, Elizabeth," Saffron said in a dignified voice, "but you're entirely wrong."

"I'm wrong to think that you've made up with your biologist and you were in here studying . . . biology?" Elizabeth didn't try to hide her grin.

"Eliza!" Saffron couldn't help but smile too. "All right—
you are very nearly correct. You did rather interrupt, though."
Saffron was actually glad of her interruption. It didn't feel right
to be so happy sitting on the couch with Alexander after discussing her father and Wesley. It had gotten easier, but that guilt was
never far from her mind, even after five years.

"Shall I recall a sudden appointment?" Elizabeth offered.

"At eight in the evening? That might be a little obvious,"
Saffron replied with a sigh. "Come along, then."

Elizabeth followed Saffron back into the sitting room.

"So, how goes the preparation for your expedition,
Alexander? Have you gotten your itinerary?" Elizabeth asked
smoothly, busying her hands with preparing tea.

Alexander accepted a cup. "We're to sail on the seventh of
next month, arriving the twenty-first."

Elizabeth continued peppering him with questions as they
sipped their tea. Saffron was pleased Alexander didn't balk at
her friend's polite interrogation, though he responded without
embellishment to each question.

Finally, he said, "We'll land in Brazil at São Luís, but our
base will be Macapá, at the mouth of the river. Several groups
will go much farther up the river. Dr. Henry seems—or rather,
seemed—very sure most of our time would be spent camping
out along the river."

Elizabeth asked, "Do you think Dr. Henry did it? Poisoned
his wife?"

Unperturbed by the shift in conversation, Alexander said,
"More likely him than Dr. Maxwell, no doubt."

Elizabeth nodded as though this was the correct answer, her
penciled brows arched.

Caught by a sudden thought, Saffron set down her teacup
and said, "But Dr. Henry would be more likely to go at her in
a rage, don't you think? Plus, he was completely drunk by the

time the poisoning happened. I should think that most murderers would want to keep their senses about them. It's hard to think on your feet and come up with alibis and all that if you're stewed."

Elizabeth nodded and said sagely, "I don't think it was Dr. Henry. I've seen his type many times, definitely not the sort for poison. I believe they say that poison is a woman's weapon. Any ladies on the scene who make good suspects?"

Saffron shook her head. "There weren't that many women there—mostly the wives of the professors and researchers. Lady Agatha wouldn't have poisoned her. What would be her motivation? They talked as if they were friends, anyway, when she suggested that Mrs. Henry try to reason with Dr. Henry about his dalliances. Unless Lady Agatha was secretly having an affair with Dr. Henry . . ." Saffron tried to imagine the muscular Dr. Henry sweeping the wispy, graying Lady Agatha off her feet and shook her head. "That is highly unlikely."

"I didn't see Dr. Henry speaking with any women." Alexander frowned. "Apart from the young woman, Miss . . .?" He looked to Saffron. "Dr. Henry followed her out onto the terrace."

"Miss Ermine?" Saffron recalled Lady Agatha mentioning something about a terrace. "Eris Ermine was very interested in Dr. Henry."

"*Eris* Ermine?" Elizabeth turned to Saffron with a scowl. "Saff, you didn't tell me Eris Ermine was at the party! Well!" She picked up her teacup again.

Alexander and Saffron exchanged a confused glance. Elizabeth huffed impatiently at their clueless expressions.

"Eris Ermine, the heiress of the Ermine fortune? They're nouveau riche, made their money in watches during the war. Their familial drama lined the pockets of the scandal sheet publishers for weeks a few years ago when Mrs. Ermine ran off with a foreign count or something. A bit cliché, of course, but the man apparently made it out of Bulgaria with heaps of jewels, and they now reside in Switzerland, of all places."

She finished her recital to their blank stares. Elizabeth shrugged. "Well, it might not have been quite so melodramatic. Scandal sheets aren't exactly known for getting all the facts right. The point is, when the wife ran off, Cedric Ermine threw himself into all kinds of charitable activities in an effort to pull his family's name from the gutter. Or just to distract himself. Eris was left to herself, more or less."

"How old was Eris when her mother left?" Saffron asked.

"I'm not sure, but part of the scandal was her coming out not too long after. She had no one but her father to take her around. As he was often too busy, he made a sordid deal with the Kentfields. Lord Tyrell—the earl, you know—he was in terrible debt because his son, James—" Her waving hand paused as she noticed she was losing her audience. "Anyway, Cedric Ermine essentially paid Lady Tyrell to take Eris around, and the gossips made a point of bringing it up whenever possible."

Saffron frowned. It would be too easy for a flashy man like Dr. Henry to charm a lonely young woman like Eris. The thought made Saffron's skin crawl.

"Perhaps Eris Ermine was going after Dr. Henry, Mrs. Henry caught wind, then Miss Ermine poisoned her?" Elizabeth suggested.

"I didn't see her in the room during the poisoning." She considered it for a moment before letting out a frustrated breath. "But we don't even know if the poison was in the champagne! It could have been mixed in with her food or something. Or she could have ingested it hours before, and the effect wasn't apparent until she fainted."

"The poison could easily not have been intended for her. Plenty of other motivations for getting rid of Dr. Henry," Alexander said.

Saffron poured herself more tea, a bitter smile on her lips. "My favorite thus far has been that Dr. Maxwell and I are in on a plot to get revenge on Dr. Henry for rejecting him from the expedition party and Dr. Berking for being . . . well." She didn't need to remind Alexander of her humiliating confession.

"You're a suspect, Saff?" Elizabeth gasped. Her hazel eyes widened with what Saffron suspected was excitement. "Who would think you'd try to kill anyone!"

"Remember, Maxwell and I have access to all sorts of poisonous things, including the xolotl vine," Saffron said. "And, according to 'a source' of the inspector's, the professor argued with Dr. Berking and threatened him in addition to Dr. Henry."

"Did he?" Elizabeth said with an approving smile.

"You and Dr. Maxwell are meant to have accidentally poisoned Mrs. Henry in an attempt to kill Dr. Henry? How does Berking play into it?" Alexander asked, frowning.

"Perhaps Maxwell was meant to poison Dr. Berking, and I was meant to poison Dr. Henry." Saffron sighed. "Or something like that. It appears we're his top suspects."

"He arrested Dr. Maxwell," Elizabeth said slowly, her spoon making idle circles in her tea, "but not you. Maybe he was trying to get you to admit something, rather than actually accusing you."

Saffron certainly hoped so. Though what further information she was supposed to have revealed was beyond her. She pursed her lips, looking down at the amber liquid in her cup. She really ought to have told the inspector about her experiment.

Later, when Saffron walked Alexander to the door of the flat on his way out, he asked, "Are you planning on sharing your experiment with Inspector Green?"

"I am," she replied with more confidence than she felt. Given the inspector's suspicions, she didn't think it was likely to go over well. Hopefully Mr. Winters had bolstered Maxwell's case.

"I'd like to come with you, if you don't mind," Alexander said. "I don't think he'll take too kindly to one of his suspects offering up evidence she created herself. I was there, I can corroborate."

A smile tugged on her lips, even if his words did make her a little anxious for the conversation with Inspector Green. "I'll feel much better about seeing the inspector with you along. Thank you for helping me. And Dr. Maxwell."

They paused before the front door. Alexander looked uncharacteristically uneasy. "Saffron, I know that you're determined to help Dr. Maxwell, but you need to consider that he might be guilty."

"You can't be serious," Saffron said, shocked. "I've already told you that he couldn't have done it. You watched me prove xolotl wasn't the poison."

"I am serious," he said quietly. "I don't want to believe him guilty any more than you do, but you must consider that he could have done it using another poison. Or that the police will find enough evidence to be convinced that it is him."

Saffron hoped for a hint of disbelief in his expression. There was none. "Why are you telling me this?"

"Henry told me what Dr. Maxwell said when they argued. Maxwell apparently told him that he'd regret not having someone versed in poisonous plants on the trip because Henry was too idiotic to see a poison when it was right before him."

Saffron's breath caught. "No!"

Alexander looked down at her with a grim expression. "It's incriminating, especially combined with a motive and convenient materials. I don't want you to get your hopes up that your experiment will be enough to save Dr. Maxwell."

CHAPTER 12

Outside the police station the next day, Saffron shifted from foot to foot. Peering down the street, she saw nothing more than mid-morning traffic. She fidgeted with her hair, in a different style today, parted in the middle, with curls tucked up to resemble a bob, rather than her usual waves and coiled bun. Although she dismissed it as silly, Elizabeth's suggestion to wear different lipstick and her hair in another style so as not to be recognized as Dr. Maxwell's "niece" wasn't a terrible idea. She didn't need Inspector Green being reminded she had been caught in a lie before.

Relief steadied her pulse as she saw Alexander, looking harassed, walking quickly down the street toward her. He muttered an apology and led her inside the police station. He spoke to the sergeant at the desk, a different man from last time, who didn't look twice at Saffron, and then they sat on the hard wooden bench and waited.

"Alexander," Saffron whispered, fingers twisting the fingertips of her gloves. "I should tell you, last time I was here, I pretended to be Dr. Maxwell's niece."

He nodded, expression unchanging. "I see."

"And Inspector Green thinks we are involved beyond what our working relationship requires," she added, cheeks heating.

Alexander frowned. "All right."

Saffron shot him a dubious look. "*All right?* I've just told you I lied to the police, and they think that we're . . . well, they think that you can't be trusted to be objective when I'm involved. We're about to give evidence to them!"

Alexander looked sideways at her, a smile tugging at the corner of his mouth. "We can't do anything about it now. Just don't bring it up. Plus, I see that you've adopted a disguise. No one will recognize you as the false niece."

They waited for ten minutes before Inspector Green marched through the doors with a small paper bag from which was emanating a scent of bread, asked the sergeant for updates, then turned with a frown to his guests in the visitors' chairs.

"Good morning, Inspector," Saffron said brightly, her nervousness dissipating at the amusing prospect of the inspector's breakfast. "Please, don't allow us to keep you. We are happy to wait."

"Thank you," he said curtly, and marched on into the din of shuffling bodies and paper.

They were shown into the inspector's office a few minutes later, where the warm scent of bread had disappeared into the musty miasma of the station. The small room was as neat as Alexander's office, though stuffed to the gills with files. They were organized with precision on his desk, and numerous filing cabinets covered the dark paneling on the walls. The paint had probably once been white, but now looked gray in the dim light from the frosted window behind the inspector's desk. When they sat in a pair of rickety chairs, Saffron looked expectantly at Alexander.

"Inspector Green," he began, "Miss Everleigh and I have some evidence regarding the poisoning of Mrs. Henry."

The inspector opened his notebook and poised his pen at the top of a page. "Go on."

Alexander took a deep breath and began. "Miss Everleigh and I had some thoughts regarding the suspected use of the xolotl plant. Dr. Maxwell was responsible for the plant originally, but since he returned from his travels with a cutting some years ago, it has lived in the greenhouses at the university, where nearly anyone could get some. I myself went into the greenhouses with no trouble the other day, although I'm not a member of the botany department. The caretaker mentioned that several people had recently shown an interest in the plant."

Here he paused, giving the inspector an opportunity to interrupt. He didn't, but merely looked back at Alexander.

Saffron's fingers were slippery within her gloves. Why did Inspector Green have to be so inexpressive? She had no idea what he was thinking.

"Miss Everleigh was distressed that Dr. Maxwell was arrested. She suggested we conduct an experiment to prove that the xolotl vine was not the plant used to poison Mrs. Henry." Alexander shifted uncomfortably, coming to the lie. "Using the guidance of an old journal Miss Everleigh discovered among Dr. Maxwell's things, we retrieved a sample of the plant, and Miss Everleigh took a small dose to see what the effects were. We recorded the experiment to the best of our abilities and brought the results to you."

Saffron passed Inspector Green her typed notes and the tattered notebook. He opened and scanned through the summary on the first page. As he read, his face was still impassive as ever, although toward the end his mouth thinned to a grim line.

"Well, Mr. Ashton," he said, leaning back in his chair and putting down his pen, "this certainly seems to point in the direction of the xolotl plant not being the culprit."

"That is what we believe," Alexander replied, matching the inspector's unaffected tone.

"You say that you agreed to carry out this experiment. I find it hard to believe that you would allow Miss Everleigh to take poison with your support."

Compared to the two men, Saffron felt ready to burst with all the tension. She jumped in. "Mr. Ashton offered to take it himself, of course. But it had to be me, the same approximate height and weight of Mrs. Henry, for the experiment to be as relevant as possible." She cursed her quick, nervous cadence.

"Even so, Miss Everleigh," the inspector said, turning his impassive eyes to her, "because of your own suspected involvement, you must see that I cannot take you at your word."

"Of course not, Inspector," she said. "You're not taking just my word. You're taking Mr. Ashton's, too, who witnessed the experiment."

"Indeed," he said, his voice utterly flat.

"I know it isn't my place to say, but there are a number of other people who attended the party who could have been the poisoner," Saffron said earnestly. "Dr. Henry, for one. Even Richard Blake could have been responsible."

It was surprisingly infuriating how unsurprisingly indifferent the inspector was. Her words dried up at his blank face.

"I hope that you will take our evidence into consideration." Alexander stood and shook the inspector's hand. Saffron shook his hand too, and they exited his office.

A dull gray cover of clouds darkened with every step, matching Saffron's downcast mood. In silence, they stepped onto the bus to the university, and the sky gave way to rain. Umbrellas swelled to life, and the streets slickened through the dirty bus windows.

On reaching the Euston Square stop, she and Alexander sheltered under an archway of one of the lodges that flanked the circle drive of the garden. Saffron leaned on the cool brick, looking out at the fresh green grass. Alexander, partially shadowed beneath the arch, faced the memorial obelisk. His hair, black with rainwater, curled on his forehead.

Saffron looked appreciatively at him for a moment before recalling herself to the matter at hand. "Now what?"

"Not sure," Alexander said, still gazing out onto the green. "I have a lot to do."

"I suppose I do too. Are you going to the North Wing?" she asked hopefully. Perhaps he was ready to continue their work from the other day.

"I have to confirm with Blake that he received my equipment orders."

"Oh, you're meeting Mr. Blake. Perhaps I'll come along and see what I can get out of him."

Alexander's brow creased in a frown. "You can't just go about interrogating people. What reason would you give for speaking with him?"

"Well aware, Ashton," she said sourly. "I don't think there's any harm in asking a few questions. I'll figure out something."

When the rain gentled, they made their way toward the tall columns of the Wilkins Building, where the administrative offices for the university had their home in the lower levels. Despite his objection, Alexander showed Saffron where Blake's office was, and they parted company outside his door.

Saffron returned to the lobby, to contemplate her strategy for questioning the funding coordinator. Alexander might not think she had any business asking Blake what he knew, but someone had to look at the other suspects if the police weren't doing it. Dr. Maxwell was still trapped in that awful room at the police station, and it didn't seem like her experiment was going to get him out. It was frustrating how right Alexander had been.

The administrative offices were more polished than the rest of the university buildings. White and black tile shone in the many overhead gilt lights, and there were elegant red chairs situated around matching rugs for esteemed visitors. Saffron claimed a seat near the window, noting that the chair looked far better than it felt. From her perch, Saffron watched a woman stomp through the center of the Quad and veer off toward the door on Saffron's left. A man scurried after her, clad in gray livery that was wet through, and holding up an umbrella, as if the woman wasn't equally wet and clearly furious.

Eris Ermine stomped into the lobby. The young man dashed after her, desperate in his dripping chauffeur cap and apologizing profusely. "The crack in the pavement caused me to trip and I—"

"Just go back to the car, Brigham. Leave the umbrella. I can't rely on you to hold the silly thing, apparently, so I'll just do it myself," Miss Ermine said. Brigham put the umbrella in the umbrella stand and walked away, tail between his legs. Miss Ermine looked furiously about her, her red hair damp and beginning to frizz beneath her wilted pink cloche.

"Miss Ermine!" Saffron called in a friendly voice. "How nice to see you again."

Saffron noted Miss Ermine's momentary slip of face before she realized who was addressing her. She saw for a moment an unsure young woman with wet hair before the ennui reassembled on her features.

Saffron smiled brightly at her. "Did you get caught in the rain too? I was just going to see what I could make of my hair. Maybe we can find the ladies' together."

"What? Oh . . ." She looked as if she were determining whether she should snub Saffron or actually go to fix her hair. Vanity won out. "Yes, I suppose, Miss . . .?"

"Everleigh, Saffron Everleigh. We met at the Leisters' dinner." Saffron showed her into the ladies' room. "I was just coming in for a meeting when the rain caught me off guard. Do you have a meeting too?" It was a clumsy attempt, but Miss Ermine didn't seem to notice.

"I'm meeting with a few of the Committee members, but they'll have to wait," Miss Ermine said. She immediately went to the mirror over the sink, where she removed her damp hat and patted her frizzing hair with annoyance.

"Have you heard anything about the condition of Mrs. Henry? I was so shocked by the whole affair, I've been thinking about it all week."

Miss Ermine shrugged. "No, I haven't. Lady Agatha called the next day to apologize for all the commotion, especially when I'm assisting my father during his illness." She sighed and pulled at a hairpin. "I suppose she's still in hospital."

"Have you been to visit her?" Saffron asked.

Miss Ermine let out an inelegant laugh. "Good Lord, no. Why would I go to see her?"

Saffron removed the pin attaching her own hat. "I thought that you were friends with the Henrys."

"Not *her*. Dr. Henry has long been a friend of my father's. My father has funded his last two expeditions. Lawrence visits him often with artifacts."

"You must know him quite well," Saffron said, taking on the attitude of a chatting girlfriend. She leaned closer and added in a gushing voice, "You're so lucky."

Miss Ermine smirked and opened a tube of lipstick, her hair repaired. "Yes, I know him *very* well. He's a fascinating man. So . . . experienced in the world. He's been all over." Her eyes grew wide with what Saffron imagined were lascivious thoughts as she swiped color over her lips.

Saffron affected a little giggle. "Oh my! I can't imagine the sorts of things he's seen and done! Does he have many fascinating stories?"

"You can't imagine!" Miss Ermine said, smacking her lips together. "He's shown me some incredible things."

Saffron wanted confirmation of what she was hinting at. "But isn't his tiresome wife rather annoyed with him sharing his *adventures* with you?"

Miss Ermine's tone turned venomous. "Given how *she* carries on, I'm surprised she cares at all. Although"—she pouted into the mirror—"she was in a terrible state at the party. She cornered me and prattled on and on. Terribly embarrassing for her. Lucky for her, no one was around to hear her pathetic braying." Miss Ermine touched a puff of powder onto her already white nose, and her eyes narrowed at her reflection. "Hypocritical bitch."

Now that was interesting. "Oh my, how dreadful! She was angry with you?"

"Oh yes, she was quite offended that I took an interest in her husband's work." Saffron rather thought it wasn't the interest in her husband's work Mrs. Henry objected to. "She's never complained about him spending time with dear old Daddy, who used to navigate the boat of cash. Now I'm in charge." She snapped her compact shut with a satisfied smile.

"Really! You're the one who made the Amazonian expedition possible, then?"

"Oh yes," Miss Ermine said, eyeing her reflection with pleasure. "Without me, it wouldn't be happening. Lawrence nearly fell over himself to get to me. I'm going to make all his plans possible."

Miss Ermine turned away from the mirror. As she opened the door to the lavatory, she said breezily, "See you later, Miss Eversby."

Saffron, not the least offended, was pleased at least one of her theories was confirmed. When she returned to the lobby, the sky beyond was once more heavy and dark. What excuse did she have to try to speak with Blake anyway? She could come up with one once she'd thought over Miss Ermine's comments.

Saffron climbed the stairs to the Flaxman Gallery and continued across the span of the Wilkins Building into the North Wing, jostled in the overcrowded halls by students avoiding the inclement weather. Saffron could believe that Miss Ermine and Mrs. Henry had argued. Did she believe that Mrs. Henry had confronted Miss Ermine out of jealousy? Or had Miss Ermine instigated the argument? It was highly doubtful that the younger woman was giving a complete impression of what had actually happened.

And what had Miss Ermine told Inspector Green? Saffron thought it probable that she wouldn't have been forthcoming about her relationship with Dr. Henry, nor the events of the party. After all, arguing with the victim before her collapse was suspicious.

Not for the first time, Saffron wished she knew more about the evidence Inspector Green had found. Was Miss Ermine even one of his suspects? Miss Ermine's likelihood of having access to a mysterious toxin was slim. Miss Ermine in combination with Dr. Henry, though—that was possible.

If Miss Ermine was to be believed, she could have been having an affair with Dr. Henry. That would resolve the problem of access to a poison and the issue of Dr. Henry not being the poisoning type. Saffron wondered just how much of her claims about her relationship with Dr. Henry were invented or exaggerated.

The storm finally thinned into a sad drizzle. Saffron stood behind Dr. Maxwell's desk, gazing through the window overlooking the Quad. She'd spent the last hour sketching out all the clues she knew of, every theory she'd come up with. Her head hurt. She was used to solving puzzles; indeed, it was the goal of every scientist to find answers and explanations. But with such insufficient information, there was only so much she could do.

She traced rain droplets on the window idly, allowing her mind to wander. Everything looked more alive and fresh after the rain. On the fringes of the concrete lay little sections of grass and garden. Red and purple tulips bowed toward the ground alongside the drooping yellow crowns of daffodils. Most botanists she knew sneered at the local, common flowers as being uninteresting. Saffron loved any flower she came across, just like her father had. They'd spent hours on long walks, quizzing each other on wildflowers. She remembered learning to cut roses with her mother; her parents weeding the garden bed together; laughing as her father teased her mother with a dirt-covered worm.

It was an unfair turn of fate that they had been taken away from each other before their time. They could have continued on so happily together. Not like Dr. Henry and his wife. Why should they remain together if they were so unhappy?

But she supposed they weren't really together anymore, anyway. Dr. Henry was cavorting with who knew how many women. It was very possible Mrs. Henry also had taken up a lover. Eris Ermine certainly had made it clear she believed that the wife was no more loyal than the husband.

In her mind's eye, Saffron saw the glittering dinner table, Mrs. Henry casting dark looks at her husband and Miss Ermine. And looking down the table, at Mr. Blake, with . . . interest. There had certainly been something between them, both at the dinner table and when Blake handed Mrs. Henry the champagne. Richard Blake was angry with Dr. Henry for stepping on his toes about the funding, and Mrs. Henry was embarrassed by his flaunting his relationships with other women. Was it possible that they were involved with each other?

Saffron straightened, her hand dropping to her side. Perhaps Richard Blake was Mrs. Henry's lover. He *had* given Mrs. Henry the glass of champagne that likely contained the poison. Maybe it wasn't meant for her. Maybe she was supposed to pass it on to Dr. Henry. Maybe his wife and her lover had botched an attempt to poison Dr. Henry and rid themselves of several problems at once. But something had gone wrong, and Mrs. Henry had drunk from the glass instead.

Body thrumming with the excitement of a new idea, she crossed to the door and made her way down the hall to Alexander's office. He knew Blake better, or at least had spoken to him. Maybe he'd have something to add.

After knocking, she opened the door at his invitation and announced, "All right, Ashton, new theory."

Alexander set down a magnifying glass on the botanical text laid out on his desk before him. "All right, Everleigh, let's hear it."

Saffron plopped into the chair across from him, eying the Marianne North illustration of *Victoria amazonica* with momentary interest.

He raised a brow. "You had a theory?"

"What if Richard Blake and Mrs. Henry plotted to get rid of Dr. Henry? She was embarrassed by his behavior with other women, even if she says she didn't care. Blake was angry that Dr. Henry had gone around him to get to the donors. They could have devised a plan to get rid of Dr. Henry—killing two birds with one stone."

Alexander narrowed his eyes. "Did you end up using your powers of persuasion to get a confession out of Blake?"

She laughed. "I didn't see him, actually. I did see Eris Ermine, however. She implied that Mrs. Henry was just as disloyal to their marriage vows as Dr. Henry. Dr. Henry had been spending a lot of time with Miss Ermine, since she's now in charge of her father's money while he's ill. I can guess exactly how Dr. Henry ensured his expedition would go forward."

"And she suggested that Blake and Mrs. Henry were having an affair?" Alexander looked doubtful.

"No, no, Dr. Henry is having an affair with *her*," Saffron said, leaning forward. "Or at least she would have me believe so. She obviously didn't come out and say that either of the Henrys were having an affair. But it fits with what you heard Berking say, that Henry got his funding in a scandalous way. Seducing Miss Ermine for money certainly would be scandalous."

"So, you think that Dr. Henry was the real target for the poisoning, and his wife and Richard Blake were trying to kill him? Why?"

"To get revenge and clear the way to be together, of course!"

"No, why do you think that's the case?"

"Oh." Saffron thought for a moment. Why had she jumped to this conclusion? "I suppose . . . well, I suppose my only reason was the meaningful looks they gave each other. Miss Ermine implied Mrs. Henry wasn't faithful. And Richard Blake gave Mrs. Henry the glass that probably had the poison in it. Maybe she didn't realize that was the glass she was meant to give her husband."

Alexander frowned. "That's rather sloppy. Wouldn't Blake have indicated to her that it was the poisoned glass, rather than allow her to drink it? He wouldn't have been able to watch her put it to her lips without a reaction. And if it was by accident, they must be terrible would-be murderers to choose a situation where they could poison the wrong person so easily."

"I suppose you're right." She sighed, slumping back in her chair.

"Probably more likely that Blake tried to kill her instead, since he poured her the glass. Did you actually see him or anyone else touch it before?"

"The inspector already knows that both he and Dr. Henry poured into the glass." Saffron stood and began pacing. She wasn't pleased that her theories were so easily discarded. Now that the idea that Mrs. Henry and Blake were lovers had taken root in her mind, it was impossible to ignore. But how to prove it?

Silence settled between them. Saffron looked up from her musing to find Alexander straightening the book atop his desk, a frown creasing his brow. "Oh, I'm sorry! Am I distracting you from your work?"

"No . . . There's just something about Richard Blake. Something about the papers on his desk when I was in his office. It's probably nothing."

"What seemed amiss?"

"He had his papers everywhere. He seemed to be looking for something; he was completely distracted from our conversation. I looked at the papers and saw what you'd expect—receipts, invoices, letters, order forms for the expedition. Quite a lot of forms were spread out."

"Did you see what they had ordered?" Saffron asked. She was curious what had Alexander so tense. Although given how he'd cleaned Dr. Maxwell's office during her experiment, and how he kept his own office, he clearly had a problem with clutter. Even now, he was prodding the book to make it perfectly parallel with the edge of the desk.

He shook his head, eyes unfocused. "No, I didn't. Dr. Berking had one or two orders, and Somerville from geology had several, Robinson, Straithway . . . Dr. Henry's name was all over the place. His signature is so large and messy, it's easy to identify."

"So, it was odd because . . .?"

"I don't know. I suppose it was odd because Dr. Henry had ordered so many things compared to the other professors, although I'm sure not all the forms were visible. Mine wasn't there, for one."

"Perhaps it was the usual materials, and they were all laid out, so it looked strange," Saffron suggested.

He stood and went to his bookshelf, straightening a book that wasn't out of place. "I suppose. But his research is about people. It doesn't require vast amounts of supplies—just crates and packing and cloth to collect artifacts, and he could get most of that in Brazil."

"He is the leader. Perhaps it's the materials for the whole team, tents and camp supplies and things."

Alexander shook his head. "He wouldn't be ordering that sort of thing himself. It wasn't his responsibility for past expeditions." He ran a hand through his hair, still curly from the rain, and said again, "It's probably nothing."

"Maybe," Saffron replied. She didn't have any experience ordering materials for an expedition and didn't particularly want to emphasize that inexperience further. She stood, walking to the door. "Well, I won't take more of your time. I'm afraid I've been quite a nuisance. See you later, Alexander."

Standing in the hall, Saffron decided she could no longer avoid her work. But when she settled down at her own desk, she found herself staring down at a pile of books and papers rather than doing anything productive with them. Her thoughts were scraping the bottom of the barrel, searching out new possibilities for Dr. Maxwell's defense. She'd just proved why she couldn't theorize based on insufficient information; Alexander had tossed out her ideas with barely any consideration.

She cast a glance over to Dr. Maxwell's vacant desk, far too empty of clutter and long-cold cups of tea. Perhaps by now the professor had heard more about the evidence against him and could give her more of an idea of what was left for her to disprove.

CHAPTER 13

The next morning, Saffron crossed the ugly tiled floor of the police station to the sergeant's desk with her chin held high despite her nerves.

"Back again?" asked the familiar sergeant, a twinkle in his eye.

There was no waiting this time, as Inspector Green himself had agreed to let her visit Dr. Maxwell when she'd telephoned the previous day. She was led immediately back through the catacombs of the station, which was a bit quieter in the early morning hours, to the same small room with table and chairs. Dr. Maxwell, looking disheveled, braced his hands on the table to stand.

"Professor!" she cried, rushing to him. "Are you all right?"

"Don't worry about me, my dear," he said, his voice hoarse. He attempted a smile under his mass of whiskers. His tired eyes had shadows under them, and his hands were shaking badly.

She rounded on the inspector, who had settled in a chair opposite the professor's. "Inspector, Dr. Maxwell doesn't look at all well! He needs to see a doctor."

"Saffron—" began Dr. Maxwell before erupting into a cough.

Inspector Green merely raised an eyebrow.

Saffron slammed her handbag onto the table. "Truly, Inspector, this is getting to be ridiculous! He clearly had no part in the poisoning, and now you're keeping him here without proper evidence, just hearsay from the guiltier parties—"

"Just a moment—" Dr. Maxwell tried to interrupt again, looking from her reddening face to Inspector Green.

Temper boiling over, she cried, "No, Professor! I proved that the xolotl vine wasn't what hurt Mrs. Henry, and that was their only reason to arrest you other than the ridiculous rumor that you threatened Dr. Henry!" Saffron faltered on seeing Maxwell's chagrined expression. "Oh no, Professor . . . you didn't actually threaten him, did you?"

He gave her a small, guilty smile and said, "I may have suggested something . . ."

"Do sit down, Miss Everleigh," the inspector said, gesturing to the chair in front of her.

She sat, her face radiantly hot. "I didn't believe it, sir, not even when Alexander told me—"

The professor looked at her sharply. "Alexander Ashton? You're not still hanging about with him, are you?"

Inspector Green cut in before she could ask him what he meant. "I agreed that you could see Dr. Maxwell today because he is no longer under arrest for the poisoning."

"Oh, but that's wonderful!" Saffron exclaimed, squeezing the professor's gnarled hand and smiling at him. Of the inspector, she asked, "What made you decide he was innocent? And why didn't you just tell me when I telephoned?"

"It is not information I want shared just yet. We need the poisoner to think that they're free and clear." Inspector Green leaned forward, bracing his arms on the scratched tabletop. "Can you think of anyone that might want to frame Dr. Maxwell? Anyone with a grudge against him, apart from his argument with Dr. Henry?"

Saffron didn't miss that he didn't answer her question about how he'd determined Maxwell wasn't responsible. She doubted he would admit that her experiment had something to do with it. She cleared her throat. "Well, no, except for Dr. Berking or Dr. Henry. Dr. Maxwell gets along with most people." She patted the professor's hand again.

The inspector nodded. "We know about those issues. If you will excuse me, I'll just make a telephone call."

When the door shut behind him, Saffron turned back to Maxwell. "Do you really think someone is framing you?"

"I can't be sure, but the inspector certainly seems to think so," he said. His brows dipped low over his glasses. "What is all this about you proving the xolotl vine wasn't the poison?"

She looked anywhere but into his eyes. She'd never had to lie to the professor before and wasn't sure she would be able to do it convincingly. Given how unwell he looked, she wasn't going to give him another shock by admitting she'd poisoned herself. "I was sure there must have been a journal or paper that was left out of the police's search, so Mrs. Maxwell and I searched through your study. And I was right. I found an old journal from your original voyage, and it had an account of xolotl poisoning. The symptoms were quite different from what Mrs. Henry experienced. She didn't have blue lines on her hands, for one thing." She smiled brightly, as if it would keep him from suspecting anything else.

Maxwell continued frowning, a hand drifting to his scruffy chin. "Now that you mention it, that does ring a bell . . ."

Relieved, Saffron patted his hand again, her smile turning genuine. "And you're to be released—that's wonderful news. I hated to see Mrs. Maxwell in such a state over you."

Maxwell cleared his throat. "Saffron, my dear, I really don't think you should be mixed up with Ashton."

Confused, Saffron asked, "Whyever not?"

"He's a good scientist. His recent work has been most impressive." Saffron waited for Dr. Maxwell to give her a good reason to avoid Alexander, but he looked unwilling to continue, eyes avoiding hers just as she avoided his. "He's done well at the university. But in the past . . . he may not have the most even temper."

Saffron nearly laughed. Alexander was the most even-tempered man she'd ever met, except perhaps Inspector Green. She'd endangered them both with her experiment, and he'd done nothing more than give her the telling-off she'd deserved and then *helped* her. In a gently chiding voice, she asked, "What about your temper, professor? Did you really tell Dr. Henry you would poison him?"

"Not in so many words, but I'm afraid that was the gist. I had just spoken with that"—Maxwell cleared his throat again, his face flushing beneath his white whiskers—"with Dr. Berking about your encounter, and I was rather hot under the collar, you see. Dr. Henry called me to see him, and I went, expecting to discuss arrangements for the expedition. Instead, he laughed at me. He said it was foolish to think he'd let an old man slow down his expedition." The professor's kind face darkened. "So I told him that if he wasn't careful, he'd find himself laid out in the jungle somewhere, choking on his own—"

"Right," Saffron interrupted. "But you were upset. Surely you didn't mean it!"

"No, no, I meant that, Saffron." He looked earnestly at her. "Dr. Henry is a foolish man, running around without consideration. For goodness' sake, he wants to make his own department just to satisfy his ego! The man pushes his way into any situation that pleases him. He has knowledge of the field, to be sure, but he tramples over people around the university all the time. I'm not surprised someone tried to remove him."

"And Dr. Berking?" Saffron asked.

Maxwell shook his head. "I'm afraid I lost my temper with him too. I suppose, Everleigh, when one gets to a certain age, one is no longer willing to put up with certain behaviors and attitudes."

Just then, the inspector opened the door, saying it was time for Dr. Maxwell to leave.

"What? Now?" Saffron asked.

"We're moving him to his other residence outside London. All done without anyone's knowledge, of course"—he looked at her significantly—"or else the poisoner might try something on the professor."

Saffron helped Maxwell to his feet. She kissed his fuzzy cheek and said a tearful goodbye, incredibly relieved he was no longer imprisoned and yet sad to see him go.

A huge weight had been lifted off Saffron's shoulders now Dr. Maxwell was safely away and out of trouble. She herself seemed no longer to be under suspicion either. Saffron wasn't satisfied, however. A puzzle was laid out before her, with only half the pieces revealed. She was confident that she could solve the rest of the mystery, no matter how many times she was told it wasn't her place to do so. The inspector must have taken her evidence to heart in order for Maxwell to be released, so he might listen to more evidence she could find.

After a restless weekend dissecting her clues with an increasingly uninterested Elizabeth, Saffron was ready with a plan come Monday. She was going to narrow down the list of suspects. She now had four: Dr. Henry, Richard Blake, Eris Ermine, and Dr. Berking. Saffron had added Berking to the list, telling herself it was because he was present during the champagne and had suspiciously forced his way into the expedition, and *not* because it gave her satisfaction to write it down on a list of possible murderers. She was trying to be as objective as possible, as any good scientist would.

Dr. Henry seemed the most likely person to try to kill his wife, so she decided to begin with him. Harry Snyder, sounding harassed on the telephone, replied that Dr. Henry was not in the office. Saffron decided that maybe Mr. Snyder needed a little distraction from whatever he was so worried about.

She carefully reapplied her lipstick and adjusted the front of her pale green dress in the lavatory mirror. With a firm nod to her reflection, she reminded herself that Harry Snyder was a far cry from Dr. Berking. Not all men were monsters.

The thought put her to mind of Maxwell's warning about Alexander. Picturing Alexander with a foul temper was difficult to do. But Maxwell had always been protective of her. Maybe this whole poisoning business was making it worse, especially since he had to go away.

Saffron put her jumble of theories aside as she mounted the steps of the history building and located Dr. Henry's office. It was the corner office on the top floor, a suite with an outer office for his assistant. Mr. Snyder looked flustered. He hurriedly detached himself from his messy desk and crossed to where she stood in the doorway. He smoothed his black hair back and blinked rapidly at her.

"Hello, Mr. Snyder," she said, smiling. "Do you have a moment?"

He hesitated before stepping back and allowing her inside.

"What a beautiful room," Saffron said, no simpering needed. The room was decorated with a lush Persian carpet in hues of burgundy and scarlet, and a massive table on which were placed a colorful selection of curios that looked like they were brought back from Dr. Henry's travels. Several large windows lit the room, with pearly gray skies beyond. It looked more like a study in a grand house, and this was only the outer part of the office.

Snyder smiled and replied, "Yes, Dr. Henry worked hard to get this space. He insisted." Saffron guessed Dr. Henry had bullied some old man out of this office and probably into retirement. "Miss Everleigh, I did tell you that the professor wasn't here, didn't I? He is still tending to his wife at the hospital."

Saffron wondered if Dr. Henry really was at the hospital. That seemed unlikely. She nodded anyway and said, "Oh yes, you did, Mr. Snyder. But I had such a curiosity about some of the things Dr. Henry had brought back from his journeys after speaking with Eris Ermine the other day . . ."

Snyder's face tightened with annoyance. "Ah yes," he said, "Miss Ermine often speaks to Dr. Henry at length about his travels. She was here just the other day to view his Mauryan coin from his Indian expedition."

So, Miss Ermine had recently spent time in Dr. Henry's office? Perhaps plotting during a tryst?

"How fascinating! I know Dr. Henry isn't here at the moment"—Saffron looked at Snyder through her lashes, and he stood up straighter—"but do you think you could . . . I mean, you must know exactly the same things as Dr. Henry, having traveled with him . . ."

Snyder's dark eyes followed the motion of her hand as she tucked a hair behind her ear. "Yes, yes, I've been with Dr. Henry for years. He's taken me on all his recent expeditions."

"I mean, people say all the time how brave Dr. Henry is," Saffron said, stepping closer to Snyder. "But they forget that, as his assistant, you've seen it all too."

That seemed to decide him. His chest puffed out, and he said, "Yes, of course. Allow me to show you. After all, I was actually . . ."

Saffron could hardly believe her luck as she walked into Dr. Henry's office. It was furnished in much the same tastefully expensive way as the outer room, except with more maps and globes littered with pins. She followed Snyder to Dr. Henry's desk, a monstrosity of polished mahogany, where he held up a little frame in which lay a small, unevenly cut square of silver.

She took it in her hands and gasped with false astonishment. "How amazing! Where did you say it was from? Perhaps you could show me?"

Snyder looked quite pleased with himself and turned to the map that spanned most of the wall, pointing to a pin in India in the map. "You see, we had just arrived in the Punjab, and we prepared to travel east . . ."

Saffron, with the occasional "Oh my" and "Indeed!" edged back toward the desk, silently sliding the stacks of paper on top of it so she could see who they were from and the first few lines of text. She found several notes that had gone back and forth with other professors in the history department, including a few mentioning Dr. Henry's petition to get another branch of the history department instated. From the few lines of text here and there, Saffron thought he wanted to head up a new series of courses in "primitive cultures" and eventually create a new degree.

"Oh dear, my shoe has come unbuckled," she murmured. She knelt down behind the desk. Quickly, she pulled at the two drawers in front of her, finding they were both unlocked. She stood up and took a few steps back to where Snyder stood, still reminiscing about the coin's discovery.

"Mr. Snyder," she interrupted, "could you perhaps fetch me a glass of water? All this talk of adventure is quite exhilarating. My heart is absolutely pounding!"

Snyder, eye on the hand which she had put to her throat, leapt to attention. "Most certainly. I won't be a moment."

He left the room. Saffron dashed back to the desk and knelt down again to the open drawers, quickly scanning the contents. Ideally she would find something about the equipment orders or missives from a murderous mistress. The first drawer contained a great deal of scrawled notes on a series of notepads. Nothing she read sounded promising. The second drawer had office supplies, but squashed in the back were some opened letters. She grabbed them, and slid the drawer closed just as Snyder returned to the room with a glass of water. Saffron smiled at him and shoved the envelopes into her bag when he gestured again to the map. He insisted she stand next to him to see the movement of the expedition team, so she stayed by his side, agreeing with him as she sipped her water, and feigned interest in another ten-minute-long tale. Just as he was about to launch into another story, she asked him the time.

"Nearly eleven o'clock? Oh dear! I was supposed to attend a meeting." Saffron added in an undertone, "You know, to discuss what to do about Dr. Maxwell. He's still under arrest. I can't imagine what Dr. Berking will say,"

Snyder, with an expression of lofty disdain, said, "I'm surprised they haven't given old Maxwell the sack yet. If anyone in our department was under such suspicion, Dr. Henry would have them tossed out immediately."

"Really?" Saffron was tempted to tell Snyder that Dr. Henry was one of the suspects, but didn't want to disrupt their rapport.

"Absolutely. We can't have people sullying the name of the university like that," he said importantly. His small eyes narrowed at Saffron. "Isn't Dr. Maxwell your professor? You're his assistant, aren't you?"

"Oh yes," Saffron said with an eager nod, "but I wouldn't go against the police. If they say he's guilty, I believe them. It is just such a baffling circumstance that someone would try to poison Mrs. Henry. Do you know her well?"

Snyder frowned. "I can't say I do. Mrs. Henry doesn't often visit the university. Although she did stop in last week."

Saffron tamped down on her flare of excitement at that significant piece of information. Keeping her voice casual, she asked. "Did she really? She spoke to Dr. Henry here, in his office?"

"I suppose. I saw her walking into the Wilkins Building when I went to drop off paperwork for Dr. Henry. He's forming his own department, you know." Snyder drew himself up. "Forming his own degree program and everything. This expedition will go a long way toward proving he's prepared for the responsibility."

Brows arching, Saffron said, "It's a pity he won't able to lead it after all." When Snyder frowned in confusion, she added, "Since Dr. Henry will have to stay behind with his wife."

Snyder shook his head, his oversized teeth on display in a patronizing smile. "Oh no, Miss Everleigh. Dr. Henry is still leading the team, of course. Who else could do it? It was all his plan to begin with. As I said, it's the way to convince the College Committee to form a new department. Anthropology, you know. It will be one of the first in Britain."

Saffron nodded slowly, assimilating all this new information. Dr. Maxwell had mentioned Dr. Henry wanting to form a new department, but she was unclear how it related to this expedition. Circling back around to Mrs. Henry, she asked, "You mentioned Mrs. Henry was on campus not long ago. Did you happen to see Dr. Henry with her?"

"No, he wasn't. But I wasn't going to ask the man about her either. Dr. Henry rages quite enough without mentioning his wife." Snyder let out a laugh that was immediately choked by a look of panic. "Oh no, I don't mean—that is to say, Dr. Henry would never—"

"Oh, of course not." Saffron extended a hand to him with a flirtatious smile. "I'm afraid I really must dash. Thank you so very much, Mr. Snyder."

Mr. Snyder's ears went pink, and he asked her to come back some time to hear about the ancient vase he had dug up. She would probably have to when she returned the letters.

Saffron nearly broke into a fit of giggles as she strode away from the history building. Was it truly that easy to flirt her way into obtaining information? Passing by the steps of Wilkins Building, she gave up holding back her amusement and actually did laugh aloud.

"Laughing at us studious scholars?" a voice said from behind her, making her jump.

She laughed again when she saw it was Alexander. "Oh yes, I always laugh when I see others working hard. Makes me feel much better about all my own hours of work ahead. You will absolutely never guess all the headway I've made on the investigation!"

"Tell me about it over lunch. I've been in there for hours," Alexander said, indicating the library. "Besides, you can't meddle in police business on an empty stomach."

❧

"So, you see, I actually have the letters," Saffron finished.

Alexander nearly choked on a sip of tea. "You took them?"

"What did you expect me to do, read them and put them back with Snyder breathing all over me?"

"Snyder was breathing all over you?" Alexander's dark eyes narrowed.

"I suppose not. To be fair, the fellow is just starved for attention. Who'd pay him any mind with Dr. Henry around? He was like a puppy when I said I wanted to hear about his side of things," Saffron said with a doting smile. "But hopefully it was worth it."

She glanced furtively about the teashop. The single room was cramped with far too many rickety tables, but the usual rush of students in search of a bite between classes was still an hour off. The young woman at the counter was paying them no mind, so Saffron took out the letters. Four slightly battered envelopes were addressed to Dr. Henry in feminine handwriting. Two had been sent to what must be his home address, and two had been sent to the university. She set them on the table in the small space between their now empty plates and opened the first one.

"'My dearest darling . . .' Oh, it's signed 'Daphne,' and not Cynthia Henry—big surprise. 'I miss you terribly . . . Do come visit me soon . . .' Oh goodness." Blushing, she passed the letter to Alexander, whose eyes widened slightly at the steamy suggestions that took up most of the letter.

"How . . . creative," Alexander remarked dryly, returning it to its envelope.

The second letter, signed "Lola," was much the same, although the writer was not as elegant in her descriptions as the first.

"No surprises there," Saffron said, batting away any lingering embarrassment at the contents. "We knew that he's a Lothario. Those were both sent to the university, not his home. Perhaps they didn't know him privately and knew he worked for the university."

Alexander agreed and opened the next letter. "'Dearest Lawrence, I must speak with you urgently,'" he read. "Oh."

Saffron paused in opening the last envelope. He passed her the letter he held.

Dearest Lawrence,

I must speak with you urgently. Please, darling, I love you so, and I know you love me too. Our dreams could be realized so

*easily if only we could meet and discuss our future. Please, come
to me soon. I don't want to come to you, lest someone discover
us, but I must speak to you.*

Your truest love,
Eris

"Well, she certainly is a lot more interested in him than I'd
thought," Saffron concluded.

Alexander took the letter back and read over it again. Saffron
sighed and frowned down at her teacup, thinking. Miss Ermine
asking to speak to Dr. Henry urgently suggested a lot of possible situations, one in particular that came to mind, especially
in reference to the future. But Miss Ermine didn't look to be *in
trouble*. It was possible that, had she become pregnant, her family was rich and powerful enough to hush it up. Or Eris could
have been mistaken and simply afraid she was pregnant. Or it
could have been something else altogether that brought out the
urgency in Miss Ermine's phrasing.

Alexander put the letter back in its envelope. "I've heard
Henry describe his collection of artifacts. There's every possibility that he has something poisonous stashed away."

Saffron watched his thoughtful expression with a mixture of
intrigue and appreciation that had nothing to do with the mystery at hand. She didn't know when Alexander had become her
collaborator in this inquiry, but she was glad of it.

He nodded to the final envelope. "Go on."

The last letter was also from Miss Ermine. Ink splattered
angrily across the small piece of paper.

Lawrence,

*After I gave my love to you, this is how you repay me? How
dare you, after all I've done? You'll be sorry.*

Eris

Saffron let out her breath, read the brief note aloud, and replaced it in the envelope.

"Does it have a date?" Alexander asked after a moment.

"No, neither of hers do."

"Unfortunate."

Saffron tapped her finger on the stack of letters. "They weren't unfriendly at all to each other at the party. Eris fawned all over him, and then Henry followed Eris like a dog to a bone. She didn't sound angry when she spoke of him. Perhaps it's an old letter, and they took up again." Alexander nodded absently. Saffron huffed and set the letter down with the others. "But it could also be an elaborate scheme to exact her revenge on him. So much for eliminating suspects."

"Did Inspector Green make you an honorary officer, then?" Alexander said, rising from his seat.

"Of course not," Saffron said, following him to the teashop's door. They stepped onto bustling Gower Street, and Saffron added, "I thought, since I had some luck rooting out some of the problem, why not try to solve the rest of it?"

His brow furrowed. "And you're not at all concerned that you are investigating a murder attempt? Your interest is bound to get attention, if it hasn't already."

Saffron waved a hand, dismissing his concerns. "Snyder was falling over himself to give me access to Dr. Henry's office. Eris Ermine couldn't even remember we'd met before. Apparently no one suspects that I would be up to something."

✤

Just as Alexander was packing up his things for the evening, Saffron appeared at his door. Fighting a smile, he said, "Yes, Inspector Everleigh?"

"Going home?" Saffron asked, looking at his bag as he placed a notebook inside.

"I was planning on it," Alexander said. "You see, those of us that actually do work during the day get to leave at a reasonable hour."

"Reasonable? It's nearly seven." She nodded to the darkened window behind his desk. "Do you always work this late?"

Alexander nodded. "I do, unless I've got somewhere to be."

"Do you often," Saffron began, a little smile playing on her lips, "have places to be in the evenings?"

Alexander leaned back on his desk as he crossed his arms, enjoying her coy question. "Yes, rather often."

"Going to dinner . . . dancing?" She gave him a sidelong glance, taking a few steps and leaning a hip against the couch.

"Occasionally." The look in her eye was intriguing.

"Really? Not recently, though," Saffron said. "Not since the party, I believe. You've been here, at least when I have been, in the evenings."

Her line of questioning made him suddenly wonder the same things about her. Why was Saffron here so late? Surely she had better things to do than hole up in an office and stare at dusty old books. Or at least, that's the way his mother put it when she asked him about his social life. He got the feeling that Saffron rather liked dusty old books, in addition to poking around in police investigations. "Taking an interest in my evening schedule, are we? Am I also a suspect?" Alexander smirked.

"Yes, of course," Saffron said lightly. "I was quite convinced that you were the would-be murderer, of course. But then you had an excellent opportunity with the xolotl, and you didn't try to finish me off."

He chuckled. "I suppose I could have let you die on the floor of the office. That definitely would have cleared my name."

With a soft laugh, she meandered toward him. "Alexander, do you think you might be willing to help me with something?"

"I thought I had already been helpful."

She took another step toward him. He was still much taller than her, even when he was leaning on the desk. "You have been, of course. I just was hoping, you know, since I don't really have anyone else at the university now that Maxwell is gone for the time being . . ."

"Yes?" What was she asking him to do?

She closed the distance between them. With her came a hint of old books and a feminine freshness like flowers. Her eyes were shining gray in the yellow light of the lamps, and her hand was warm where she'd placed it on his bare arm, his sleeves still rolled to his elbows. Her soft words practically brushed against his cheek, she stood so close. "And it's been so difficult, trying to solve this mystery. You're so clever, and so I was wondering if you could maybe help me get into Dr. Berking's office."

Alexander's mind was on all the other possible favors he might do for her, favors he could do right now, with the door closed and the hall beyond quiet, so it took him a moment to realize what she had asked him to help with. "You want me to do what?"

Saffron placed both hands on his crossed arms, leaning her weight gently on him. "Please, Alexander. Dr. Henry's office provided such important information; surely Berking's would do the same. I need your help." She bit her lip, adding, "You're the only person I can ask. You're the only person I can trust here."

If he thought Saffron would actually drop this idea if he refused to help her, he would. But he doubted it. Better he help keep her out of trouble instead, especially where Berking was concerned. "Of course I'll help you."

"Oh, thank you!" Saffron smiled and leapt into his arms. "I knew I could rely on you!"

There was a brief moment where Alexander considered not letting her go, but he somewhat grudgingly released her waist, where his hands had automatically gone. He gave her a stern look. "You can't use your wiles for your investigation."

"Well, it's worked twice today, so you certainly can't say that I *can't* do it," Saffron replied briskly, those blue-gray eyes alight with amusement. "If you don't like it, Alexander, don't be so easily manipulated."

He was allowing himself to be manipulated. It would be disappointing to find it was all for her misguided investigation, he realized. He sighed. "Fine."

"You'll do it?" Saffron's whole face lit up with a delighted smile.

"Yes," he replied, frowning with extra annoyance to counteract the effect of her smile on him. "But if we're caught, I'm going to say you threatened me and forced me to help you."

Saffron's eyes widened, scandalized. "You wouldn't! What am I meant to have threatened you with?"

"Your copious poisonous plants, clearly."

The arch of her brows gave her a haughty expression to match her words. "It's your job to make sure we don't get caught, so unless you want to sully my name and yours, you'll do a proper job."

He shook his head again, and she told him the plan. She was mad, no doubt about it, but he was finding it increasingly hard to be upset about it.

CHAPTER 14

The hallway was silent as Saffron removed a pin from her hair and inserted it into the lock on Dr. Berking's door. She had never picked a lock before but was familiar with the process from a very loquacious man she'd met at one of Elizabeth's more daring literary circles a few months ago. He had been a poet by name but had bragged about all the other skills he had. Luckily, they had been skills like lockpicking.

Smiling to herself as she thought back to the drunken man, she heard his slurred voice in her head talking about sliding the pin in and moving it until one felt it move sideways. Then, it was about catching all the pins with the second hairpin. Saffron struggled for five minutes before she caught any of the pins, but eventually got it. She pushed the door open and popped her head around into the stairwell where she'd stationed Alexander to listen for approaching footsteps.

"Got it!" she whispered with a grin, then ducked back around.

It was well past eight o'clock now, and Saffron knew all the other professors on the floor had cleared out, either to go home or to go to a gathering to which Saffron had declined Maxwell's invitation a week ago.

Saffron stole across Mr. Pierce's little office, casting a glance at the assistant's desk and chair, and into Dr. Berking's office.

She paused on the threshold. The meager glow of the street-lights below the window created a haze of golden light that barely illumined the room. It was eerie, to be sure, but the sudden pounding of Saffron's heart and dampness of her palms had little to do with the shadows cast by the multitude of plants, a mere glance into Berking's extensive personal collection, on the office's walls.

She crept forward, her feet padding across the thick carpet to Dr. Berking's desk. All Saffron could think of was Berking's horrible smile, his slimy voice. She could almost feel his wandering hands and the feel of his breath on her face, her neck. She shuddered. That was precisely why Saffron was in his office now, despite her fear of what had happened and what had almost happened. Berking was a horrible man who it was very easy to believe would be part of a crime. It was not as if she wanted him to be guilty. Certainly not.

After a moment of debating the risk of turning on the desk lamp, Saffron clicked on the small green lamp at the corner of the desk. No one would find it strange to see a light on in the North Wing; people worked late all the time. The expanse of polished wood was tidy and almost bare. She read through the messages in the letter tray next to the lamp, hoping to recognize handwriting or names. There were only two notes, one from Dr. Aster about the budget for the coming academic year, and a note from someone called R. Glass, reminding Berking to bring a sample to their meeting.

She placed the papers carefully back where she had found them, then moved on to the desk drawers. Unfortunately, Berking didn't seem to be as careless as Dr. Henry; his drawers were all locked. Saffron frowned. She didn't want to attempt to pick each one open. She had spare keys for Maxwell's desk—not that Maxwell ever remembered to lock his drawers—so perhaps Pierce had another set for Berking's desk. She hurried into the outer room, sliding her pins into the lock on Pierce's top desk drawer. After a struggle, she pulled the drawer open and smiled at the key nestled among a handful of pens.

Back in the gloom of Berking's office, Saffron opened the bottom right drawer. She sorted through files and files on the botany department's recent studies, with notes from each researcher. She flicked through and paused at her own name across the top of a file. Frowning, she fished the paper out and saw that it was her study proposal, the one she'd presented when she'd met with Berking and he'd attempted to get at her. Saffron turned a few pages, wondering why he'd bothered to file it.

She moved to the next drawer. Nothing but budget records.

After twenty minutes of unlocking drawers, revealing nothing of interest apart from Berking's checkbook, full of random names and sums, and a bag of sweets containing only licorice, Saffron looked to the cabinets behind the desk. The first cabinet was a fast job. It had Berking's work clothes and boots, evidently stored in case Berking ever deigned to do some work in the greenhouses. A few personal effects, like a bottle of cologne, lay in a shallow drawer.

Her hands began to sweat. There had to be something here, something to make this worth manipulating Alexander into an illegal activity. Surely she hadn't broken into Berking's office for nothing.

She went to the second cabinet, unlocked it quickly, and looked around. She glanced over the various boxes of files and folders of what appeared to be very old botany department business, and shuffled through a few of the papers, recognizing names from her father's or Maxwell's stories.

Her fingers stilled as they passed over a familiar script. She slipped the yellowing folder from between the papers and looked down at her father's handwriting elegantly rolling across the page, describing something relating to breeding and heterosis.

Thomas Everleigh had died several years before Berking even joined University College, but several of the names she'd seen belonged to men no longer at the university. It really wasn't so strange, even if it felt wrong that Berking had something of her father's.

She was just contemplating taking the file with her when a sound froze her entire body. It was the worst possible sound she could imagine in that moment. Dr. Berking's voice booming from the hall.

Saffron replaced the file back in the stack and closed the cabinet as silently as her shaking hands would allow. She nearly cried out when the door to Pierce's office outside banged open. Her heart pounding in her throat, she heard Alexander's voice speaking loudly. She couldn't make out what they were saying, but she hoped it would stall Berking long enough for her to conceal herself. There wasn't enough room in either cabinet for her to hide. She dropped to her knees and crawled out of sight, moving aside Berking's enormous chair and diving under the desk. Just as she resettled the chair in front of her, the door to the room opened.

Saffron pressed her hand against her mouth, barely breathing. She was both terrified and furious. How had Berking gotten past Alexander? Why was he in his office so late? He was supposed to be at the dinner party with the other professors. He never missed the chance to drink and gossip.

Saffron tried to focus on what Berking was calling to Alexander rather than the fact that his voice was getting closer.

"Oh yes, yes, Ashton." His loud voice was a little slurred. "Can't say that it won't be tricky! The natives of any country can be dangerous. No use getting upset about the possibilities."

"I just mean, sir," Alexander's tight voice said, "that Snyder implied there was some trouble to be had. Dr. Henry apparently always carries a knife and a gun. Surely that isn't necessary."

Dr. Berking's footsteps shook the floor beneath her as he drew closer to the desk. Her fingers curled around her mouth, digging into her skin as she prayed her breathing wasn't as loud as it seemed to her own ears.

"Ashton, my boy, don't worry about Henry. He might think he's in charge"—Berking let out a barking laugh, causing Saffron to jump in her hiding spot; he was standing right in front of her now—"but his part to play in the whole expedition is small. Growing smaller every day! Now, where is it!"

Alexander's tense voice asked, "Can I help you find something, Dr. Berking?"

"No, no," Berking huffed. "Just needed to get my checkbook. I lost a bet to Anderson at his dinner party down the street. Left it here." There was a jingle of keys as he unlocked a drawer. Saffron hoped she'd put everything back in its correct place.

"Pen?" Berking mumbled and his large body shifted in front of her.

"I have one, sir." Quieter steps approached the desk.

Berking grunted in thanks. "Don't you worry about the expedition." There was the sound of a pen scratching against paper, then a rip. "Though it's never a bad idea to be traveling with protection. I, myself, will be bringing a pistol, of course." Laughing merrily, Berking shoved his desk drawer shut with a snap and a sound like tearing paper. Two pairs of feet left the room, the lock of the door flicking behind them. A moment later, the outer door shut and locked.

Under the desk, Saffron slumped. She might have the nerve to flirt with a few men and pick a lock or two, but hiding under a desk while her harasser stood inches away—she did *not* have the nerves for that. And she didn't even have anything useful to show for her attempt to unearth something in Berking's office.

She didn't dare move, even if she believed that if Berking came back, Alexander would stall him again and she'd be able to hide. Her ears strained for hints of his return. Her neck, twisted into a strange angle by her hunched position, began to cramp. She finally forced herself to move, and as she pushed aside the heavy chair blocking her, she saw a piece of paper had been caught in the corner drawer from which Berking had retrieved his checkbook, wedging it in the back of the desk. Saffron tugged on it, and it ripped, the sound so loud and shocking in the silent office that she jolted to her feet. Holding her breath, she waited for sounds of approaching footsteps.

When nothing came, she stood up, stretching her neck this way and that, then rubbing at her knees, which burned from crawling across the carpet. Her stockings were likely ruined. She switched off the lamp and crossed the room to leave. Her hand had barely touched the door when she stopped, glancing down at the corner of paper she'd ripped. The letters and numbers on the paper didn't mean much, but it was clear that it was a formula of some kind. Where fear had been a moment before, suspicion crept back in. Pursing her lips, Saffron frowned at the desk. Could she risk another few minutes?

She'd already come this far.

Saffron turned around and hurried back to the desk. With the light back on, she unlocked the top drawer and slid it out, feeling the catch of the paper as she did so. Carefully, she inched her hand as far back into the drawer as it would go. Her fingertips met the scrunched paper. She tugged and wiggled, but she got nothing but another torn edge, frustratingly blank, and feathered bits. Disappointed, Saffron looked to the checkbook, flipping through his receipts. She found it odd that Berking left it in his desk drawer, but he would not be the first to try to keep his spending habits in control that way. Her uncle had done the same thing—kept his money stashed far away when he was drinking.

She found the check from today. It wasn't addressed to Dr. Anderson, but to Rupert Glass. She quickly nabbed a sheet of paper from the second desk drawer and copied the information; then, remembering Glass's note she had found earlier, she copied it onto the piece of paper too. It was too coincidental not to be the same person. Now that she thought of it, Glass was a name she'd heard around campus before. She would check.

She replaced everything except the torn formula, which she folded into the paper, and checked each drawer to make sure they were all locked. She replaced Pierce's spare keys, but after two failed attempts at picking his desk drawer shut, then the office door, she gave it up as a bad job. The cleaners would find the office door unlocked in the morning and likely think nothing of it.

Back in the hallway, she silently made her way to the stairwell.

"Well done, Ashton," she hissed at Alexander with a mocking glare. "I was nearly caught!"

He pressed a finger to his lips, and she followed him down the stairs and to his office. Just as she turned to him with a triumphant smile, ready to share her discoveries, Alexander closed the office door, enveloping them in darkness before he crossed to his desk and flicked on the lamp.

He sat in the middle of the couch and nodded next to him in invitation. Saffron, unsure of his enigmatic half smile, sunk onto a cushion. He stretched an arm behind her.

Clearing her throat against the sudden nerves she felt, Saffron began to describe what she'd found, but the look Alexander gave her effectively dried up her words.

"Saffron . . ." Alexander said, his dark eyes on her face.

"Yes?" Saffron was very aware of his nearness, the warmth of his arm not quite touching her neck. She hadn't expected to go from breaking into an office to being stashed away in a dimly lit room with Alexander. She certainly didn't mind.

His steady gaze was intense, confident. Alexander reached to her face and brushed back a lock of hair come loose from losing her hairpins. He tucked it behind her ear, looking at her mouth.

"I just wanted to say . . ." His face, golden in the dim light, drew nearer to hers.

"Y-yes?" Anticipation made her voice shake.

Inches from her, Alexander murmured, "That was a stupid thing to do." A switch clicked on behind her, flooding the room with light and extinguishing the spark of want he'd so effectively fanned to life.

Saffron blinked at him with an open mouth. Alexander fell back onto the cushions behind him, a look of satisfaction on his face.

"Are you *serious*?" Saffron hissed, hitting him on the arm.

Alexander chuckled. "Not so funny, is it?"

"Oh, shut up—it was your fault I was nearly caught to begin with!" Saffron huffed, face hot. It was only fair that he got her back, but she didn't have to admit it any time soon. "Do you want to hear about what I found or not?"

"I do," Alexander said with a grin, "but not tonight. I need to concentrate."

"Concentrate on what? I thought you were finished working for the night."

"I am. I need to concentrate on cementing the look on your face into my mind. I never want to forget that."

CHAPTER 15

Alexander's flirtatious revenge had utterly distracted Saffron. When she and Alexander parted ways, her head had been filled with the melting look he'd given just before scolding her. That look had helped Saffron put from her mind the unease she felt whenever she remembered that Berking had some of her father's papers. However, walking to work through cool mist the next morning, it was all Saffron could think about.

She'd never gone through her father's things, having been just young enough when he died that her mother deemed it inappropriate and locked all his papers away. At the time, her fourteen-year-old self had scoffed at the idea that journals detailing plant growth and disease could be inappropriate, but considering how affected her mother had been by his death, she hadn't risked upsetting her by asking. Now, she wished she'd taken the folder from Berking's cabinet. Plant breeding, the subject of the document she'd barely skimmed, would not have been a new concept to Violet Everleigh when her husband had died—especially since she was a botany enthusiast herself—but perhaps the concepts of sexual reproduction in plants were what made her keep Saffron from reading her father's papers. Researchers spent years on work that never saw publication, and Saffron hadn't had any idea what her father had been working on before he left for war. Apparently, it was related to creating hybrid plants. That line of research held as little interest for her as plant pathology did, unfortunately. It would have been nice if her father's work had been something she could continue for her graduate studies.

There would be another few years of work and study, all under the uncomfortable gaze of Dr. Berking. At least he would be absent for the next few months. Maxwell had encouraged her to wait a year or two to apply, but she didn't see why she should. She simply needed a topic that captured her interest and for Berking to approve it.

Alexander, like Berking, would be leaving in less than two weeks, she thought with a sigh. She hadn't fallen madly in love yet, but she certainly liked the man. Maybe she should do what Elizabeth suggested and set something up between her and Alexander, though she didn't know what that would look like considering he was leaving England for six months.

Her thoughts carried her all the way to the university, her mind full of swirling possibilities.

Wedged in her office door was a note from Dr. Aster requesting her assistance that morning, forcing her to postpone her plan to immediately go to the library to decipher the few legible parts of the formula on the torn paper. It was lunchtime before she managed to find time to get to the library.

Clear blue skies and the clock indicating the lunch hour meant that the Quad was buzzing with life. She had to dodge students sitting in clusters on the steps to the portico to get inside the Wilkins Building. She'd barely crossed into the Flaxman Gallery when she heard her name.

She tempered her smile when she saw that Alexander was not alone, but flanked by two other biology researchers. They stood to the side of the gallery, just beneath the relief of a Roman soldier with an arm lifted and shield resting beside him.

"Yes, Mr. Ashton?" she said politely.

"I had a question for you regarding Dr. Maxwell's study," he said, his voice equally polite. He wore another gray suit, with a slight pinstripe that made him look even taller today, and a green tie. "About one of the samples you mentioned. I'm sure I saw it listed as one of the specimens in the greenhouses. I'd appreciate it if you showed me which one."

Saffron nodded, though she was quite sure she'd shown him nearly every specimen in the greenhouses already, and definitely all the ones related to Dr. Maxwell's work. "Are you available this afternoon?"

One of the biologists smirked. Clinton McGuire had been one of the first to come sniffing around her when she began at the university. He was as tall as Alexander, with light brown hair and eyes. If not for his perpetual contemptuous expression, he would have been handsome. Saffron resisted the urge to fidget under his gaze. He'd been a friend of Archie Davis's and took offense to her stepping out with Archie instead of himself. McGuire had spent the better part of their brief relationship trying to provoke Saffron with comments about her father and family, suggesting she'd only been admitted to the university because of her father's position. It was thanks to McGuire that Archie found out about her grandfather's title, though it had backfired spectacularly since Archie had been excited at the prospect of Saffron's connections to nobility, rather than offended by it as McGuire was.

Saffron hoped he'd given up bothering her, but apparently McGuire couldn't resist the temptation to sneer at her now. The other man, Geoffrey Kent, was bent over the book in his hands, oblivious.

Alexander nodded. "I have an appointment now. Around two in the greenhouses?"

Saffron agreed and left the trio a moment later. She could practically feel eyes on her back as she crossed the wood floors of the gallery. She glanced over her shoulder and saw McGuire and Alexander were both watching her leave. She didn't want to consider what snide comments McGuire might make to Alexander. But even if he did say something rude, surely Alexander wouldn't listen. He'd told Berking off at the dinner, after all.

Ignoring the too-familiar feeling of living under a magnifying glass, Saffron entered the library and headed straight for the chemistry section.

The afternoon was pleasant; a blue sky peeked from behind fluffy clouds, and birds swooped from tree to tree. The weather didn't match Alexander's mood as he descended the steps of the library. Saffron had still been in sight when McGuire started mouthing off. He was a pain to work with on a good day, and Alexander had no patience for him scoffing at Saffron, so he'd walked away before he lost his temper.

Only a handful of people were in the low-ceilinged lobby of the administrative offices, and their conversation filled it with murmuring. The receptionist sat at her little desk against the wall, an older woman with a mouth that looked puckered from lemon juice, adding her steady clattering to the ambience as she typed on her ironically named Noiseless.

Alexander passed through and went straight to Blake's office to see if he was in. He wasn't, as Alexander had hoped.

"Excuse me," he said with a nervous voice as he approached the receptionist. "Look, I know that Mr. Blake isn't in the office, but you see, I, uh, turned in the wrong form, and my department head is already in quite a state over my completing another wrong form last week, and I was hoping I could, er . . . go in and collect it before Mr. Blake confirms with him." He rushed his words and looked down with shame.

The receptionist, gray-streaked hair in a severe bun, gave him an unexpectedly kind smile. "Yes, dear, I'll just pop in and fetch it for you."

"Oh, you needn't trouble yourself," Alexander said eagerly. "Please, I promise I can be quick about it."

"Very well, I'll just let you in." She got up and shuffled down the hall, to the door of Blake's office. "He files equipment forms over in the drawer to the right. I had to get into them just the other day . . ."

Alexander crossed the room swiftly and scanned Blake's newly tidy desk. Remembering he had to be anxious since the receptionist was still standing at the door, he let his hands shake more than usual as he opened the filing cabinet against the far wall and began to comb through the files of equipment forms.

Perhaps Saffron's relentless interest in Mrs. Henry's poisoning had gotten to him. There was something going on, something with Berking and Henry and now possibly Blake. But damned if he would admit that to Saffron.

He saw his own name at the front of the row of files, as it always was, and moved on to Berking. He pulled out his ten or so forms, flicking through each page as quickly as he could while still taking in each item. Nothing odd there, just plates, a travel microscope, some general supplies.

"Not this one then," he said with an embarrassed smile, looking at the receptionist. She wasn't watching him particularly avidly, but instead looking at a map on the wall, idly running a finger along the blue line of the Amazon.

"You're going on the expedition, then, dear?" the receptionist asked in a dreamy sort of voice.

Alexander looked up from his shuffling through the papers. "Yes, I am."

She smiled at him. "How very exciting! Must be a grand sort of adventure."

Alexander returned her smile and went back to the "H's" and found Dr. Henry. His file was thick with forms. He quickly found all the forms for this expedition and found that there were nearly thirty, all of which had already been marked as fulfilled.

Odd, he thought, then odder still. Rather than one telescope, Henry had requested five. He'd also ordered two dozen bags of emergency supplies, two hundred boxes of pens, and at least ten more exorbitant amounts of supplies. Perhaps it was a realistic amount of supplies for the six months in the jungle. But that wasn't right; his department head had said they'd order more supplies from locals once they got there and settled in. They definitely had pens and bandages in Brazil.

Realizing he was lingering, he chose a few of the forms with more ridiculous amounts to take with him.

"Did you find it?" the receptionist asked.

"Thank you, yes," Alexander said, now anxious to get away. "You've really saved my neck."

"Now, don't make it a habit!" She locked the door again and started back down the hall, imperturbable sour expression firmly back in place. "That's twice in as many weeks that I've had to let someone in to Mr. Blake's office. He'd be furious if he knew I'd let that woman in, let alone you, but I try to do what I can . . ."

Alexander barely heard her, hardly believing his luck. According to the forms, Dr. Henry was making unreasonable orders of supplies. That could mean one of two things: Henry was a wildly incompetent leader and possibly losing his grip, or he was doing something with the supplies. Perhaps selling them on the side or giving them away for some reason. Selling was more likely. Dr. Henry had faced pushback for this expedition and therefore had trouble funding it; maybe he was going to stash the money for the next one. Or he was simply greedy. Either seemed possible.

Perhaps this was what he'd overheard Berking speaking about. This could be the unsavory way that Henry got his funding, not by seducing Miss Ermine, although that had apparently happened regardless. It had to be connected to the poisoning. Blake and Henry's involvement left no doubt in his mind about it.

Saffron reached the greenhouse before Alexander. She traded out her gloves for a working pair and went to check on the saguaro cactus in greenhouse three, which had unfortunately developed more spots. Kneeling near the base, where a new dark circle marred its prickly green skin, Saffron considered telling Mr. Winters to perhaps move it to a drier area, or maybe water it less. Really, Dr. Parson should have given better instructions to the caretaker for the care of his specimen.

A pair of polished black oxfords came into view. "What seems to be the problem, Doctor?"

Saffron stood up quickly, brushing dust and dirt off her skirt. "I'm not sure. A mystery for another day, I suppose. Now, why did you want to meet in the greenhouse?"

"I thought it might be prudent to speak away from the North Wing, considering how often eavesdropping has revealed interesting information." Alexander started through the crowd of cacti, and she followed.

"You think we might be overheard in the office?" Saffron asked, suddenly worried. They'd discussed the whole investigation in the North Wing.

He shrugged. "Better safe than sorry, especially in light of what I've just discovered."

"Well, go on!"

Alexander told her about the forms as they made their way into the next greenhouse, then the next. She was pleased he'd taken the initiative to sneak into Blake's office, and relieved that someone else was taking her ideas seriously. When they stopped in front of the wall of xolotl, he offered her several folded papers from his pocket. Saffron quickly doffed her gloves and examined them, her lips pursed in thought.

If Dr. Henry was amassing a considerable number of supplies, or made it seem like he was, there was only one explanation that made sense to her. "Embezzlement!"

Alexander gave her a searching look before tucking the papers back into his pocket. "It must be. Either he's found a way to get the money for the supplies directly, or he's planning to sell them off. Was the poisoning an attempt to cover it up? Perhaps Blake realized too late and was going to get in trouble for not spotting the embezzlement, so he tried to get rid of Henry as revenge?"

"Perhaps." Saffron tapped her chin, looking hard at Alexander. "It can't be as simple as handing in a couple of extra forms, can it? That's far too easy."

"I've no idea what other financial arrangements Henry or Blake make for the journey. But it could be extensive. Excessive equipment purchases may be only part of it."

Saffron nodded. She had no idea what the financial side of the expedition would be like. But she was sure that few people were involved deeply enough to catch it, and that made for a perfect opportunity to scheme. "If Dr. Henry found out that Mr. Blake knew about the embezzlement, and his wife was having an affair with him, *that* is a perfect motive. And Henry argued with Dr. Maxwell, who studies poisonous plants. Henry framed Maxwell!"

"Henry tried to poison Blake, but got his wife instead?" Alexander raised his eyebrows.

Satisfaction suffused through her, and her face broke into a wide smile. "I think we've got it, Alexander."

Alexander was not so easily convinced. No matter how many times Saffron said she felt confident that they had solved it, he was unmoved. "It doesn't explain the champagne. Dr. Henry poured the champagne into Mrs. Henry's glass, not Blake's. Furthermore, we don't actually know how Mrs. Henry was poisoned. It might not have been the champagne. We also haven't fit together how—or if—Berking is involved."

Annoyed her theories were once again proven to have holes, Saffron tugged a book from her bag and set it on a nearby rolling cart. She flipped to the relevant page, a colored illustration of inky purple blooms hanging from a green stalk.

She gestured to the flowers. "*Aconitum*, the genus collectively and commonly known as wolfsbane. Aconite contains the toxin aconitine, which is annotated"—she unfolded the paper on which she'd copied the formula from Dr. Berking's office and tapped on part of it—"like this."

His dark eyes jumped up to hers, making her stomach flutter a little with his intense focus. "And this is in the formula you showed me?"

She nodded, biting her lip as she came to the bad news. "Unfortunately, aconite is very well known. It's been used as a poison for thousands of years, and poisonings from it are still common enough as aconite is still considered a pretty addition to gardens. A doctor would likely be able to identify the symptoms and could probably find it in her blood or stomach."

Alexander closed the book. "But that wasn't the only thing in the formula." He took the paper from her hands and frowned down at it. "I was never any good at chemistry."

"Nor I," Saffron said with a sigh. "It's the only class I ever failed. Worse than Greek."

Alexander let out a sudden laugh, and Saffron looked at him curiously, but he shook his head with a small smile. "I can't make any of this out."

"This is a preservative," Saffron pointed out. "But that's all I could discover this afternoon. It's possible that the other components could alter the effects of aconitine, and so the doctors or police wouldn't know to look for it, if this is what Mrs. Henry was given. So, what does it all mean?"

When Alexander didn't respond, Saffron poked his shoulder. "It means Dr. Berking had something to do with the poisoning, of course!"

Alexander checked his wristwatch and glanced at the fogged door. "Saffron . . ." he began.

"Alexander . . ." she said, mimicking his tone.

"Look, I know how important this is to you—"

She felt him trying to temper her enthusiasm, and fought not to become frustrated. She couldn't have him backing out now, not just when things were getting more serious. "And you. Don't forget, if Henry and Berking are let off the hook for the poisoning, you'll be traveling with a treacherous murderer— maybe two. They know that we've been spending a lot of time together, and they know that I'm loyal to Maxwell. That might put you in danger too."

His eyes narrowed, though she saw the ghost of a smile on his lips. "All right. What is it that you want to do about this formula?"

CHAPTER 16

The dark house across the street was large and well-appointed, sitting comfortably in the center of a rectangular property at a respectable address. In the wee hours of a windswept Wednesday morning, curtains were drawn across dark windows up and down the street. Saffron and Alexander leaned casually on a stone wall, their eyes on the gate.

Glancing to the left and right, Alexander muttered, "Are you sure you want to do this? This is completely different from the university. We have absolutely no business showing up here at this time of night."

The honest answer was no, Saffron wasn't sure. But she couldn't think of another way to determine if the formula was a fluke. Saffron took a deep breath, her face set. "Yes. Now, you go over first and unlatch the gate. Then, we search. Do you remember what aconite looks like?"

He nodded, slipped his jacket from his shoulders, then jogged across the street. When she gave him a quick wave, indicating that no one was coming, Alexander set his jacket onto the top of the wall, grabbed the top of the tall stony ledge and pulled himself up. He disappeared onto the other side. Saffron was impressed by his physical acumen, but quickly reprimanded herself for being distracted. She looked up and down the street, shivering slightly in the wind.

Saffron rushed across the street toward the gate when it opened. It was nearly pitch black in the garden. The moon had not yet risen, and the high stone wall and voluminous foliage blocked most of the orange glow of the streetlights. They crept nearer to the house to ensure it was silent and still. Then, as agreed, Alexander remained in the front to keep watch while she circled the house in search of the conservatory.

It was well known that Dr. Berking had amassed a personal collection of plants that rivaled that of the university, but his collection was restricted to plants of Southeast Asia, where Dr. Berking focused his studies. Another reason Berking's interest in the expedition was suspicious, since he had never worked on plants from South America.

Aconite was not a plant native to that region, but Saffron couldn't imagine that, if Berking required plant for a nefarious purpose, he wouldn't grow it himself. A botanist was still a botanist, even if they did want to poison someone with the fruits of their labors. It was likely he'd cultivated it in a place he could tend it and harvest it without notice rather than at the university. Camouflaged among his other plants seemed the most logical place.

Before approaching the fogged windows of the glassed conservatory, she took a quick look around the garden and the barely visible houses beyond. A sweeping breeze rushed through, making all the trees and bushes shake and sway. It was as if the world was undulating around her. Closing her eyes to the vision of blackness, she visualized aconite's hooded blooms and deeply lobed leaves. It should be easy enough to identify if Berking had it inside.

Saffron crept toward the clouded glass door, wondering where Berking's servants were, for a grand house like this certainly warranted multiple servants. Not even the lights from the kitchen were on. Perhaps it was their night off, if Berking was also absent as the calendar on Pierce's desk had indicated he would be.

Holding her breath, Saffron tested the wrought iron door handle to the conservatory. It squeaked slightly, but gave. She carefully stepped inside the warmth of the greenhouse.

A faint glow from an interior lamp provided meager light, and Saffron didn't need more to know that Berking was right to be proud of his conservatory collection. The large room was crowded with verdure. Heady floral scents made her light-headed, both with the smell and excitement. She could detect the scent of a blooming member of the *Hedychium* genus nearby, and followed her nose to an enormous potted plant emanating a heavenly smell like honeysuckle.

She glanced about the dark room. She couldn't very well follow her nose to aconite. Saffron determined the most likely location for Berking to grow it would be under cover of a larger plant, as aconite would grow without full light, and that would reduce the chance of any fellow botany enthusiasts seeing it and asking questions. Outdoors, it ran the risk of being noticed by a gardener who might spill Berking's secret.

She considered how easy it would be for Berking to have poisoned Mrs. Henry with several of the plants in the room. But surely, if Berking were a suspect, the police would have searched his home and logged all the poisonous plants he had, like she had done for the university. Did the police force have a botanical expert to do such things?

She made her way beneath an exorbitant monstera, was only momentarily sidetracked by a collection of small hanging flowers she was sure were *Clematis repens*, then managed to duck beneath the larger palms and potted bushes, only to see that her query was nowhere to be found. She slowly crept around the perimeter of the room, dodging under vines and branches and leaves as she looked for gangly stems with heavy flowers, circling closer and closer to the center of the room.

A long, soft creak interrupted the humid silence.

Saffron crouched beneath an aggressively pointy palm and peered across the room to the door. She saw nothing but the faint waving of a disturbed frond. If Berking had entered the room, there was no way he'd only disturb just one palm frond.

A familiar figure stepped from behind a sheath of leaves, and Saffron let out a huff. "Do you have to be so stealthy?"

Alexander whispered, "Did you find it? You've been ages."

"No luck in here."

"Do you think it could be in the garden outside?"

Though the notion of searching through the bushes in the dark was not a pleasant one, Saffron agreed that it was possible, considering aconite seeds required cold treatment prior to germination. She should have thought of that before, but it hadn't occurred to her that Berking might be working with an immature plant.

Saffron didn't speak again until they were well out and away from the conservatory, where they once again agreed to split up. Saffron took the back, Alexander the front.

She considered the organization of a typical English garden. Surely Berking wouldn't have planted something so dangerous close to the kitchen garden where his cook might accidentally pick it. No, it would be far away. She started toward the darkest corner, furthest from the kitchen door. Saffron squinted into the black of the dense foliage and began her search.

Half an hour passed, revealing nothing more than a few long-forgotten garden ornaments half-covered in natural debris and a handful of rather nice tulips that an overgrown boxwood obscured from view. Her stockings were stained and torn from crawling about on her hands and knees, and her fingernails were doubtless similarly ruined. The ceaseless wind smarted against her cold ears. Saffron sat back on her heels with a huff and pushed aside a lock of loose hair. Hopefully Alexander had discovered something in the front.

Just as Saffron resolved to find him, a ringing clang broke through the ambient rushing of the wind. Saffron's heart stuttered as the sound of the gate opening followed, then the rumble of an automobile and the crunch of gravel. Headlights flashed along the far side of the hedge. Saffron pushed through the bushes and dashed to the side of the house, pressing her back against the wall.

The engine cut out. Saffron searched the darkness for Alexander. She saw no sign of him, which was a mixed blessing. The driver wouldn't see him, but neither could Saffron.

Gravel crunched as feet moved forward on the drive. A long silence followed. Just as Saffron moved to make for the gate, lights flared suddenly from within the house, illuminating the small lawn Saffron had just set her foot onto. She leapt back with a gasp, pressing her back to the cool stone of the building again. Her eyes searched the garden. Her partner was still nowhere to be seen.

There were no good options. She could move along the back or front of the house and pray that Berking wasn't looking out any windows. She could make a run for it, counting on that she likely could run fast enough to not be caught, but risk being exposed.

She took the last option and sped back into the garden beds, shoving past a bush into the line of cypress trees all the way to the wall. Saffron picked her way through, suddenly grateful for the wind disguising her movements through the shrubs and trees. She made it to the end of the length of the wall and crouched to hide beneath the low hanging branches of a weeping pea shrub, whose fringed leaves tickled her face. No noise had come from the house, and with any luck she would make it to the gate and out without notice. But what if she didn't come across Alexander? What if he'd gone to find her and was stuck in the bushes, too?

There was not a clear path along the wall. Several cypress trees hugged it to the extent that Saffron could not maneuver behind them. Just as she'd wiggled her way past the last in the line, her foot became tangled on something and she fell roughly on top of something that definitely wasn't a shrub.

Before she could shriek out her dismay at suddenly being pulled to the ground, a hand smothered her mouth. Relief overtook her at the sight of Alexander's dark eyes searching her face in the faint light seeping through the leaves.

"*Sorry,*" he mouthed. His face was partially obscured by shadow but his expression of concern was clear as day. She nodded to show she was all right.

He moved his hand from her face. They were sprawled in a small gap between the cypresses and a collection of thickly leaved bushes. His warm body was beneath hers. Saffron shuffled slightly so she lay next to him. Leaning close enough for her lips to brush his ear, she whispered, "What do we do now? Was it Berking in the car?"

Alexander inclined his head to hers, his breath warm on her cheek. "It was Berking, he went inside ten minutes ago. We'll have to stay in the bushes until he turns off the lights or make our way like this."

With a sigh, Saffron let her head rest on the hard ground beneath her. "I suppose crawling along the ground is not the best option."

Alexander relaxed into the same position, and for five minutes they lay in the dark bushes, facing each other. Wind continued to batter the trees overhead in great, swirling gusts. Faint hints of blooming flowers and the deep scent of fresh soil mixed with something warm and clean, which Saffron realized must be the man laying not a foot away from her.

Was it odd that she found lying in this dark garden with Alexander a little romantic?

She forced herself to consider their next move. It seemed that there was nothing hidden in Berking's garden but two wayward scientists. Where would they look next? Could Berking have stolen aconite from another garden? Or perhaps it was simply growing in a pot in his house. Or a friend grew it for him.

The minutes ticked on with no change in the house. Saffron was growing cold on the chilled earth. Shadows from the glow of the house swayed around in the wind. After fifteen minutes, they agreed to try to move. Alexander crawled forward through the brush with Saffron following. Before long, they reached a naked patch of dirt surrounded by large rhododendron bushes. The earth there was recently tilled.

Saffron stilled and she scanned the area. It was shaded by a broad Chinese Juniper that had littered the ground beneath with berries. On a sunny day, this area would likely receive dappled light—

A rapid shuffle in front of her brought her back to the situation at hand. Alexander had turned around—somehow managing it with so little space available for his tall form—and was crawling back to her rapidly. He moved past her with surprising agility and paused in the far corner near the base of the tree and the rhododendron. With one hand, he reached into a pocket.

The door to the house banged open. Heavy footsteps sounded across the threshold.

Saffron sucked in a breath and Alexander tensed, then raced back to her on his elbows, grasping her arm and pushing her ahead of him. They scrambled into the rhododendrons bordering the bald patch. Thorns bit into her arms and legs, grabbing at her hair. They'd just reached cover when the unmistakable sounds of the lumbering Berking crossing the lawn in their direction. They had no hope that the shadows would obscure them, not at this distance and not with the house lit up.

Saffron curled her legs up just as Alexander flattened her to the ground. Then he was next to her, his eyes locked on hers. They lay still as the sound of rustling met their ears. A torch flickered on. The rustling grew louder, a light passing just over Alexander's face. His mouth was a line, his eyes narrowed.

Saffron's heart pounded wildly, the urge to spring up and run away overpowering. Her fingers dug into the dirt and she forced herself to remain still. She flinched as something passed very close to her foot. Alexander took her hand. She squeezed it with the full power of her anxiety. What would they do if they were found? Berking could have them arrested, or force them into his house for questioning or send Alexander away and then she'd be alone with him—

The torch went out.

Berking's booming voice swore, then came the clatter of him shaking the torch aggressively. "Blasted thing!"

He stomped off. Alexander and Saffron didn't wait to hear the door open and close. Once Berking had cleared the stairs to the house, they crawled back to the gate through the bushes, catching more rhododendron thorns as they went. Alexander opened the gate as quietly as possible, and they fled.

They ran down the street and into an alleyway, far into the rubbish bins.

"You're covered!" Saffron gasped, breathless but laughing. She was a little light-headed. She dusted leaves and dirt off Alexander's shirt with shaking hands.

"You are, too," Alexander chuckled, pulling a twig out of her hair. He grinned down at her. "You'll want to look at this."

"What is it?" Saffron asked, frowning at the long rectangle of linen Alexander passed her.

"I snatched this just before Berking came out. Is this what we were looking for?"

Saffron opened the handkerchief and squinted in the half-light of the alley down at the small, flowered stalk within. "Alexander!" She looked up at him in disbelief. "You found it!"

Saffron cradled the small shoot of aconite in her shaking hands, nearly dropping the handkerchief. Alexander met her hands with one of his, steadying it with warm pressure.

"Adrenaline." His murmur was quiet and utterly enticing, until Saffron registered what Alexander had actually said.

"Adrenaline?" she repeated.

He dropped her hand. "Adrenaline, you know. The hormone responsible for certain physiological responses in mammals. The fight or flight response. Hyperarousal as a result of a perceived threat. Cannon's hypothesis states—"

"I see," she said, fighting a smile. His biology talk was endearing, if not exactly romantic. She held up the handkerchief. "You make quite the botanist, Ashton. Well done. Now what?"

Looking down at her with his small smile, he said, "Now, we find a taxi and hope that no one asks us why we're covered in dirt."

⤞⤝

Alexander scrutinized the plant under the glare of the light. It was no more than five inches tall, a pale green stem interspersed with clumps of small purple hooded flowers. Botanical references opened to illustrations and entries covered the small kitchen table alongside the lamp Saffron had removed the shade from. The naked bulb's light cast harsh shadows on her face, enhancing the smudges of dirt she had missed in her rapid wash-up moments ago.

With a hand cupping her chin, she stared down at one of the illustrations, then back to the specimen from the garden. "It certainly looks like aconite . . . But it's not quite right. See here?" She used a pen to indicate the cavernous, violet flowers. "It has clusters of flowers rather than single ones. *"Aconitum* species have single flowers along the stem. Not to mention the blooms are about three months too early. Aconite flowers in the summer."

He ran a hand over his face. Now that they were safely settled in Saffron's kitchen, the late hour and recent nights of poor sleep were catching up to him. "Could this be a different species? One you haven't encountered?"

"The genus is widespread and varied, so I suppose that's possible . . . But this specimen has foliaceous stipules, here." She gently prodded a pair of leaves from which a stem was emerging, "Yet the entirety of the *Aconitum* species can be characterized as lacking stipules altogether." She leaned toward one of the texts and confirmed her statement with a nod. "But the structure of the flower, the hooded opening with clearly defined veins . . ."

Alexander left her to it. As he watched her lean on her elbows and frown in concentration, he wondered how exactly he'd ended up in a woman's flat in the middle of the night, covered in dirt, studying a potentially dangerous plant.

He apparently drifted off, hand supporting his head, as Saffron had to rouse him to declare that she was satisfied that what they stole was at least in the same genus as the well-known poisonous species, but she couldn't absolutely conclude that the plant was a species of poisonous *Aconitum.* Improvising with what she had in her kitchen, she did her best to preserve the various parts of the plant and tucked it into the ice box.

With utmost solemnity, she said, "Alexander, I think we need to go to Inspector Green and tell him everything."

"And tell him what?" Alexander wasn't looking forward to explaining to him how they had gotten the plant.

"That we found Dr. Berking created his very own breed of a highly toxic plant, of course!"

"Is that what this is?" Alexander asked, eying the quick sketch Saffron had done of the plant.

"I can't think of any other explanation. I'll have to look at some other references, of course, but a man of Berking's experience would be able to cross-breed until he got something like this." She paused, discomfort flashing across her face. She sighed and shook her head, her enthusiasm waning to make her look pale and tired. "I'm not sure what he bred it with, or what chemical properties it has, but the features of aconite are definitely there."

"Inspector Green will have to send it to a lab to be tested." Alexander ran a hand through his hair, dislodging a scrap of leaf and frowning down at it. "The results might not be ready before the ship sails. He can't arrest Berking for breeding a new plant, even if it is poisonous."

Saffron bit her lip. "He arrested Dr. Maxwell for less, didn't he?" She looked up at him, eyes pleading. "We can't *not* tell the inspector, Alexander."

Sighing, Alexander agreed. They'd see the inspector tomorrow. Hopefully, by then Saffron would have found something useful in her references.

Quietly, they made their way down the hallway, not wanting to wake up Elizabeth nor the landlady in the flat below.

On the street, the wind had died down and the sky was clear. A slender silver moon had risen over the neat rows of flats. They spent the time walking to a busier street for a taxi comparing cuts and bruises. Saffron won the count contest. Her venture through the length of the garden had punctured not only her arms, but had left a long scratch down the side of her throat. Alexander won for the worst, a long scrape from the rhododendron crisscrossing his arm, right over his scar.

"Alexander," Saffron said, giving him a sidelong glance, "how did you get that scar?"

He was tired, covered in dirt, and had already crawled through a dark garden with Saffron. Why not tell her?

"It's from the War." He stopped there, looking at her. Saffron pressed her lips together like she wanted him to expound on his statement, but didn't. Alexander smiled at her torn expression. "I told you that I was in Fromelles. My unit was stuck in our trench. We fought, many of my friends died. Someone threw a grenade and it hit near me." He paused, pushing back against images of mud and blood flashing through his mind. "I was knocked out. When I woke up, I had a concussion, and my arm and back were in bad shape. Second and third degree burns, limited range of movement, concerns about lasting nerve damage. My arm healed, my back healed. I had to learn to write with my left hand, but compared to most, I got off easy. I have no reason to complain."

He glanced at Saffron but her face was shadowed.

Alexander contemplated telling her more. The horror of waking with half his body burning, the gut-wrenching sensation of being a stranger to himself when he looked at his scarred body for the first time. How the sight and the smell of smoke or a book dropping to the floor used to cause him to slide into terror so complete he would forget where he was.

He'd spoken to his older brother, a former pilot, concerned he was going mad. His brother and several of his friends all experienced similar things on their return from the war—night terrors, shaking hands, aversion to loud noises, even unprovoked violence. Some of them had fled to the country, the survivors of horrors worse than his. Some turned to alcohol or something harder, as he had before finding a better strategy. It had been months since he'd had a slide, as he called them, and more than a year since they'd been a regular problem.

Feeling emboldened by his progress, or perhaps the lateness of the hour, Alexander continued. "I'm sure you've heard of soldiers returning with shell-shock who can't handle loud noises or sudden changes. That was me, too."

He could recall his temper splintering one day after his shaking hands had dropped yet another plate in the lab.

The plate fell to the ground, and a hot wave of shame and anger had caused him to shove a tray of samples to the floor. Between his heavy breaths, he'd heard the sudden silence from the hallway outside. He'd not seen anyone witness his misery, but he was sure someone had noticed and he'd be out of the university without a second chance. That was the day he'd finally gone to Dr. Avery for help. He'd learned a form of Tibetan meditation from the professor and had never looked back.

That was nearly three years ago. He was a different man now.

He cleared his throat. "I use that breathing technique, you know, the one I mentioned."

"You tidy things, I've noticed," Saffron said gently. "Your office is always so neat, too. After the xolotl," she stopped him, hand on his arm, "you put right the whole office. Even after I'd made it such a mess."

Alexander looked intently at her, unsure if he wanted her to continue.

"But now," she said, gesturing to their dirt-streaked clothes, "you don't seem bothered."

"I don't always . . ." He sighed, shaking his head more to himself than her. "It doesn't always work in the way I expect it to."

They walked past another flat in silence.

It was true that his need to have things tidy was not a constant obsession, considering it came and went with varying degrees. It was frustrating, the unpredictable way his brain now worked. But at least it allowed him to work in the field. Nature's chaos rarely bothered him like humanity's did. He had never bothered trying to do something about it. In fact, no one, not even his brother, had ever commented on his aversion to disorder.

Unsure how he felt about Saffron noticing that part of himself, he said, "You seem to have a passion for detective work." He slanted her a teasing glance. "Maybe you should change fields?"

Saffron's expression was troubled. "My only interest in it is making sure they don't succeed in framing Dr. Maxwell. Or me, for that matter. And that Berking doesn't get away with it." She seemed ready to say more, perhaps about why she wanted Berking held accountable more than the others.

Alexander stopped, his hand on her hand. "Berking won't get away with anything."

She looked at him for a long moment, eyes searching his. "Why are you helping me? Truly?"

Alexander considered all the excuses he'd come up with for why he was so willingly roped in. He chose the simplest one. "I'm a scientist, same as you. I like solving puzzles."

Just then, a lone taxi turned onto the street, saving him from a closer examination of his motivations. The driver, puffy eyed and dragging on a tiny cigarette, raised his eyebrow at Alexander and Saffron's disheveled appearance.

Back at his own flat, Alexander took off his stained and torn clothes and ran a bath. He winced as his cuts twinged in the soapy water. The evening replayed over in his mind. It was rather intoxicating, playing detective with Saffron. Dangerous, to be sure, with lethal plants and almost getting caught by Berking . . . but intoxicating. But he could hardly have told her that.

CHAPTER 17

Saffron was already outside the police station when Alexander arrived, buzzing with nervous energy. She'd agreed to put off coming until the early afternoon. He'd had appointments and errands for the expedition he couldn't reschedule, and she grudgingly agreed. But it meant she'd spent hours that morning in Maxwell's office, unable to focus on work. The realization that had come to her looking at the aconite the previous evening had shaken her deeply. Berking had created a crossbreed of a dangerous plant. In his office, she'd found a folder containing notes suggesting her father had worked on hybridization. There was no further evidence than that, the logical, scientific part of her mind insisted, but her chest filled with ice each time the pernicious thought crossed her mind, wondering if the two were connected.

Saffron spent the morning researching aconite in the library, in part to avoid the North Wing where she might run into Berking, and trying to determine what to say to the inspector. Their meeting about the xolotl vine hadn't gone well at all, but she believed her evidence had contributed to clearing Maxwell. Hopefully, Inspector Green would trust her more today.

Alexander looked no worse for wear after their late night adventure. His navy suit was in perfect order, his jaw smooth from a fresh shave. Only his right hand was marred with a scratch. Saffron had her lavender coat buttoned to the top, and her hair was arranged in a lower twist than usual, to conceal the red scratch still along her neck.

They settled into Inspector Green's office in the same uncomfortable chairs as they had the last time, then waited in silence while the inspector opened his notebook and prepared his pen. Saffron counted the number of cracks in the wall; there were seven, unpleasantly reminiscent of the spread of the xolotl vine over the wall in the greenhouse.

When she couldn't take the tension any longer, Saffron spoke. "Inspector, Mr. Ashton and I have been looking into the poisoning of Mrs. Henry, and—"

The inspector looked up with a frown and said, "Have you?"

"Y-yes," she said, hesitating at his hard tone. "I happened to find something in Dr. Berking's office. It was part of a formula that included the chemical aconitine, the toxin found in aconite. Aconite is wolfsbane, the poisonous flowering plant."

Inspector Green's mouth thinned. "*Happened* to find?"

Saffron was grateful Alexander continued, for her mouth had gone dry at the unamused look on the inspector's face. "After further research, we discovered that one of the other compounds in the formula is a preservative."

Dreading their next piece of information, Saffron drew her fingers together tightly. "So we went to Dr. Berking's house and in his garden was a plant."

The inspector looked up and cocked an eyebrow. "Most irregular. A plant in a botanist's garden."

Saffron almost smiled at his dry tone. "It is a member of the *Aconitum* genus, although it isn't formed like any species I've seen before. I have the specimen here." She removed the carefully cushioned handkerchief from her handbag and put it on his desk. She opened the folds to reveal the plant, now sadly shriveled as she hadn't dared utilize any of the department's resources to better preserve it.

"How did you obtain this plant, Miss Everleigh?"

Saffron cleared her throat and met his eyes. "I took it from Dr. Berking's garden, Inspector."

"That would be illegal."

Numerous ill-advised responses crossed her mind about how no one would have known about it if not for her illegal snooping and stealing. "I think you'll find, in conjunction with the formula, it's relevant to your investigation. The plant is a new species of aconite, one that doesn't appear in any books I've been able to get my hands on."

Saffron pointed out some salient features, to which the inspector nodded minutely and notated. When Saffron asked about the type of poison used on Mrs. Henry, he glanced at her warily. His silence was confirmation that they still hadn't identified it.

After another pregnant pause, Saffron added, "The only reason we've brought this to your attention is because it seems likely that this plant is connected to the poisoning. It's possible that Dr. Berking needed a new kind of aconite to camouflage a crime. It would be well within his skills to breed a new species. This new species might have a different chemical composition, perhaps included in that formula. The garden bed where we found the plant had recently been cleared, so there were likely more plants that were taken and perhaps used." She glanced at Alexander, who gave her an encouraging nod. "It would be easy enough to have it tested, Inspector. If the toxins in the plant match what was in Mrs. Henry's blood, then you could be sure about Dr. Berking's involvement."

Saffron was rather at a loss. The deadpan policeman didn't seem at all interested in their evidence. She was ready to get up and leave when she realized they hadn't said anything about the equipment forms.

"We also discovered"—now Inspector Green showed the slightest hint of exasperation as she continued—"that Dr. Henry has submitted requests for an outstanding amount of supplies for the expedition, running to hundreds of pounds. The other members of the expedition have asked for only a fraction of what Dr. Henry asked for. We wondered if he was perhaps involved in embezzlement of the expedition funds. That would set him up to be either a target of someone trying to cover up their mistake or involvement, or as someone with something to hide."

This seemed to mean something to the inspector, who paused in his writing and looked up. "Where did you obtain *this* information?"

Alexander explained his observations when he'd visited Richard Blake's office.

Leaning forward in her chair, Saffron asked, "Do you think Mr. Blake might be connected to both the poisoning and the embezzlement? He is known to have had a quarrel with Dr. Henry about joining the team and the funding. And he was possibly having an affair with Mrs. Henry."

The inspector gave her a piercing look. "I beg your pardon?"

With another glance to Alexander, whose expression said she was on her own with that particular theory, Saffron said, "Well, I . . . I saw them speak together at the party, and they exchanged some significant looks. Mrs. Henry, in the conversation I overheard during the party, was well aware of Dr. Henry's various, ah, *friendships*." She contemplated sharing the letters they'd found, but her theories about Miss Ermine seemed unimportant now. "Miss Ermine mentioned to me that Mrs. Henry was not exactly faithful herself."

"I see." Inspector Green finished his notes, then shook Alexander's hand and then Saffron's, whereupon he said, "No more investigating. If I hear of further misconduct, from either of you, I shall have to place you under arrest for interfering with a police investigation. If you learn further information, please refer it to me." He said the words firmly, without his usual disinterest.

Saffron and Alexander stepped into a teashop down the street to recoup. They settled at a small table and soon had a fresh pot of tea before them.

Alexander shook his head, saying, "I never have any clue what Inspector Green is thinking."

"Ha! Now you know how it feels! You can be just as cryptic."

"I do more than frown and write. He must be a very successful interviewer. We didn't get a thing out of him."

"Alexander, I rather think you've caught the bug!" Saffron grinned.

His eyes warmed over his teacup. As he set it back down, he said, "I think we know that the embezzlement idea is relevant, at least. That was the only part he was interested in."

"Yes." Saffron patted her mouth with a napkin, frowning. "But what connection is there between the aconite, Dr. Berking, and the embezzlement? Berking was in on the embezzlement? Perhaps the conflict between Berking and Henry is a ruse to disguise their alliance. Dr. Henry used Berking's skills to create a mysterious toxin to poison his wife or perhaps Blake?" Saffron mused, stirring her tea. "There are simply too many possibilities."

"The inspector has far more information than we do, and now we've given him even more to consider. I'm sure he will figure it out. After all, he is trained to solve crimes."

Saffron, curiosity still burning, said, "But it could be weeks before he solves it! You could be stuck in the Amazon with a murderer by then!"

"Plants and poisons may be in your wheelhouse, but an embezzlement scheme is better handled by the police." Alexander smiled, his tone softening. "If we see or hear anything else, we can let Inspector Green know."

The bus jostled Saffron and Alexander together and apart in turn as it trundled back toward Fitzrovia. As they entered the Quad, Saffron paused, asking, "Should I have told him about Eris Ermine and the letters? It could be important, and the inspector might not know about her involvement with Dr. Henry."

"I can't imagine that didn't come up in his interviews with the other witnesses," Alexander replied. "And it would necessitate you revealing you looked through Dr. Henry's desk in addition to—"

Saffron was nearly knocked to the ground when a blur of a figure pushed into her. Alexander caught her arm and Harry Snyder, with pink cheeks and an overwrought expression, gasped, "Terribly sorry, Miss Everleigh."

"Mr. Snyder? Whatever is the matter?" Saffron asked.

"Just was running to collect you," Snyder said to Alexander, panting. "Dr. Henry has called a meeting of the expedition crew, and I have to gather everyone quickly." He gulped and mopped his brow with his handkerchief, further mussing his black hair. "We're meeting in South Quad Hall in the conference room on the third floor. Could you come now, please? The meeting is at two o'clock, and I've got six other people to find!"

Alexander quickly agreed and Snyder turned to leave.

"Mr. Snyder," Saffron said sweetly, stalling his rushed departure, "I don't mean to be intrusive, but would you like me to come and take notes for the meeting? I'm sure you usually are tasked with it, but why should you have to sit scribbling what everyone else says? I know you have so much to contribute."

Snyder, clearly overwhelmed with the urgency of the meeting, merely stared at her for a moment before babbling, "Oh yes,

Miss Everleigh, how kind of you. I usually do have to take notes during such meetings as Dr. Henry's assistant, but it would be nice to be able to participate for once."

Over his shoulder, Alexander smothered a smile and said, "Very well, Miss Everleigh and I will go to the hall and see you there. Third floor?"

They watched Snyder scamper off in the opposite direction.

"Well done," said Alexander. "Poor man was completely taken in."

"He actually rather reminded me of you," Saffron replied lightly. They changed direction and headed toward the other side of the Quad. "I couldn't just let you go without me. I'm dying of curiosity. What could be the emergency?"

Alexander shrugged as they continued, crossing onto the green. Alexander turned toward the administrative offices.

"I thought we were going to the hall?" Saffron asked, indicating the black door to the South Wing just a few feet away.

Alexander stopped in his tracks, looking as though he was confused that she was asking. Then he nodded. "Right."

Saffron led them toward the South Wing, which they could pass through to get to the South Quad where the hall stood. When they entered the South Wing, a mirror image of its partner, with beige tiled floors and dark wood bordering white-washed walls and tall windows, Saffron caught sight of lines of photographs along the walls. The weak sunlight of a gray midday glared off the glass frames, obscuring the faces Saffron knew were looking out solemnly from the dozens of photographs. Students, professors—those whom the Great War had taken from the university community.

A glance in her companion's direction confirmed her suspicion. Alexander was looking determinedly ahead, with his mouth fixed in a tight line. Did he really completely avoid the South Wing's main floor to stay away from the memorial? She went out of her way to pass by it, if only to catch a glimpse of her father's blurry face in the middle, right at the top. But perhaps she, too, would avoid it if she'd fought alongside these men and lived like he had.

They emerged on the other side of the South Wing and into the South Quad. On the far side, the ramshackle carpenter's shack, wreathed in a thick layer of sawdust, detracted from the pleasant view of the small green. University College was always in a state of improvement, with new properties on Gower Street and around it being bought up and adapted to academic uses all the time. It was easy for her to forget the constant expansion, being constantly cooped up in the North Wing, the library, or the greenhouses.

The sun made a half-hearted appearance behind clouds, casting great swaths of shadow on the ground. Saffron and Alexander climbed the winged stairs on either side of the ground-floor entrance to the hall and entered the quiet building.

They walked down a long corridor of polished wood to the conference room, where about twenty men waited. The noise level matched the restless nature of the assemblage. Some sat around the long table, but most stood around in small groups, and all were talking with enthusiasm and curiosity.

Alexander walked to a group of other researchers. They stood by a window that had been cracked, letting a cool breeze into the stuffy room.

"Robinson," Alexander said to a burly, dark-haired man in a green bow tie, "what's all this about? Snyder nearly knocked me over trying to get me to this meeting." Out of the corner of his eye, he saw Saffron slip into a corner and draw a chair to the side, where she pulled her notebook and pencil out.

Robinson chuckled. "You know how Snyder is. Henry sneezes, and it's like the whole building is collapsing around him." Robinson shrugged bulky shoulders. "Adams suspects the old man will turn in his boots since his wife is still in hospital."

The short man next to him—Adams, Alexander presumed—nodded vigorously and said in a hushed voice, "Can't very well up and leave his wife in that state. Even if things were . . . you know." He raised his eyebrows with exaggerated meaning and looked about as if Dr. Henry would hear him, though he wasn't in the room.

Crowley, a bespeckled assistant researcher from the history department, sidled over. "Any news, chaps?" His brow was damp and his pale eyes wide. "My professor says that Henry is out. I wonder who they'll get to replace him."

The men chattered for another moment, suggesting people who might take over the leadership role. A handful more people joined the group, including Dr. Berking. When Dr. Henry and Harry Snyder walked into the room, a hush fell, and the men quickly took seats around the long table. Alexander thought Saffron was rather determinedly not looking at him. Her blue eyes steadily marked all the people along the table, skipping over him, then rested on Dr. Henry as he sat heavily at the head of the group.

His face was gray and his dark hair greasy. Even his brawny physique seemed diminished from the last time Alexander had seen him. He said a few words to Snyder as the group settled round the table. Berking sat opposite, at the foot of the table, his small eyes narrowed. Alexander sat mid-table, facing Saffron, whose eyes leapt to Berking as he leaned to Blake on his right and murmured something. Probably avidly noting her suspects were conversing.

"Well," Dr. Henry began, his voice heavy, "our expedition is just a few weeks away, and we have much to do. My prolonged absence, I'm sure you are aware, was due to my wife's unfortunate illness. You'll excuse me for being away in the midst of our preparations. Snyder has kept me abreast, so I am aware of what needs to be attended to before we depart. Today, we are meeting to settle some details."

At this, whispers and sidelong glances erupted all along the table. Alexander locked shocked eyes with Saffron. Dr. Henry still planned to go on the expedition?

Dr. Henry could not have ignored the whispers, nor did he try to. His ice-blue eyes, darkened by deep shadows beneath, glared up and down the table for a good thirty seconds before they abated. Dr. Berking and Richard Blake were still whispering together as he began to speak again. He said rather forcefully, "We are here to review the schedule of the entire expedition, in addition to making some adjustments to the docket of projects and who is responsible for what."

Many continued looking dubious, and several made the occasional side comment to their neighbor, but the meeting progressed. It was a blur of dates and names for thirty minutes. Alexander listened and wrote some notes, his mind working furiously to figure out why Dr. Henry would go on with the expedition. He must have realized how suspicious it was for him to leave the country in the midst of the investigation. Had Inspector Green already cleared him to go?

"Ashton!" Dr. Henry barked down the table. Alexander was suddenly aware that all faces were turned toward him. "Ashton, what's the update about Dr. Maxwell?"

Remembering that Dr. Maxwell's release was not yet common knowledge, Alexander said, "We are still unsure if his study will, uh, need to be completed. We're continuing to prepare as if it is going forward, so the supplies have been ordered and the preparatory research is nearly complete."

Dr. Henry grunted and nodded to Snyder, who he apparently thought was taking notes, though he had nothing to write on in front of him. Henry moved on, growling at the next researcher. From opposite him, Saffron made an amused face at Alexander, who grimaced.

Dr. Berking cleared his throat. Henry ignored him and turned to the next researcher, but Berking said, "Dr. Henry, the botany department—"

With a look of utter annoyance, Henry looked at him and said, "We've heard from botany, Berking."

Affronted, Berking's face colored a deep red. "As the head of botany, I would think that I should get a say in whether or not Dr. Maxwell's study will go forward."

With an eye roll and a huff of frustration, Henry waved a hand. "Go on then."

"As Dr. Maxwell is currently *indisposed*," said Berking, his eyes slipping over to Saffron with a malicious glint, making Alexander grit his teeth, "we are still in consultation over whether we will continue on with the chlorophyll study or press into the next available research project, which is a study on exotic poisons. You must be *well* aware of all the possibilities the Amazon offers for such things, Dr. Henry. We wouldn't want this opportunity to pass by."

Henry, who was letting his attention wander obviously, stiffened as Berking spoke. His eyes narrowed at the window. "Indeed," Henry replied gruffly, nodding again to Snyder. With amusement, Alexander watched Henry realize Snyder hadn't been taking notes. He looked ready to reprimand him when he caught sight of Saffron just behind Snyder, writing notes studiously. His eyes lingered on her momentarily.

After a few more comments about studies and supplies, the meeting concluded, and the group began to break up. Dr. Henry stood talking to several men as they passed on their way to the door, his old swagger seeming to come out as he laughed and clapped them on the back. Robinson, who insisted they discuss how biology would be coordinated with entomology, shuffled Alexander down the hall.

Saffron finished her notes and stood, taking a very long time to close her bag and prepare to leave. She was trying to overhear Dr. Berking and Richard Blake. Blake had remained completely silent throughout the whole meeting. His face had stayed the same too. She was beginning to wonder if his face made any other expressions than indifference and a bland smile. Blake and Berking had their heads together and backs turned, and their conversation was far too quiet to hear.

Dr. Henry strode over to her. "Miss Everleigh, I believe."

"Yes, sir," said Saffron, somewhat surprised he knew her name.

"Snyder says you stepped in to take notes to free him up for the meeting. Very kind of you to humor him," he said, his voice as loud as when he had addressed the whole room. "He gets in quite a tizzy if he's forced to do his job and write things down. Some assistant!"

Saffron offered a tight-lipped smile.

Dr. Henry dropped his voice to a normal volume and gave her an evaluating look. "I want to get a copy of these notes so I could look over them this evening. Type them up and bring them to my office at the end of the day."

"Yes, sir, I can do that," Saffron said, stomach fluttering. She'd just been given the perfect opportunity to question the top suspect. "Is five o'clock all right?"

"That'll be fine," he said, eyes narrowing slightly. "See you then."

CHAPTER 18

Saffron hurried along the hallway, heels clacking as she passed researchers from the meeting chatting in the hall. She needed to type up the notes for Dr. Henry, but more than that, she needed to plan what she was going to say to him.

A frisson of nerves slid down her spine at the prospect—he could have tried to kill his own wife. But she would be careful. A few questions about his wife being in hospital would be a natural lead into more serious questions. She could always plead curiosity, since she obviously had nothing to do with the Henrys or the expedition funds.

At the bottom of the stairs, Saffron looked about the hall, hoping to see Alexander amid the students milling around. She needed to get his advice about how to handle Dr. Henry. Instead of Alexander, she saw Dr. Berking's hulking figure making his way through the door at the far end of the hall, Mr. Blake behind him.

Caught between impatience to question Dr. Henry and the desire to know what Berking and Blake were talking about, she found her feet moving toward the retreating backs of the two men. They were already almost to the racquetball courts to the north of the building when Saffron exited the hall, but Saffron could hear Berking's loud voice echoing across the green.

"Why announce it to the whole bloody group then?"

Blake must have made a reply, because Berking shook his head and said, "No, no, you're right."

They turned into the door leading into the Wilkins Building and began up the stairs. Saffron waited until they'd reached the first landing before she followed. She hadn't heard a word Blake said, his voice was too quiet, but Berking's side of the conversation sounded promising. They were at least discussing Dr. Henry.

"This should have been cleared up days ago," Berking growled. "Getting close to the departure . . ."

Saffron crept up the deserted stairs after Berking's voice faded. There would be more students to disguise her following them in the main halls, so she dashed up the remaining steps and promptly ran into someone standing at the landing. She dropped her bag, sending her pen, pencils, powder compact, keys, and notebook scattering across the black and white tiles.

"Oh, excuse me," said Richard Blake, his low voice cool and even.

"I'm so sorry!" Saffron gasped, her voice high with dismay. Her eyes darted around, looking for where Berking might be lying in wait, but saw no one.

Blake stooped to help her pick up her things. He handed her pencils and her notebook, pausing to look at her as she placed them into her bag. "You were at the expedition meeting, weren't you? Just now."

"Yes, I was taking notes for Harry Snyder. I just . . ." Considering she had smashed into him in an otherwise lonely stairwell, she needed a reason to be following him. "I saw that you were there, Mr. Blake, and er, wanted to speak to you."

He raised his brows in polite expectation and they rose to their feet. "I see. How may I assist you?"

"I wanted to ask you about, er . . ." Saffron cast around for something benign and landed on the photographs she'd passed by with Alexander earlier. "My father."

Blake's lips tipped up in a smile that didn't reach his eyes. His eyes were blue, she noticed, but rather a watery blue. "Your father?"

Saffron cleared her throat and nodded, her idea forming quickly. "You see, my father was a professor here and died in the war almost five years ago and I'd been thinking that perhaps my family might want to make a contribution in his honor."

"I see," Blake replied.

His eyes flickered down her body, though not in the way she'd become used to. She realized that he was looking at the dust clinging to her skirt. Nervously, she brushed at it.

"Could I set up an appointment, perhaps? I can telephone my mother and grandparents this evening to get more specifics."

Blake nodded. "Of course. Best to have one's information prepared upfront, that way there is no delay in honoring your late father. Simply contact my secretary to find a time."

Saffron smiled and nodded.

"May I ask his name?" he asked.

"Oh," Saffron said, hitching her handbag farther up her arm. "Thomas Everleigh. He was a botany professor. I work in the department too."

She thought she saw a flare of recognition in his eyes at the mention of her father's name, though she couldn't think of why his name would mean anything to Blake, especially as he wasn't involved in the botany department apart from his apparent friendship with Berking. Had he heard about the disagreement between her and Berking? The thought made her teeth clench in a strained smile.

"Thomas Everleigh, my goodness," Blake murmured with a slight smile. "I am sorry for your loss, Miss Everleigh. His heroic sacrifice does a credit to the Easting line. Well, we will ensure he is well remembered. Come to my office now, if you will, and we can get started."

His disinterested tone soothed her concerns over Berking's influence on him. If she went with him now, she'd perhaps get to snoop inside his office. But she also had no idea what she might say to him. How could she ask if a crime had been committed right under his nose? And she still had to prepare for Dr. Henry. One suspect at a time, she decided.

"I'm afraid I have some work to get done this afternoon," Saffron said quickly.

Blake inclined his head. "I understand. If you please, come tomorrow, around two in the afternoon. I always make time for special bequests such as yours, Miss Everleigh."

Saffron nodded and watched Blake walk away, disappearing around a corner in a rush of students exiting a classroom.

Flush with success, Saffron hurried off toward the North Wing. She had an appointment with yet another suspect.

Her feeling of victory was short lived. Like Dr. Aster's note this morning, she found another tucked into the office door when she returned. She read it through and, her hand holding the paper so tightly it tore in her fingers, she walked slowly to the top of the stairs and down the hall. Full of dread, she entered Pierce's office.

"Yes?" Pierce said from his desk, not looking up.

"Is Dr. Berking available, Mr. Pierce?" Saffron asked, holding up the torn note. "He wishes to speak with me."

Pierce looked up and his near-black eyes immediately narrowed. With a sneer, he asked, "Do you have an appointment?"

Frowning at his odd question, she shook her head. Wasn't he the one who'd left the note in her door?

With an exasperated air, Pierce went to the office door and called in to Berking. A moment later, Saffron stepped into his office, hands shaking and heart pounding. There were several reasons Berking might want to see her, but each one made her want to insist that the door stay open. If he'd found out that she'd broken into his home, or even his office, he wouldn't confront her now, comfortably sitting behind the same desk she'd hidden under, would he?

Dr. Berking's vast face stretched into an unctuous smile that revealed nothing of his intentions as she passed through the door. She imagined him as a red-haired spider, waiting for a fly drawing ever closer to his web. Had she really thought she was no longer afraid of him?

"Why, hello," he said with a leer. "You're very smart not to leave me waiting today, Miss Everleigh. I'm an impatient man."

Saffron's lips trembled as she forced a polite smile on her face.

His grin widened as if he sensed her turmoil. "Why don't you sit down?"

Saffron took a few steps forward to give the impression of compliance, though each step toward him made her stomach clench.

"Well, this is quite a turn of events, is it not? You must feel triumphant, I'm sure," Berking said, his voice loud and jolly.

"I'm sorry?" Saffron inched another step forward.

"The study, my dear!" Berking leaned back in his chair, his smile fading slightly as Saffron blinked blankly at him. "Surely you remember. It was not even a month ago, when we had our little misunderstanding."

Confusion stilled her steps. "My proposal?"

"Yes, my dear, for your study." He chuckled. "I'm afraid I might have misrepresented it to Dr. Henry at the meeting. But it does include a few poisonous plants, does it not? I looked back over the notes you left behind about comparing pigmentations of tropical plants. Your study will round out our department's docket nicely." A sly smile crept across his features. "With Dr. Maxwell being unavailable for the foreseeable future, I thought you might want a chance to take the lead."

Her mind was numb, shock blanketing all other thoughts. "Take the lead?"

Berking's booming laugh jolted her. "Yes, my dear—your own study."

"But sir," Saffron stammered, her mind fixating on what was really a minor problem, "the expedition leaves in just two weeks. How can I—"

"You'll have to get to work, Miss Everleigh, in order to make sure Mr. Ashton will be able to carry it out properly. I understand you two have been working closely on Maxwell's project. I'm sure you won't mind putting in a few extra hours." His smile turned malicious. "Come to me tomorrow evening with your final proposal, and be ready to explain it *thoroughly*. You'll get your study if I'm pleased with what you have to offer."

The excitement that had begun to hum in her mind dropped off immediately. Her skin crawled. She forced out the words, "Thank you, Dr. Berking," before turning around and leaving, practically running back to Dr. Maxwell's office in a fog of confusion and concern.

Saffron arrived at the door and realized the keys to the office were missing from her bag. Had she dropped them in the stairwell? She dashed across the North Wing and into the Wilkins Building, but when she reached the stairwell where she'd spoken to Blake, they weren't there. She exhaled slowly, trying to focus when all she could think about was Berking's last words. *"You'll get your study if I'm pleased with what you have to offer."*

One thing at a time. She didn't have too long to get the typing done before meeting Dr. Henry—that was the priority. Alexander would probably let her use his typewriter if he was in his office.

Luckily, Alexander was inside. She entered at his word and sat on the chair opposite where he stood at his desk, sleeves rolled up and pouring over files.

Her heart was still pounding from her jaunt back and forth across the Quad, but she forced her voice to be steady. "I just went to see Dr. Berking."

He looked up quickly, concern sharpening his eyes as he looked her over. "What happened?"

Saffron still felt dazed, like the last ten minutes had been a bizarre dream. Running her own study *was* a dream, but being indebted to Berking would be a nightmare. "He offered me my study."

"Your study? Which one?"

"I proposed a project when he, you know, bothered me, and he hadn't said anything about it, and I never thought he would agree to let me do it—not after what happened. It's regarding the pigmentation of different kinds of tropical plants. He mentioned it at the meeting, but not very accurately. I think he said it like that to bother Dr. Henry. Didn't you notice how he got all stiff and annoyed when Berking was speaking? It's because some of the specimens are rather poisonous, and I wanted to determine what differences there were in pigmentation since Dr. Maxwell will already be working on chlorophyll. Except that now Berking says his study is off." Saffron realized she was rambling. "Anyway, he said I could do it if I could get it ready in time."

Alexander frowned, leaning his knuckles against the surface of his desk. "Dr. Maxwell's project is scrapped, and yours is going forward?"

"It seems so," Saffron said, a little hurt at his complete lack of enthusiasm. Was he angry that hours of research had been wasted? "I know you've already done so much work for Maxwell's study, but I'll be able to do most of the work myself, so you won't have to—"

"I'm not concerned about the work," he said impatiently. "I'm curious why he's allowing you to do it now, just before we're leaving. And why is he giving you your project rather than one of the professors or researchers?"

"Well, it was a rather good proposal," Saffron muttered, put out at his inference.

"What did he say you have to do?"

Her stomach dropped at the prospect of being in that office with Berking again. "He said I have to finish my proposal and discuss it with him tomorrow to finalize it."

"You have to go speak with him?"

"Yes," Saffron said slowly.

"In his office?"

Saffron nodded, excitement replaced entirely by anxiety.

Alexander crossed his arms. "Don't you think he'll use this situation to his advantage? You're going to him for approval for a project you shouldn't even get the chance to do—"

"Shouldn't get the chance to do?" Saffron repeated, her voice rising. "What is that supposed to mean?"

Alexander grimaced. "That isn't what I meant. I mean that there is a reason he's offering it to you and not to an actual researcher with more experience. You're just an assistant."

Even if she knew what he was saying was true, that he would say it hurt more than she would have thought. "Maybe it's because my design was *good*. Maybe it's because—"

"Maxwell is now gone and Berking knows you badly want to get ahead in the department? He's already targeted you once."

"I don't have a choice!" She was on her feet in an instant, unable to sit still with the roiling anxiety in her stomach. Saffron hated that she knew how right he was. But even though she knew Berking was scum and might have a mind to repeat his prior actions, how could she say no to the possibility of her own study, one that might possibly be published? This might be her only chance. If she said no, she doubted the offer would be repeated.

"Of course you have a choice," Alexander said, his voice more gentle. "I don't understand—"

Saffron blinked away furious tears. "You *clearly* don't understand, Alexander. You've no idea what it's like to come in here every day and feel inadequate, to feel like an imposter. You don't know what I gave up to study here, let alone work here. You came to the university and found your place and thrived. You have no concept of the daily struggle that I have just to *be* here."

Alexander's face turned stony, though his eyes burned hotter. He just stared at her, jaw clenched.

"Thank you for your concern," Saffron said stiffly, looking away, "but I'm quite sure I have it under control. May I use your typewriter? I need to prepare the meeting notes for Dr. Henry, and I've lost the keys to Dr. Maxwell's office."

Alexander went to the cabinet behind his desk. He lifted the heavy typewriter from within and set it on the desk, then left the office without a word.

Saffron finished typing the notes much sooner than she expected, spurred on by Alexander's voice in her head with each punch of a key. *"You're just an assistant. You shouldn't get the chance."* It infuriated her that he would say something that could have come from the mouths of any of the cynical men she'd worked with. She'd thought he was different.

Alexander returned just as she stood up with her stack of notes.

"Thank you," she said, not looking at him. "I'll let you know what needs to be done to prepare for my study, if it's approved."

Saffron was still angry when she reached Dr. Henry's office ten minutes later. Snyder was gone and Saffron was early, so she paced around the fine carpets in small outer office. Better to be angry than afraid. She'd feel plenty of fear tomorrow when she walked into the room with Berking, and the anger would fuel her work more effectively now.

"Miss Everleigh, do come in!" Dr. Henry called from his office, his brusque voice making her jump.

Saffron stepped inside, making sure to leave the door opened. The hall outside the office was still bustling with students and staff, so if things went awry, someone would hear her calls for help. The thought made her insides squirm.

Dr. Henry stood at the glass shelf by the nearest window on which stood a collection liquor bottles. He poured a good amount of scotch into a glass that had the dregs of a prior drink. He lifted the glass to his lips and caught her looking. "Damned gossips will drive a man to drink, you know. Will you join me?"

"No, thank you."

Either he didn't hear her, or he didn't care, as Dr. Henry brought her a small glass of chartreuse from a nearly empty bottle. The terrible thought that the drink could have been laced with poison crossed her mind, and she sat it on Dr. Henry's desk, untouched.

Dr. Henry settled behind the large desk and said, "I brought that back from a conference in Marseilles. Waste of bloody time." He took a long drink from his tumbler. "Good liquor, though."

Saffron smiled slightly and put her notes on his desk. He didn't look at the file, just continued looking at her, his eyes narrowed.

"Snyder says you assist old Maxwell. What's he got you doing? Typing and shuffling around books? Or out in a field, pulling up plants?" He chuckled and took a drink.

Despite herself, she was gratified by his question. Usually people assumed she just typed things and stood around like an ornament. "I do a bit of everything. Dr. Maxwell usually gives me work in the greenhouse or research to do. I've been helping to gather his materials for the expedition."

Dr. Henry nodded and finished his drink. He swaggered back to the bottles for another, his eyes still on her but perhaps a little unfocused. How many drinks had he had? Maybe enough to talk.

"There seems to be so much to do for the expedition. I can't imagine how you're coping with your responsibilities on top of caring for your poor wife. I was at the party when she was taken ill," Saffron said sadly, her eyes innocently wide.

Dr. Henry made an impatient noise and looked off toward the window. "Yes, it's been challenging. Can't even go see her without . . ." He cleared his throat and took another gulp of his drink. "But that doesn't matter. Expedition is on. I've got work to do."

Saffron shifted in her chair, attempting to get a view of his face. "It's got to be such a burden, trying to get everything straightened out before your departure. You know, arrangements for your wife, sorting out equipment and finances . . ."

Dr. Henry drained his glass and clunked it down on the shelf, causing the glass panels to tremble and Saffron to jump.

Hurriedly, she said, "I'm sorry, Dr. Henry, I didn't mean—"

"No, no," he said gruffly, looking about the room disconsolately. "She hasn't woken up after that blasted drink. I don't know what to do. Poor girl is right out of it, and I'm going off . . ." His throat bobbed as he swallowed.

Saffron was rather at a loss. Dr. Henry was surprisingly emotional at the mention of his wife. He didn't seem to even hear her obvious reference to the embezzlement.

His hand shook as he refilled his glass, and his face was clouded.

"I didn't mean to upset you, Dr. Henry. I'm sure you're doing what she would have wanted you to do," Saffron said softly, aware that her words were absolute rubbish. She had no idea if Mrs. Henry wanted him to travel and explore.

His gulped his drink, then looked sadly into the bottom of his glass. "I just want . . . I just wanted to do it all, you know. Explore the wilds of the world, bring back treasures . . ."

He sounded so lost, Saffron stood and gently guided him back to his chair. "Please don't be upset. I'm sure before long she'll be right as rain and be there to welcome you back from Brazil."

"That's just it," he said with a crack in his voice. He sunk into his chair. "She's not going to be there."

"What do you mean?" Saffron asked cautiously.

"She gave me the papers just before the party," Dr. Henry moaned. "Cynthia—she's going to divorce me."

Saffron fought to hide her shock, both at the news of divorce and Dr. Henry's utter misery. To give herself something to do, she took up his glass to refill it. She walked back to Dr. Henry, who had buried his face in his hands. This was not how she'd expected this meeting to go at all.

He lifted his face from his hands and drained the glass in one. She patted his shoulder again. "She asked for a divorce just before the expedition?"

He squinted up at her, his handsome face crumpled. "She always stood by me, even though I treated her rotten. All those skirts . . ." With a groan, his hands hit his desk, and he stared straight ahead, looking shocked. "The Committee. That's why she was here. Oh God." He let his head hit the desk with another thunk.

"It's all right, I'm sure she'll come around after all this." Saffron patted his shoulder awkwardly. "What about the College Committee?"

"What if . . ."—his voice cracked again—"she dies?"

He buried his face in his arms atop the desk, his enormous shoulders shaking. Saffron sat quietly as he sobbed. He was already drunk and crying; perhaps she could ask him a few more questions.

Saffron cleared her throat. "Did . . . did your wife know about Miss Ermine?"

"Eris?" He raised his head to look at her as if he'd only just recalled he wasn't alone. His eyes were bloodshot. "I don't know, I don't know if she knew. She was furious during the party; she had that look . . . Did Eris—she talked to you?" Saffron lifted a shoulder noncommittally. "I'd hoped that . . . being gone for so long, she might forget. Eris too—that she'd forget about me. She's so young." His face disappeared into his arms again. Saffron sat in her chair, trying not to watch him cry. She thought she heard him mumbling *"What have I done?,"* but couldn't quite hear him. After a moment, his voice grew stronger and she caught him say, "Just as well, everyone knows I'm a useless husband. If Cynthia does wake up, she'll never forgive me."

Wondering aloud, Saffron said, "It sounds like you care very much for your wife. Why not just be a useful husband?"

"I don't know, I don't know," he mumbled, sinking lower and lower into his arms on his desk.

"Well, when she wakes up, you could apologize," Saffron suggested.

Dr. Henry said nothing. In fact, he snored. Saffron sighed and looked around the room, wondering what had become of her meeting with a rumored rake. She carefully removed his glass from his slack grip and replaced it on the glass shelf. There was a loud snore behind her. Realizing her opportunity, she sidled over to the desk and managed to open his desk drawer to replace the letters she'd taken.

Gazing down at the snoring man, Saffron considered what he'd said. Mrs. Henry had gone to see the College Committee. Had she planned to reveal her husband's liaison with Miss Ermine, possibly getting him kicked out of the university? Or perhaps just interrupt her husband's plans to create a new branch of the history department? Dr. Henry knew of her meeting. Did that give him further motive for killing her?

Dr. Henry might be unfaithful, but she didn't believe he had it in him to murder his wife. He was crushed about the divorce and Mrs. Henry's continued incapacity. He'd been sobbing over her. Saffron tiptoed from the room, leaving the mess of a man sleeping on his desk.

She was just closing the door when Snyder came rushing into the room, directly to his desk. He sorted through a stack of papers and looked relieved to find one before he looked up and saw Saffron standing next to the door. "Miss Everleigh?"

"I was just dropping off the notes for Dr. Henry," she said in a loud whisper. "I'm afraid he's very upset. We spoke about his wife, and he was really quite overwrought. You might want to look in on him in a bit—he's fallen asleep."

"His wife? He's asleep?" Snyder gaped at her. "He talked to you about his wife and he fell asleep? Are you a miracle worker?"

It was Saffron's turn to be astonished. "Whatever do you mean?"

Snyder took off his glasses and hurriedly wiped them on a handkerchief, blinking as he replaced them. "Miss Everleigh, I've been trying to get the man to sit down and rest for days! He's been roaming around the hospital like a mother hen worried about her eggs. He won't admit he's concerned about her."

"But he said she'd filed for divorce—"

"Yes, yes," he said, waving his hand absently, "she did file the papers and have them delivered, but she probably just did it to get under his skin before the expedition. She's already done it once, just before he went to Spain two years ago. Henry nearly skinned the messenger alive! But a week later she called it off. I don't know the sort of games she plays, but in all likelihood it wasn't serious."

Saffron didn't know what to make of that. "But I heard Mrs. Henry talking at Sir Edward's party, and she seemed very angry with him."

"I wouldn't trust what you overhear, Miss Everleigh," he said, looking about conspiratorially. "I overheard the argument between Dr. Maxwell and Dr. Henry, a completely overblown argument with so much shouting and carrying on, but it didn't mean anything. Just blowing hot air, the two of them."

Saffron stared at him. "Did you tell Inspector Green about the argument?"

"Well, yes, he asked about any recent arguments Dr. Henry had. Hard to remember them all, of course." He smiled sheepishly.

Her fists balling at her sides, she hissed, "Mr. Snyder, that argument between Dr. Henry and Dr. Maxwell that you seem to think nothing of is the reason that Dr. Maxwell was—*is* under arrest for the poisoning!" She was furious. "Who else knew about the argument?"

"D-Dr. Berking was also here, I believe. He had the next appointment," Snyder stammered, nonplussed by her vehemence.

Dr. Berking had probably also recounted the fight, and possibly the threats Dr. Maxwell made, to the inspector. At the door, Saffron turned to the baffled Snyder and said, "Sorry, I must dash, Mr. Snyder. Please do take care of Dr. Henry."

Chapter 19

Saffron sped back to the nearly deserted North Wing, hoping Alexander was still there. Their argument utterly forgotten, she burst through his door, ready to spill Dr. Henry's revelations.

He looked up with raised brows. "Saffron, I was just leaving—"

"Not yet!" Saffron exclaimed. "It's important! I just finished meeting with Dr. Henry."

Alexander set his bag down on his chair. "What happened?"

"The poor man was terribly overwrought. He was drunk and in tears."

Alexander stared at her. "Good Lord, Everleigh, what did you do to him?"

"I asked about his wife, and he cracked like an egg. After he had a few drinks, he told me that she had filed for divorce and he had no idea what to do," she said, wide-eyed and still breathing hard. "I was absolutely shocked. I mean, he's a world-renowned scholar and explorer, and he totally fell apart. I think he really does love her. I don't think he poisoned her."

"It's still possible he tried to poison Blake but got his wife by mistake. That would make him miserable and guilty."

"Blake!" Saffron exclaimed, hands raised in aggravation. "I didn't ask Dr. Henry about the equipment forms. How could

I have forgotten? Key evidence!" She shook her head at her missed opportunity. "Oh well. I'll have the chance to find out more tomorrow."

Alexander glanced at his watch. "I'm sorry, I really must go."

Face heating at the realization that her interruption was unwanted, she said, "Oh, of course."

He slipped on his jacket, without doing up his cuff links, and slung his bag over his shoulder. Saffron followed him out of the office and stood awkwardly as he locked it.

"Goodnight," he said with a brief smile.

"Goodnight," she replied, forcing one of her own.

He disappeared down the stairwell, and Saffron wondered if he had someone to meet. He had said he went out in the evenings sometimes, though it disgruntled her a bit to consider that he might be out with some beautiful woman who wouldn't be buried shoulder-deep in botanical tomes and frantic revisions. It was fine he wasn't available for her investigation discussions, she forcefully thought as she went into her office to collect her things. Even if the playing field of suspects had been significantly narrowed. But that tantalizing thought would have to wait for the next twenty-four hours. She had a study proposal to revise.

～✦～

The pub off Gower Street was smoky and noisy. Alexander's shoes stuck to the floor as he crossed the crowded room to where some of the fellows from the university sat. He shook a few hands before being pushed into a chair.

"Guess that means the old man didn't do it then," one of the researchers was saying.

Alexander's ears perked up. Were they talking about Dr. Maxwell?

"Can't be him, if they're letting him go," Robinson said. He sipped his beer. "Can't sail off if they think you tried to do your wife in."

Dr. Henry, then.

"Nah, they arrested that old chap," called someone from down the table. That was clearly in reference to Dr. Maxwell.

"Right!" Robinson nodded, nudging Alexander's shoulder with his meaty elbow. "You're stuck with botany. How do you like a new project coming up two weeks before we leave? Nice to have all that prep work for the murderer go out the window?"

"Don't go jumping to conclusions." Alexander shrugged. "It won't be bad. The researcher in charge won't give me too much to do."

Robinson looked doubtful. "A whole study? With two weeks to prepare? Who's in charge?"

"It's Everleigh, Dr. Maxwell's assistant," Alexander said, waving off the serving girl who stood waiting.

"Everleigh?" Adams slid into the chair next to Alexander. "That fellow with the mustache?"

"Have you been under a rock, Adams?" Robinson nudged him, smirking. "Everleigh—you know, the girl taking notes at the meeting today."

"Oh! That's right, the gel with the eyes," said Adams, taking a gulp of beer.

"Well, if she's in charge, at least you won't have much to do," said a blond man with a crooked grin from across the table. "You won't have to do half of what she says."

Irritated, Alexander said, "I'm not going to put off responsibilities."

Adams grinned, eyes darting to the other fellows around them. "Come off it, Ashton! She won't know what she's doing anyway. Just let it run its course, and you save yourself some work."

Now truly annoyed, Alexander glared at him. "She does know what she's doing—"

"Oh, does she?" Adams crowed, and a handful of the others laughed.

Fists clenched beneath the table, Alexander said coolly, "Yes, she does. That's why she's been given a study as an assistant. How many studies have you done, Adams?"

There was a chorus of laughter and taunts up and down the table. Adam's ears turned red, and he busied himself with his drink.

Robinson wiped foam from his mouth thoughtfully. "She's an assistant, though. How'd she manage to swing her own study? Decided to play nice with Berking after all, did she?"

The group laughed. Alexander didn't. Ensuring he was speaking loudly enough to be heard down the table, Alexander said, "If that's your first thought about a colleague advancing in their department, Robinson, I have concerns about how exactly you got your position."

Robinson, to Alexander's relief, let out a laugh. These men were his friends, his close colleagues for the next six months. He didn't want to alienate them just before setting out, but he couldn't stand to hear Saffron's name sullied as the punch line in their drunken jokes.

Robinson nodded and waved a hand to settle down the laughter around them. "Quite right, quite right. Not even the most desperate of *colleagues* would submit to that cretin. Did you hear him making digs at Dr. Henry during the meeting?"

Alexander nodded, glad the subject of Saffron's credibility was off the table.

"It'll be fireworks on the journey over, you mark my words. Actually"—Robinson swatted at McAllister's arm next to him— "mark my words, Mickey. Take down bets. Who says Henry and Berking will have it out before we reach São Luís? Two quid on Berking ending up chucked in the sea, I say."

Amid more laughter, a few raised hands, and Mickey did indeed take names down on a bit of paper.

Adams, who appeared to have recovered his nerve, said, "My bet's on Henry duking it out with Blake."

Robinson scoffed. "Over what?"

Adams glanced around, suddenly unsure. "Well, I—er, you know, his wife . . ."

"Spit it out, man. I need to know if there's another few quid waiting for me."

Adams's pale eyes darted to Alexander as if worried he'd get another tongue-lashing. "Well, I saw them, didn't I? Mrs. Henry and Blake."

Nerves on high alert, Alexander asked with forced calm, "When was that?"

"Just a few days before that party. My mum's been ill so I went to visit her at lunch . . ." His words dried up and his ears went red again at Robinson's impatient eye roll. "Anyway, I was coming back to the U when I saw them on the street, walking and having a grand old time. Her hand on his arm, smiling and talking. Looked cozy, that's all."

Robinson stroked his chin. "That might be worth putting another bet on. You know Henry won't stand for that, even if he chases after anything in a skirt."

Alexander left a few hours later, the stink of smoke and beer clinging to his clothes. He'd have to get his head on straight before the ship sailed. They'd hassle him every day about having a drink, and he'd give in if he wasn't careful. He always regretted it when he did, when one led to another, and he found himself barely able to stand. Better not to even start.

The street was damp from an early evening shower, the brisk air blissful after the rowdy, close air of the pub. He'd kept his ears peeled for any further mention of the investigation but heard no more than a handful of doubtful mutterings about Dr. Henry's leadership. Nothing particularly helpful. Adams seeing Blake with Mrs. Henry just gave more credence to Saffron's theory they were lovers.

He usually enjoyed talking shop, even with his tipsy friends, but tonight it felt like a wasted evening, with Saffron and her impending meeting never far from his mind.

He'd have to try speaking to her again tomorrow, Alexander thought as he unlocked the door to his flat and stepped inside. Convince her to rethink accepting that meeting, even if it meant accidentally insulting her again.

He sighed, leaning his head back against his bedroom door. Saffron was right. He didn't understand why she would go to meet with the man who'd not only forced his attentions once, but whom they suspected was involved in the poisoning. The other thing she'd said, him not understanding the struggle to simply be at the university . . . well, he did understand that. Every day had been a struggle for him for years.

He shucked his shoes and smoke-ridden clothes and sat on his bedroom floor, already taking deep breaths to erase his worries from his mind. It would be a long time before he'd be able to sleep.

Saffron awoke early, her mind having buzzed all night with ideas for her research project.

The previous evening, Elizabeth had told Saffron to take Berking's offer and put it somewhere unpleasant. She'd agreed that Alexander was absolutely right about being wary of Berking's intentions, but she was just as sure as Saffron that it was all but impossible to say no. It didn't comfort Saffron, but at least she felt understood. To bolster her confidence that morning, Elizabeth gave Saffron her favorite lipstick and promised a gourmet supper before sending her friend out the door with a smacking kiss on the cheek.

Saffron arrived just before eight o'clock at the North Wing. Her hands shook with anticipation as she searched her bag for the keys only to recall they were still missing. She never had found them. Wincing at the prospect of a run-in with the disagreeable maintenance man of the North Wing, Mr. Tummel, she set off to find him in his basement office. He unlocked her office door for her with something that shockingly resembled politeness and promised a replacement key would be forthcoming. She arranged herself in Dr. Maxwell's office, with reference books on all sides and her original proposal in front of her, and started back where she'd left off the previous evening.

Her hair ruffled and her fingers smudged with ink, at midday she had a new version of her proposal. She wished Dr. Maxwell was there to advise her, or that Dr. Aster was not so intimidating. The three other botany professors were unlikely to give her any help. Saffron sighed and admitted her best option for advice was Alexander, who, though not in her department, was very familiar with research proposals. She fixed her hair quickly and attempted to scrub off the ink on her fingers before knocking at his office door.

"Hello," Saffron said from the doorway, not willing to feel uncomfortable that they had parted ways awkwardly last night. "I'm sure you're very busy, but would you mind looking over my proposal?"

He agreed and beckoned her inside. Alexander looked a little worse for wear. His hair was slightly tousled, and he had shadows under his eyes. She tried not to wonder why he looked like he'd spent the previous night climbing through another garden.

He accepted her file and flicked through pages, frowning in concentration. She sat on the couch at first, then stood to examine his bookshelf. Then she went to the chair and sat.

"There's no need to be anxious," Alexander said after she'd made another circuit of the room. "This is fine."

"But what is 'fine'? What does that mean?" She went and stood next to him, leaning over his shoulder and pointing. "Like this—you've put a mark. What does that mean?"

"It means I have a question about what you wrote," he said, a smile in his voice.

"About what?"

"You wrote 'pigmen' rather than 'pigment.'"

Saffron scowled at him. "Fine, a typing mistake. I can fix that. I can't fix it if the whole thing is wrong. What do I need to change?"

"Apart from the typing, which I'm sure is because you felt rushed, and a few changes in wording, this should be fine," Alexander said, still examining the file.

"This is the most important thing I've done yet in my career. Could you maybe find more to say apart from that it's fine?" Despite herself, she could hear the edge of panic in her voice. She sat down heavily in the chair opposite him, clutching her hands together.

Alexander took pity on her and gave her half an hour of slight wording adjustments and encouragement, both of which she needed. The moment he was done, Saffron rushed to the library to see if there were any other species she wanted to include in her experimental design. She had begun to worry that she wasn't giving Alexander enough options, since he would be the one collecting the specimens.

Finally, at five o'clock, Alexander poked his head into Dr. Maxwell's office. "How does it look? Do you feel prepared?"

Behind him, scads of high-spirited students were clearing out for the evening. They only served as a reminder that she'd soon be alone in a quiet building with Dr. Berking.

"Yes, I think it looks all right," Saffron replied, trying to sound confident. Her hand shook slightly as she passed him her final copy.

"This is very well done, Saffron," he murmured, thumbing through each page.

She grimaced. "I really don't know if it'll make a difference. Dr. Berking will be looking to see if I'm charming—that's all he cares about."

"I can come with you, you know." His dark eyes looked at her steadily over the pages.

She tried to smile at his offer but found her lips weren't quite willing. "Thank you, but no. This is something I have to do myself. Even if he rejects the proposal, I'll know I did my best work."

⚘

Although he told himself that he really should make better use of his time, Alexander couldn't settle himself in his office once he'd left Saffron. He didn't like that she was meeting with Dr. Berking. But he knew he had no right to tell her not to go, so he hadn't done so.

Resolving to go back to the North Wing when her meeting began at six o'clock and wait until she was finished, Alexander walked slowly across the Quad, intending to go to the library to attempt some further research. The sun had dipped below the dome of the Wilkins Building, casting long, cool shadows over the emptying Quad. Just as he was about to mount the stairs, he caught sight of the kind receptionist from the administrative offices. She was wearing a large brown hat and matching coat, fumbling with keys to the office doors.

Thinking of Adams's comments the previous evening, he approached her. "Good evening."

She turned around with her usual pinched expression, which lit into a smile when she registered him.

"Oh, hello, dear." She shoved the key forcefully into the lock and turned it. "I do hope you don't need to get in, I've already stayed far later than I intended today."

"Not at all," Alexander said. "I wondered if I could ask you something. The other day you mentioned you'd let someone into Mr. Blake's office."

She frowned, her lips puckering. "Did I? Oh dear."

"Yes, you did. I was wondering who that was. It wasn't Mrs. Henry, was it?"

The receptionist looked thoughtful. "It was, actually. She'd been to Mr. Blake's office a few times to discuss funding for the Amazonian expedition on behalf of her husband, since he was working with patrons of the university himself. She had left her handbag inside."

Alexander nodded slowly, taking in that new information. Mrs. Henry often meeting with Blake would not be surprising if they were lovers, but her returning to his office when he wasn't there was suspicious.

Realizing he was frowning at the now confused receptionist, Alexander said, "I see. Did they work together long, Mr. Blake and Mrs. Henry?"

"No, but the expedition was planned in just a few months, wasn't it?" She smiled indulgently. "I'm sure you were thrilled when you learned of it."

Alexander gave her a brief smile. "Of course." He wracked his brain for an elegant way to ask his next question, but he came up blank. "I suppose you only let her into Mr. Blake's office once. She wasn't as forgetful as I was." He forced an awkward laugh. How on Earth did Saffron find charming information out of people so easy?

"Just the once. I remember because she cancelled their next appointment the very next day. It was memorable, you see, because she actually requested a meeting with the College Committee instead. It isn't often that the wife of a faculty member wants to meet with the Committee."

Alexander swallowed his excitement. This was what Saffron had told him in a rush the day before, that Mrs. Henry could have been out to sabotage her husband's chances of creating his own department. "And did she mention what the meeting was to be about?"

"Well, yes. They won't let me just put anyone down on their schedule," the receptionist said. "It was about the funding for the expedition."

Saffron found that six o'clock came upon her surprisingly quickly. She smoothed her navy-blue skirt, reapplied Elizabeth's lucky lipstick, and collected her papers, then went up to Dr. Berking's office. Pierce admitted her to the large office and said that Dr. Berking had not yet finished his last appointment but would return presently.

Heart pounding, Saffron sat in the chair before the desk at first, then, nerves getting to her again, walked around the room. The light had faded from the windows, and the street below was filled with a steady stream of students. Their energetic chatter seemed miles away from where she looked down on them from the window.

After five minutes passed, curiosity got the better of her, and Saffron wandered to Berking's desk to casually try the drawers. They were still locked except for the top one that contained his checkbook. The drawer slid open easily this time. He must have retrieved the paper that had been jammed, the one with the formula on it. She picked up the checkbook and flipped through it again, noting that he'd written another check to R. Glass since the one he'd written when she had broken into the office. It was for a large sum; together both checks totaled five hundred pounds, which was rather a lot for a bet.

At a sound from the outer office, she shoved the book back into the drawer and closed it, clearing the edge of the desk just as the door swung open and Dr. Berking's belly came through the entrance. She gripped her hands together tightly, hoping Berking didn't notice her rapid breathing.

"Sorry to keep you waiting," he said loudly. "Have you prepared your proposal? Let's get right to business."

To Saffron's great surprise, Dr. Berking went straight to his desk and began reading her proposal. He asked a few questions, without a hint of flirtation or menace, and she answered them best she could. By the time the clock struck quarter 'til seven, he closed her file and set down his pen.

"Well, Miss Everleigh, this has vastly improved. I'm inclined to approve this project. However," he said, standing, "we have a few points we must clarify."

Leaving her in suspense, he lumbered across the room to the door. Saffron, not looking at him, heard an ominous click as the door locked. Her palms began to sweat. "Sir, I don't . . ." she stammered as he came back toward the desk.

"No need to be jumpy, just business." His expression was rather devoid of feeling, which was more alarming to Saffron than his unpleasant grin. He stopped beside his desk and remained standing. "This business of Dr. Henry and his wife, it's been very disturbing to the university and all those involved. Dreadful, dreadful." He shook his head and reached into his pocket, withdrawing a pipe. "I am aware that you've been poking around, asking questions and making inquiries. Quite natural, I say. Dr. Maxwell is your mentor, your friend for years now." Dr. Berking filled the pipe, looking thoughtfully at it as he patted the tobacco into the bowl. "Unfortunate, of course."

Saffron was rather at a loss. She just looked at him as he lumbered back around opposite her and sat heavily in his chair again. He lit the pipe and took a long puff. The smoke escaped his lips in a hiss as he continued. "I also know that you've been in this office." From his pocket he pulled out two hairpins.

Saffron stared at them, then looked to Berking. He had a hard glint in his eye. They were just hairpins, she reasoned. There was no proof they were hers. "Sir, I didn't—"

"No need to lie, Miss Everleigh. You've been snooping around, no doubt in an effort to clear your beloved Dr. Maxwell." His voice turned falsely downcast, as if he were telling a sad story to a child. "Through my own work with the police, we've determined his guilt. Old Maxwell used the xolotl vine to try to kill Dr. Henry, but instead got his wife by mistake. They've arrested him. The inspector telephoned me just this afternoon to thank me for assisting him."

Saffron's mind scrambled to make sense of his blatant lies.

He sighed melodramatically and continued with another puff of bitter smoke. "It's tragic to see what old age can do to a person. Poor Maxwell was so distraught over his rejection from the expedition team that he tried to poison a man. Such an unfortunate episode. Surely, Miss Everleigh, you've seen the signs also, that he was losing his grip on reality. Irrational thoughts perhaps, or strange moods."

"What are you saying?" Saffron asked, her heart pounding now.

"I'm just expressing my support of you, my dear, as you try to help the police close the case. Whatever you need"—his eyebrows rose—"to feel comfortable to go to the inspector to tell him your side of the story. You have a great opportunity for your pigmentation study, and surely you can't carry it out with this great weight of information on your shoulders. You're as close to Maxwell as anyone, and the police would find your story most compelling. A young woman being terrorized by her advisor, a family friend. Highly sympathetic."

Saffron stood, her face pink and her fists clenched. "You're the only one terrorizing me, Dr. Berking," she said, her voice shaking. "How dare you try to use me against Dr. Maxwell?"

Dr. Berking set his pipe down and lumbered to his feet. As he stepped slowly toward her, his voice was calm and quiet, almost hypnotic. "Miss Everleigh, I'm not using you *against* the man, I just want to make sure that a madman is put away so our university community can rest easy again. Of course, if you find loyalty to Dr. Maxwell, a *murderer*, more important than the safety of your colleagues, I'm sure you can't be trusted to remain in the employ of the university. Furthermore," he said, taking another slow step toward her, "I hate to say it, my dear, but the inspector had several questions about your relationship to Dr. Maxwell and your own state of mind. After our appalling altercation last month, when you most unfairly assaulted me—"

"I assaulted *you*?" She took a step away from him, her eyes on his slow advance around the desk and across the carpet.

"A most unfortunate choice you made to attack me rather than agree to work with me." His small eyes were slits. "I'm sure not a choice you'd want to repeat again." He lunged forward, his large pink hand clutching at her arm, drawing her closer. "Now, Miss Everleigh . . ."

Her breath was frozen in her lungs, and she couldn't breathe, let alone cry for help. Berking forced her back into her chair and put a piece of paper in front of her. He placed a pen in her hand and transferred his oppressive grip to her shoulder. "You will write of the unfortunate unraveling of Dr. Maxwell, and then we can go about our business. Your study will move forward, and I don't have to tell the inspector about your own complicity with Dr. Maxwell's plans to kill not only Dr. Henry, but me. No doubt you both plotted against me after I rejected your last proposal. Dr. Maxwell was even overheard threatening me."

Hand shaking, wondering how she could possibly get out of this mess, Saffron began to write.

At seven o'clock, Alexander yet again opened his office door and glanced down the empty hall. He'd been pacing his office for forty-five minutes, trying to piece together how Mrs. Henry's meeting with the College Committee fit into everything else.

Saffron must be nearly done with her meeting. Perhaps it hadn't gone well, and she didn't want to speak with him. Regardless of the outcome of her meeting, she would want to know what he had discovered about Mrs. Henry's meeting with the College Committee and her getting into Blake's office. He walked slowly down the deserted hallway and tapped at the dark door of Maxwell's office. Nothing. He returned to his office.

Half an hour later, after failing to distract himself by reading a chapter on caladiums that Saffron had included in her study design, Alexander roved around his office once more. She should be back by now, protesting or celebrating the results of the meeting. If he was right about Berking's intentions, she would no doubt be embarrassed, possibly very angry. Or worse. It was a mistake not to push for her to at least postpone the meeting to a time when the North Wing was crowded rather than deserted. What good was he doing her down here?

Running a hand through his hair, he wondered for the twentieth time if he should go to Dr. Berking's office. She would be furious if he interrupted the meeting, but there might be something wrong. Still itching with indecision, he walked down the hall.

Alexander first went back to Dr. Maxwell's office and knocked again, wondering if she was inside, silently fuming or even crying. He knocked again, then tried the door, which was unlocked. Wondering if he was about to be scolded, he walked inside, eyes adjusting to the darkness. Just as he reached for the light switch, a click went off next to him. The sound rooted him to the spot. A soldier, even one long out of service, never forgets the sound of the safety of a gun being cocked.

CHAPTER 20

Saffron sat, numb with shock and self-loathing, wondering how she could fix what she had done. She knew that Berking was lying, and the inspector himself had said Maxwell was no longer under arrest. But her confession might muddy the waters long enough for Berking to finish out his scheme and make his escape.

"Up you get, Miss Everleigh," demanded Berking, his voice gruff. With a bruising grip, he forced her to stand.

"Where are we going?" Saffron asked as he dragged her out of the room. She almost didn't want an answer.

"We'll just pop down to Maxwell's office."

Saffron stumbled slightly when they reached the hall. "Why are we going to Dr. Maxwell's office?"

"We need to collect your things, of course."

She prayed that someone would be out in the hall, but she was disappointed. The hall and the stairwell were silent and dark.

Was Alexander still there?

Saffron tried to think of a way to get to him, but Berking's grip was strong on her arm. If she called out, Berking might panic, and who knows what he would do to her then. He might just be walking her to the room for her things and would then let her go. After all, she'd done what he'd asked. But why risk her going to the police immediately? No, he would likely keep her somewhere safe until he sailed away. But what would happen to her in the meantime?

Bone-shaking fear wracked her body, weakening her knees. Two weeks of being stashed away by Dr. Berking? She'd never survive that. She'd have to risk calling out for Alexander. Mustering a breath to scream, it withered into a whimper as Berking jerked the door to Dr. Maxwell's office open.

Saffron and Berking stood in the doorway, staring at Richard Blake standing behind a seated Alexander, a pistol trained at the back of Alexander's head.

All the dread she felt at her own situation drained away. "Alexander?" she whispered.

He said nothing. His eyes, one swollen and purpling, swept over her, then to Berking.

"You missed our meeting this afternoon, Miss Everleigh," Richard Blake said, quiet and cold. He nodded to the chair next to Alexander. "Have a seat."

She sat.

"Sure this is necessary?" grumbled Berking as Blake handed him a length of rope.

"It is," Blake replied, wincing as he pressed his finger to his mouth and frowned. His face, too, was bruised. His lower lip was split and swollen, and his left cheek was darkening. Alexander must have tried to get away from him.

Berking tied Saffron's wrists together behind her and then bound her to the back of the wooden chair. The rope bit into her skin, ensuring she had no space to wriggle her wrists. The remaining rope secured Alexander. When Alexander resisted Berking's touch, Blake sighed impatiently and turned the gun on Saffron, who felt her heart stutter in response. Alexander stilled, his dark eyes on the gun.

"What's going on?" Saffron said, again trying to hide the fear in her voice. This was difficult, as her whole body was trembling.

"I don't care for your interest in the poisoning of Mrs. Henry," Blake said calmly, the muzzle returning to Alexander, though he faced her. "Between you and Mr. Ashton, you've poked around just a bit too much for my comfort. Berking, lock the door." He tossed Saffron's keys to him.

"How did you get my keys?" Saffron asked.

"They fell out of your bag yesterday. That's how I decided, you know, when I found you following Berking and me yesterday. Breaking into Berking's office, Miss Everleigh, so sloppily done, leaving hairpins on the floor. Mr. Tummel even saw you and Ashton dashing out of the building like lovers into the sunset. And lurking in the stairwell . . . It didn't look good for you." Blake smoothed a hand over his tie, the nondescript gray matching his slightly rumpled suit. "And Mr. Ashton, going into to my office. I nearly fell over when I was told a young man of your description needed to be let into my office to retrieve forms."

"This . . . this is about forms? What forms?" Saffron asked, trying to sound bewildered. "What do they have to do with the poisoning?"

With shocking quickness, Berking's hand crossed her face in a vicious slap. Saffron cried out, and beside her Alexander lurched forward.

"Leave her alone," Alexander growled. "She doesn't know anything about this. Let her go. I'm the one whose been looking into the forms and—"

Her eyes watering, Saffron barely made out the blur of Blake hitting Alexander across the face with his gun. Alexander slumped forward against the ropes. Blinking to clear her eyes, she saw that Alexander's temple was bleeding, his eyes closed.

Cool as ice, Blake said to Berking, "We need to discuss the plan, now that it has changed."

He looked around the small room and frowned. Saffron flinched as he grabbed her chair and dragged her toward the wall. Berking jerked around Alexander's chair, so both now faced the wall. She turned to him, hoping she could coax him into waking up. She opened her mouth to speak, and behind her Blake said softly, "One word and I will shoot you, Miss Everleigh. You are to sit quietly."

Saffron closed her eyes against tears. She couldn't believe the situation she'd gotten them into.

How was it possible that Richard Blake, the bland, boring man, was casually threatening to *shoot* her? Was she about to die? Her breath came fast and shallow, sending her blood pounding through her body as if trying to make the most of what she thought might be her final minutes.

She'd never figure out how to get out of this if she was panicking. Behind them, Berking and Blake spoke quietly. She took a few determined deep breaths, and their words came into focus.

"—can't shoot them here," hissed Blake.

"Why do we have to?" Berking huffed. "Why can't we just tie them up and leave?"

"No loose ends, Berking. I've learned that much in my years of playing this game."

A long pause. "All right. Let's just shoot them quick. We leave them and make it look as though Maxwell came back . . ."

Saffron stifled a sob and looked frantically around. Alexander was unmoving beside her, still knocked out. If she could manage to get out of the chair, she might make a run for it, but she wouldn't be able to drag him away too.

"A gunshot would be overheard," Blake's cool voice said. "No, we'll have to do something else. Do you have any of the solution on you?"

The hope that came with the promising idea of causing a loud sound—she could throw something at the window and break it—was drained away at the mention of the solution. The solution that caused Mrs. Henry to go into a coma.

"In my office. I just have one left, not enough for them both."

"Damn," Blake murmured. "Don't want to use it anyway, not the same thing. What else is available? What would Maxwell have nearby? If we're sticking with him, it should be poison again."

Next to her, Alexander stirred. His eyelashes fluttered, and his head rolled as he emitted a soft groan.

Berking said, "Ah . . . We could use the original weapon, the xolotl vine. Appropriate, isn't it?"

Xolotl! Alexander opened his eyes and looked at Saffron. Her wide eyes caught his slightly unfocused ones. Hope battled with logic. Saffron had survived the first dose, but they might force them to have more than what she'd taken.

Blake didn't seem as keen. "Would it work? I thought it wasn't clear what exactly it did."

Berking laughed. "Maxwell was too afraid to touch the thing once he brought it back. Even Winters won't go near it! Oh, it'll work."

"Fine. What do we need?"

Saffron wasn't sure whether to be relieved that xolotl was their weapon of choice. What would they do when they found it didn't kill them?

Berking paused and thought for a moment. "Too hard to force them both to eat the leaves—we'll need a solution."

"Injection?" Blake asked.

"It's highly toxic, so an infusion should do it. We'll need the kettle from downstairs and glasses. The plant is in the last green-house. Giant yellow thing. Can't miss it."

Blake moved toward the door into Saffron's line of vision and caught a set of keys from Berking. His pale eyes slid to

Saffron and Alexander. "If Berking tells me you've communicated, you will be sorry. Whoever speaks will have to go last and watch the other die."

The utter coldness of his words convinced Saffron of his promise. Blake unlocked the door and locked it again from the outside. Alexander, face completely impassive but for the flare of his nostrils, closed his eyes. Perhaps he was finding courage in the meditation he'd spoken of. Or coming up with a plan. With two of them and just Berking in the room, they might be able to manage an escape, if they were given the opportunity.

Behind them, Berking's heavy footsteps paced. He jerked open the drawers of Maxwell's desk, muttering and shoving things around inside. Then he paced again, his labored breathing marking his place in the room. Without warning, he strode over to Saffron's chair and flipped her around roughly. Saffron bit her lip on a cry of surprise as she came face-to-face with him.

"How did you know about the plant?" he demanded, his voice reverberating in her ears. When Saffron didn't respond, he tilted her head back with a rough hand grasping her chin so she had to look at his flushed face. "The aconite! How did you know where it was? I won't tell Blake, girl—I want to know! How did you find it? It was hidden! How did you know?" He smacked her smartly across the cheek.

The sting of his palm burned her cheek, sending tears flooding into her eyes. Saffron could hear Alexander straining against the rope next to her. Her cheek throbbing, she shook her head.

This didn't satisfy Berking. His face red and his eyes bulging, he grabbed a handful of her hair and jerked her face up to his. "But how did you know about the aconite? The other plant went missing from my garden. That must have been you!"

The hand pulling at her hair tightened viciously. Gasping in pain, Saffron opened her mouth to reply, but Alexander spoke.

"I did it, Berking. Let her go."

Berking maintained his grip on her hair, but his raging eyes darted to Alexander. A sneer stretched across his face. "Really, Ashton? You expect me to believe you had something to do with my plant going missing?" He wrenched her hair again, eyes back on her. "What did you do with it?"

"I tried to give it to the inspector, but he laughed at me. Said it was just a plant in a botanist's garden," Saffron cried, praying he'd believe her and let her be.

Berking let go of her and went to the other side of the room, glaring at her and breathing hard. "What else do you know?"

"N-nothing," Saffron whispered.

"She doesn't know anything, Berking," Alexander said, his voice loud and brash. His jaw was set, eyes flashing. "You're mad if you think that you and Blake will get away with this scheme."

Berking's nostrils flared. "What do you know of it?"

Alexander, indifference gone and replaced by a cold look of anger, said quickly, "You've been embezzling and want to pin it on Dr. Henry. Saffron had nothing to do with this—it was all me. I've been the one trying to figure it all out. Don't touch her."

Berking seemed to consider Alexander's words. "I don't believe you, Ashton," Berking said quietly. He took a step over to Alexander and moved his chair, too, to face him.

Saffron's stomach tightened at the sight of his darkening bruised eye, the blood on his face.

Berking's voice was a venomous hiss in Alexander's ear. "I don't believe that you figured out where my aconite strain was growing. The two of you have been huddled up together—"

With a shocking crack, Alexander smashed his head into Berking's. Berking fell back with a grunt, his body thudding to the floor. Alexander, still bound to the chair, struggled to his feet. Saffron tried to do the same but only managed to fall back and push her chair a few inches toward the wall.

Berking was already getting to his feet, blearily rubbing at his head. "You're a dead man, Ashton," he growled.

Saffron struggled against the rope. She had only a second to try to help Alexander do something, anything—

But Berking was on his feet. With a grunt of effort, he sent his fist careening into Alexander's temple, the same place he'd been hit by Blake before.

Alexander fell, the back of his head cracking against the wood floor with a resounding finality that brought a cry from Saffron's lips.

Berking stood, breathing heavily and gazing down at Alexander's still form. Then, he laughed. The sound lifted the hairs on the back of her neck.

Saffron realized she was shaking all over, her teeth chattering in her skull. Blake was cold-blooded, and Berking a madman. Even if the xolotl didn't kill Alexander and her, the two men would find a way to keep them quiet.

"Oh, Miss Everleigh"—Berking wiped a hand over his eye, turning to her—"it's a pity Mr. Ashton won't be awake to watch what happens next."

Berking slowly moved to stand over her. A terrible smile stretched his features. His knee roughly shoved hers apart, and she cried out in alarm. He grabbed Saffron's hair again and jerked her chin back, exposing her neck. With agonizing slowness, Berking ran a thick finger down the column of her throat. The furious gleam in his eye turned to something more evil.

Berking leaned forward, his hands settling on the chair on either side of her head, making her feel even more trapped than the ropes she strained against. "It could have been much easier, Miss Everleigh, and so much more pleasant for you if you'd accepted me weeks ago," he said. "You might have even enjoyed it, but now . . ."

With a chuckle that made bile rise in Saffron's throat, Berking stroked a finger along her collarbone. "Blake might be no nonsense, but I won't look a gift horse in the mouth. Such a delicate creature, just waiting for me to teach her why she can't tell me no." His finger trailed lower, taking the tie of her blouse and slipping the bow loose. Her attempts to jerk away from him were futile. His small eyes were locked on hers, enjoying the absolute panic he was causing.

"P-please," she whispered.

Her ears rang so badly with alarm that she barely heard Berking's next words, hissed into her ear. "Maybe I'll wait, so Mr. Ashton can watch."

Gasping, hands fighting the rope at her wrists, Saffron whispered, "No, *please*—"

Berking shoved Saffron back, making her head smack against the wall behind her and the chair wobble dangerously. He demanded with a terrible voice, "Then what do you know?"

"N-nothing," Saffron whispered, eyes darting from Berking's horrible face to the door. When was Blake coming back? Would he put a stop to this? It was ridiculous to hope for Blake's return, so ridiculous she wanted to scream—

Good God, why didn't she?

She drew in breath, but Berking anticipated her. He closed his hand over her mouth and whispered, "You don't want to know how I used his method to improve my aconite yield?" He leaned forward until his hot breath was in her ear. "You don't want to know how your father helped me create my poison?"

He leaned back to watch her face. The malevolence in his eyes caused dread to collect in her belly. Something in her eyes must have satisfied him, for his hand slowly released her mouth.

Almost against her will, Saffron asked, "What are you talking about?"

Berking studied her, then guffawed, throwing his head back in sudden and absolute delight. "You don't know? You stupid girl, you didn't recognize your father's hand in my work?"

Saffron gaped at him. Part of her mind, the part interested in her survival, demanded her to be silent, to ignore his baiting. But a louder part, the one that had gotten her into this mess to begin with, wanted to understand. Had she been right to fear this connection?

"My father had nothing to do with your . . . experiment," Saffron choked out.

"Oh, but he did." Berking's voice dropped into something soft and insidious. "When I joined the department, I inherited all of the previous head's items, including mounds and mounds of paperwork. And what did I find in those stacks one day? A lone file, forgotten and unimportant, at the bottom of the pile, and a request for a meeting regarding a proposed study about breeding programs to enhance natural chemicals found in plants." His smile grew at the look of apprehension on Saffron's face. "I wonder, whatever was his purpose for such experiments? It wasn't in any of his published work. Strange, isn't it?"

Again, Saffron was silent. She had nothing to say, only questions.

Berking must have mistaken her silence for insubordination. "Not going to tempt you, Miss Everleigh? Fine."

Berking's thick hands flew to her neck, causing her to gasp as they closed on her throat. His palms dug painfully into her neck, closing around her airway. "You baited Blake with your family's money. You know who he is, don't you! Tell me what you know, or—"

Dots danced in Saffron's vision, but she saw Blake enter the room, carrying glasses in which bright yellow leaves floated in steaming water. He didn't look surprised at the scene in front of him, Berking choking Saffron while Alexander, still tied to his chair, remained unconscious on the floor. He looked annoyed.

"Berking, enough of this melodrama. Let her go."

Berking's hands remained on her throat, and she gasped for breath. He was panting slightly and looked completely insane, eyes wild and face flushed with excitement.

Blake sighed and put the glasses down on a small table next to the couch. He pulled out the gun and pointed it at Berking. "Berking, let her go now."

Berking blinked at Blake, nonplussed. He slowly removed his hands, sending Saffron into a paroxysm of coughing and sputtering. "No need for that. Just checking to see how much they know," Berking muttered.

"It doesn't matter what they know; they'll be dead in a few minutes. We'll be off with our money and with our scapegoat in place," Blake said, gun still pointed at Berking. With his other hand he smoothed his hair.

Desperate for a hint of humanity, Saffron spoke with a rasp. "Mr. Blake, please—"

Blake, his eyes flashing, took a step toward Alexander and pointed the gun to where he lay on the floor. He cocked the hammer.

"Next time you speak," Blake said coldly, "it'll be a bullet through his body, Miss Everleigh. Berking may have no discipline, but you'll find that I do. I've waited a long time for this, and I find myself a little impatient. I'm not going to torture you for answers, nor will I tolerate anything further from you."

Saffron believed him. Her hopes of convincing Blake to let them go, or simply tie them up while he and Berking escaped the country, were silenced. Tears streamed down her face as she looked between Blake, who'd gone back to examining the yellowing water in the glasses, and Alexander, praying for his eyes to open.

"We can give it to her first," Blake said to Berking. "Then when he wakes up, we can give it to him."

Berking nodded, apparently cowed by his cold partner. Saffron watched them, her heart pounding, as they brought the glass near her. She desperately tried to remember what shade of yellow her own infusion of xolotl had been. She had put in three leaves of medium size. There were four in her glass now, and she didn't know how long they'd been steeping. Alexander's would likely steep until he woke up. What would that strength of infusion do to him?

The two men stood over her. Berking wrenched her hair back once again, forcing her mouth open with his other hand. Her breath caught in her throat when Blake touched the hot glass to her lips. She sputtered and his eyes narrowed. He took the gun from his waistband and pointed it toward Alexander once more. Saffron stopped struggling. The hot, bitter liquid poured into her throat, and she gagged.

"Drink it," Blake demanded.

She drank. The lightning strike of pain hit, and the world around her went dark.

"It is supposed to be incredibly toxic."

"Check her heartbeat."

The voices, quiet as they were, echoed and rang in Alexander's aching head.

"Very fast," Berking's voice reported.

"Looks almost the same as our little concoction. No wonder they believe xolotl nearly did in my dear Cynthia."

They'd given xolotl to Saffron?

Footsteps, then there came the swish of fabric on leather.

His head throbbed from all angles. How much longer would they wait before they started hitting him to wake him up? He could withstand a lot of pain, but Berking was clearly blood-thirsty, and Blake indifferent.

"Did you get the rest of the aconite?" Blake asked from across the room, sounding as if he was merely asking about the weather. "We might find it useful before long."

"No, the damned girl took it," Berking said. "Had to give the other two plants to Glass to make more of the solution, but he said it wouldn't be ready for another few days."

"We'll have to leave it behind then," Blake replied. "We can't wait around for another batch. After we're done here, we're leaving. You're quite sure Glass has been paid off well enough to keep him quiet?"

Alexander's mind was roused at the mention of Glass. Who Berking had written the check to? Not a bet, after all, but for making the poison.

Berking grunted unhappily and agreed. "He came back for more after he heard of the investigation, but I've paid him half a fortune. He should keep quiet."

"And there's no one else?" Blake's voice was quiet, but razor-sharp. There was a huff from Berking. "If you try to cross me, Berking—"

"You'll what?" Berking growled. "You'll trick me out of my money, Harper?"

Blake's name was Harper?

Blake let out a laugh, a cold, humorless sound. "You can think that I'm merely a con man, if it puts your mind at ease."

A long, quiet moment passed, interrupted only by Berking's heavy pacing footsteps and inaudible grumbling. Alexander's mind worked to make sense of what he'd heard. Blake, or Harper, was a con man. Being in charge of the university's funds must have given him ample opportunity. How much had he swindled from the school?

He heard only their breathing and shifting about. Surely by now, Saffron should have been waking up and getting sick. How long had he been unconscious? How much xolotl infusion had they given her? How strong was it?

Berking was pacing around again, cursing the xolotl and its damned yellow leaves.

"Fine, Berking, wake up Ashton," Blake said, as though he were telling a child he could have a treat after all. "Wake him up and let's be done."

Rough hands grabbed his shirtfront and hauled him upward in a nauseating rush. Alexander opened his eyes and blinked away the sting of the slap Berking had dealt him. He caught sight of Saffron, slumped in the chair and still bound to it. He opened his mouth, but Blake took a step nearer to Saffron and pointed his pistol at her. "Not a word, Ashton, unless you want to see her die right now."

He wasn't going to beg for them to see reason, though it appeared Blake wouldn't give him the chance to, anyway. If Saffron had survived her first dose, then maybe they would both live through this. Resigning himself, Alexander closed his mouth and glared at Blake.

Berking's fingers dug into his scalp as he forced his head back. Blake poured the liquid down his throat. Alexander's eyes watered at the bitter, tangy taste. They forced the entire glass down and were just picking Saffron's unfinished glass up when the lightning strike shot through Alexander. His back arched against the chair and he gasped for breath before falling into darkness.

CHAPTER 21

Elizabeth Hale, Detective Inspector Green was told, had telephoned five times in the past hour and several times the hour before that. He was told she was threatening to come down to the police station at midnight to "raise hell" for all those police officers who were "too good to be bothered about a woman who had helped them far more than they deserved." The inspector, who had just finished assisting in a large-scale arrest and was trying to complete his paperwork before going home, sighed heavily when the telephone interrupted the relative peace of his office.

He agreed to take the call without enthusiasm. "This is Miss Hale? Saffron Everleigh's flatmate, I understand," he said into the receiver.

"Yes, this is Saffron Everleigh's flatmate. This is the twelfth time I've called—"

Her shrill voice sounded especially loud. Stifling a groan, he rubbed a hand over his tired eyes and said, "I apologize for the holdup, Miss Hale, but there is more than one set of criminals to contend with in the city. What can I do for you?"

And so began a lengthy rant about public servants not serving the public unless convenient to them, which then slipped into a one-sided argument about men not taking the concerns of women seriously, during which the inspector completed three forms and said nothing until she paused to draw breath. "Yes, Miss Hale, your concerns are quite valid. What did you need to speak with me about?"

"What I've been telling your *useless* minions, Inspector, is that Saffron hasn't returned from work. She left quite early this morning and was supposed to come to tell me about a meeting she was having with—"

The inspector withheld a sigh. "Isn't it possible that she is out with a friend or colleague and lost track of the time? Have you tried telephoning her friends and acquaintances? Perhaps she and Mr. Ashton—"

"Saffron said that she would come right after her meeting, and that's what she would do. She knew I was waiting for her"—here the inspector was sure he heard a sob, but Miss Hale quickly recovered—"and she would have telephoned me to say if her plans changed. You know she has been investigating this poisoning business on her own because you lot—" Rather than a sob, Miss Hale apparently was refraining from embarking on another rant. Her voice returned with a tone of forced calm. "Now, if you insist again that she is safe and just merely forgetful, I will come down to that police station in my nightgown and wreak utter havoc until someone goes to look for her."

The inspector, sure by now that this woman was a different kind of touched from Saffron Everleigh, thought she might just do that. "If she's only been absent a couple of hours, I'm afraid we can't allocate resources to finding someone who may not be missing."

"She *is* missing," snapped Miss Hale. "She told me she would come straight home after her meeting with that wretched Dr. Berking—"

The familiar rush of instinct pulled the inspector from his exasperated exhaustion. "What time was the meeting? And where?"

"Six o'clock this evening, and I'd assume it was at the university in Dr. Berking's office."

"We will send someone to the university and surrounding haunts. What was she wearing when she left?"

Miss Hale told him and then demanded that she be called back, no matter what the hour, if and when they found her friend. The inspector, wary of her showing up in a nightgown, agreed reluctantly.

"Simpson," Inspector Green called into the next room, where Simpson stood next to a ruffian in handcuffs. "We need to get a couple men over to the university."

"Why, sir?" Simpson asked.

Irritated at Simpson's time-wasting question, he barked, "What do you mean, 'why,' Simpson? Just get someone over there. Saffron Everleigh is missing. She had a meeting with Dr. Berking and didn't return home."

His eyes widened in understanding. "Berking, sir?"

"Yes, Simpson, get on it! You go, since you have so many damn questions!"

The sergeant immediately took off down the corridor, tripping over his own feet. Inspector Green pinched the sharp ache between his brows. The boy had as much coordination as a newborn foal, but he'd been following him around long enough to know how not to mess this up. Hopefully.

Saffron stirred. She was unaware of anything except the extraordinary pain shooting through her spine into the base of her back, and a rising nausea with which she was too familiar. There was a singular thought in her mind: that she not be sick all over herself. It was coming, if the watering in her mouth was any indication.

Her eyes fluttered open to see a ceiling lined with shadows. Sweat broke out on her brow. She tried to lift her arms, to roll over to her side, but found that her arms were too heavy, like they'd been filled with cool sand. It was bad enough, memory flooding back to her, that she'd gotten herself in this stupid mess, but dying choking on her own vomit would be a particularly gruesome way to die.

Just as the wave of nausea overtook her, she threw all her strength into moving her body, and she rolled just enough.

She panted and moved her head away from her vomit. The office was quiet but for her panting and illuminated only by the hazy orange-gold glow of the lamps in the Quad. She was alone. Hopefully that meant that Berking and Blake thought the job was done and had fled. Relief made her body feel even heavier, like her limbs were sinking into the floor.

She squinted down at her arms and saw streaks on her hands. The paralysis had already begun, which explained why she was flopping around. With grunts of effort, she tried to roll to her other side, which proved too much for her equilibrium. She sputtered and spat, acid burning her throat and nose.

When she finally managed to reposition herself, she saw Alexander lying faceup on the floor a few feet away. She gasped.

"Alexander," she croaked. "Alexander, wake up!"

He didn't move. She couldn't tell if he was breathing. Saffron put her face toward the ceiling again, taking gulping breaths against the new wave of feeling coming over her, not of nausea, but of fear and guilt. Maybe Berking and Blake had forced him to drink a lethal dose of xolotl. Or maybe they'd used the solution they'd mentioned on him after all, and he'd fallen into a coma like Mrs. Henry.

"Alexander!" she cried, louder. "Alexander, please wake up!"

She forced herself to concentrate on movement. If she could move, she could see if he was alive, maybe somehow crawl her way to help.

She gave herself a great internal push and moved forward just a few inches. Alexander was about an arm's length away, but her own arms were now underneath her, and her legs were useless below her knees. And she was exhausted. Cursing, she tried to inch her way over to him, but barely moved.

One particularly bad attempt left her in a fit of panicked giggles. Tears streamed down her face as the stress of the situation overtook her, and she let herself cry until she had only determination left over. It was no use lying where she was. Any moment Alexander would wake up, she assured herself.

It took her long minutes of concerted effort, each movement making her muscles in her torso, back, and neck burn. She had even less control over her arms or legs, but she managed to inch her way to Alexander. She pressed her head against his chest. The sound of her own labored breathing and thundering heart was loud in her ears, making it impossible to hear his heartbeat, if it was there. Her breath froze in her lungs when her eyes moved from his chest to his neck. Threading blue lines reached toward his face from his collar.

His entire body was paralyzed? What if the blue lines didn't recede or there was lasting damage?

"Alexander," she whispered, "I'm so sorry. This is all my fault. If I hadn't tried to—"

Alexander's eye, still closed, twitched. Saffron gasped and called louder in his ear, "Alexander, if you can hear me, I'm here. Please wake up!"

Hoping she hadn't imagined it, she leaned against his chest, waiting for him to move. Her eyelids, heavy from all her exertions and illness, closed.

With every step across the wet green, Simpson begrudged the inspector sending him off to tap on dark, locked doors at the university. To be honest, he hadn't wanted to hang around the station either; it was currently overrun with criminals from the mass arrest earlier, and endless sleep-deprived officers ready to snap at a lesser officer without call. Even Inspector Green had lost his temper at him.

Simpson and the officer he'd snagged to come with him, Giles, stepped up to the center entry of the North Wing. If Saffron Everleigh was on campus, this is where she would likely be. Perhaps they'd find her in the arms of Mr. Ashton, as the inspector seemed to think they were a couple. Simpson would be terribly embarrassed if that was the case. One didn't just walk in on things like that, even if one was a policeman.

They waited only a moment for the university caretaker with the keys to meet them, and once the door had been unlocked, Simpson and his deputy climbed up the dark stairs, using their torches for illumination. They made their way toward the only office with a light on within. From his scrawled notes, Simpson saw it belonged to Alexander Ashton. Dread filled him; he really was about to interrupt something, wasn't he?

Giles glanced at him with a raised brow. Simpson straightened up, recalling how the inspector was never embarrassed, even when he had to ask questions that made Simpson's toes curl in his boots.

Simpson knocked smartly, but there was no reply. He tried the door and found that the tidy office was deserted. He didn't let Giles see the relief on his face.

He and Giles turned and strode down the hall toward the other office, Dr. Maxwell's. He knocked, and at no reply, tried opening the door to the unlit office. It was locked. Simpson screwed up his face and cursed his inspector. He was about to break down a door and no doubt find Mr. Ashton entangled with Miss Everleigh and be in all sorts of trouble. Sighing, he motioned for his man to move aside. He should have told the caretaker to stick around. Using the technique he'd mastered after being caught out without a key one too many times, he kicked the door open, keeping the frosted glass panel intact.

Inside, Simpson did indeed find Mr. Ashton and Miss Everleigh entangled on the floor, but in a very different way than expected. Giles flipped the light switch, and Simpson rushed to Mr. Ashton, whose eyes were narrowed against the sudden glare of the lights.

"What happened?" Simpson gasped, noting Saffron Everleigh next to him, eyes closed and motionless.

Alexander Ashton's brow was damp with sweat and his breathing labored, but he managed to say "Bin."

"What? Bin?" Simpson was confused and looked up at the other officer, whose mouth was agape as he scanned the wrecked office.

"Get me a bin, man!" Ashton groaned. The young deputy snatched up the waste bin and put it under him just in time. Simpson helped him up and held him in place for several minutes while he retched. He was heavy and seemed not to be able to hold himself up.

As Mr. Ashton was ill, Simpson told his deputy to call for the inspector and a doctor from University College Hospital across the street.

"Mr. Ashton, what happened here? What's wrong with Miss Everleigh?" Simpson demanded weakly, lowering the oddly slack man back down onto the floor.

"We've been poisoned by Berking and Blake," he managed, gulping breaths. "I'll be all right for a moment. Get Miss Everleigh off the floor."

Simpson blinked at Mr. Ashton's pronouncement, then dashed into the hall and shouted to Giles to include that information in his message to the inspector. He returned to the room and, his nose wrinkling as he stepped between the pools of sick to pick her up, brought Miss Everleigh to the couch.

As he set her down, noting proudly that he'd managed to carry her without too much effort, he caught sight of her hands. "What the blazes is this about?"

"From the poison," Mr. Ashton replied. "Can't move when they're present. Paralyzed."

Simpson looked from Miss Everleigh, whose arms were covered in blue marks, to Mr. Ashton. He rushed to his side, gaping at his neck. "Y-your neck—"

Mr. Ashton frowned. "Yes, I can't move. Tell the inspector that Berking and Blake were making a run for it with the money. They're probably going out of the country. And Blake's real name is Harper."

Simpson, alarmed at the cool way Mr. Ashton declared he couldn't move and provided all this new information, said, "The money? Blake is Harper? You can't *move*?"

Simpson, avoiding the vomit on the floor, began to pace around the room, then thought better of it. He'd probably trip and wind up with vomit splattered on his uniform. A paper on the desk caught his eye. He picked up the paper and saw a signature at the bottom: Alexander Ashton. "Mr. Ashton, did you write a note?"

His eyes were closed in a grimace. "No."

Simpson scanned the note, which explained that Dr. Maxwell, crazed, had forced them to drink a xolotl infusion, whatever that meant, at gunpoint and that Mr. Ashton was sorry he couldn't have done more to stop the professor.

Despite himself, Simpson snorted. "Not exactly masterminds, are they? We cleared Dr. Maxwell ages ago. He's not even in London. And considering you're just paralyzed and not in a coma, I guess it really wasn't that xolt—xlot—er, that foreign plant after all."

Simpson looked up from the note to see that Mr. Ashton was still, his eyes closed. Alarmed, he hopped across the room and checked his pulse. It was steady and strong. Poor bloke must be exhausted, Simpson mused. Must be tiring, being poisoned and all.

Chapter 22

"Glad to see you looking well, Miss Everleigh," the inspector said as he and Simpson entered the plain hospital room.

"Thank you, Inspector Green," Saffron said. She rather doubted she looked well. No one put their best face forward in hospital pajamas and messy hair. It was barely ten hours after she'd been admitted to the hospital, according to Elizabeth, who hadn't left her side since she'd woken up a few hours ago. Though Saffron was fatigued from the xolotl dose, not to mention the marathon of tests and doctors' visits that curiosity about her poisoning had incited, she was eager to hear news. "Have you caught them?"

"We have Dr. Berking in custody. I need to take your statement."

"Not Richard Blake?" Elizabeth asked, frowning at him. Her shadowed eyes moved to the door involuntarily, as if Blake would walk in any moment. Saffron knew Elizabeth was exhausted, having spent hours in the waiting room while Saffron was being poked, prodded, and questioned by a parade of doctors. Despite her dramatic claims that she was going to kill Saffron for nearly giving her a heart attack, Elizabeth had been her fierce advocate, demanding she be left alone to rest when still another round of doctors came to observe Saffron's recovery.

Of course, that was twenty minutes before the inspector had arrived, and now Saffron wasn't resting, but preparing to relive what had been the worst sort of nightmare.

"Dr. Berking was apprehended a few hours ago, and we have men out searching for Blake. The relevant services have been alerted and are on the lookout for him too," Inspector Green said.

"And Alexander?" Saffron asked impatiently. She'd heard nothing about his condition or recovery, not even whether he'd woken up. Elizabeth had tried, but not being family, she hadn't been able to get any information.

"I haven't seen him yet," the inspector replied.

Swallowing rising panic, she gripped her blanket with fingers no longer tinged blue. "But what happened? He must have been paralyzed far worse than I was—he had blue lines to his neck!"

Simpson piped up, stepping forward with a hesitant glance at the inspector. "I found him, miss. He looked as though he'd woken up just a moment before. First thing he said was 'bin,' which"—he frowned at Saffron's brief laugh, which sounded more strangled than amused—"I was confused by, but luckily my deputy understood. He told me about Berking and Blake right away, then passed out a few minutes later."

"But he hasn't woken up since? It's been nearly twelve hours! They could have mixed something else into his infusion." Beside her, Elizabeth sighed. These were the same concerns Elizabeth had heard fourteen times since Saffron had woken. Saffron ignored her. "What if he's gone into a coma, like Mrs. Henry?"

"Mrs. Henry woke up this morning."

Saffron and Elizabeth gaped at the inspector.

"*What?*" Saffron asked. "She woke up? Is Dr. Henry with her? What did she say?"

"We'll update you on her condition as appropriate." One eyebrow raised, the inspector lowered himself to a chair a few feet from Saffron's bed and removed a notebook and pen from his coat pocket. "I'm afraid our time is limited. According to your nurses, I'm only allowed a few minutes. Your statement, if you will."

Saffron began her story at the meeting for the expedition. The inspector interrupted a few times to clarify; all the while Simpson attempted to stand unobtrusively behind him in a corner of the room. His own pencil flew across paper until he knocked into the wash basin and nearly sent it to the floor when Saffron described finding Blake with the gun trained on Alexander. When Saffron came to the point in the story when Blake had gone to get the xolotl leaves and Berking began to question her, she felt the too-familiar build of panic in her chest.

When her voice grew wobbly and finally broke, Elizabeth said imperiously, "Give her a moment, please."

Inspector Green disappeared with a disappointed-looking Simpson into the hallway.

When the door clicked shut behind them, Saffron's face, which she'd held steady and calm, crumpled. "Eliza," she whispered, reaching out for her hand and clinging to it, "when he came for me, the look on his face . . . I was sure—I thought Berking would—would—" She took a shuddering breath. Berking's fingers stroking her neck, his breath on her ear, were memories too easy to recall.

"What, Saff? What did he do?"

Saffron gripped her hand still tighter, eyes smarting with tears. "My hands were tied up and he was over me . . . and I was sure . . . He said he would make Alexander watch." Her last words came out in a taut whisper.

Elizabeth swore and sat on the bed, reaching for Saffron. Shaking her head, Saffron pressed a hand to her mouth to prevent a sob. Her next words were shaky and rushed. "But he didn't. He grabbed my hair and demanded to know what I'd found out. He hit me, but that was all."

Elizabeth wrapped her arms around her. "I'm glad that was all, Saff. I'm so glad."

As if the embrace gave her permission to release the fear she'd felt, Saffron let out a great racking sob and buried her face in Elizabeth's shoulder. She couldn't contain the rush of fear, guilt, and relief. She'd been so wrong and so right about Berking and Blake and the whole mess, and had come very close to the worst fate she could imagine. Berking was a monster after all, and she'd put herself right into his clutches.

"Don't forget darling, he's going to prison. He can't touch you ever again," Elizabeth said, her hand making consoling circles on Saffron's back. "*You* did that, Saff. You found him out. That inspector might have never figured it out. But you did it. And now he's going to go away for a very long time."

Her tears subsiding, Saffron nodded and sat up. Elizabeth was right. Saffron had found Berking out and would help send him to prison. But she had to finish her story for the inspector first.

Elizabeth mopped her up, then recalled the policemen from the hall.

Inspector Green's careful eyes took in Saffron's reddened nose and watery eyes. "If you're ready?"

Saffron kept Elizabeth's hand tightly in hers as she told the inspector what had happened in Dr. Maxwell's office. Remembering Elizabeth's words, her voice didn't shake once.

"But I still don't know how it connects with Dr. Henry," she said. She ignored her friend's eye roll. Elizabeth could hardly blame her for wanting to finish solving the mystery. "We were sure Dr. Henry was the one embezzling, not Dr. Berking. It appears Mr. Blake was in league with Dr. Berking, but why?"

"We're still waiting to hear all the details, but Berking is singing like a bird, as they say," Inspector Green replied with some semblance of humor. "If you could finish?"

She concluded her story with waking up alone, but for Alexander, and being sick, which tempted her to ask that the inspector force the nurses to let her see Alexander. She refrained, just barely.

He stood up. "We have men stationed in the hospital in case Mr. Blake turns up here. You are to stay put and heal."

Then the policemen left. Elizabeth humored Saffron's ideas for a while, theorizing what was happening with Berking at the police station and guessing where Blake was, but soon both their eyes were drooping. They turned off the light and closed the curtains. Though she was exhausted, Saffron's head whirled with villains, poisons, and a biologist with an uncertain fate.

CHAPTER 23

When Saffron had recovered enough to leave her room, she asked to see Alexander—demanded, really—and was finally wheeled down the long corridor when she'd worn down the doctors responsible for her care.

With white walls, a window dressed with faded yellow curtains, and a dark wrought iron bed frame cushioned with an uncomfortable little mattress, Alexander's room was a mirror of her own, including the policeman stationed outside. The curtains were opened, allowing sunlight to spill into the room and over the bed, making the room look welcoming rather than drab.

Alexander's face was pale, his olive skin darkened with stubble. Bruises had bloomed to a deep purple on his left eye, forehead, and cheek, but his lips tilted into a little smile as the nurse settled Saffron next to his bed. Saffron thought he looked rather nice despite his injuries, his dark hair curled and messy on his head. It made him look quite a bit younger, especially in combination with the plain pajamas he wore. A man shouldn't look so handsome with his face bashed up.

"Good afternoon," she said with a shy smile.

"Good afternoon. How are you?" Alexander said, eyeing the wheelchair.

Saffron brushed off his concern, saying, "I woke up feeling almost normal, but they've insisted I be carted around." She held up a hand and wiggled her fingers. "I've been line-free for ages, but they're being cautious. I actually had movement in my fingers when they were still a little blue. I wonder if it's related to dosage or secondary exposure or perhaps some chemical interaction—"

With a grimace, Alexander said, "Let's not discuss poisons." He took her hand in his. His grip was a little weak, but his eyes were earnest and open, the usually dark color a striking mahogany in the sun. "I'm glad you're all right."

Saffron swallowed, guilt eating at her. "I'm sorry. I'm so sorry I put you in danger—"

Alexander shook his head. "*I'm* sorry. I did nothing to protect you, and . . . I wouldn't have been able to protect you, had Blake not come back."

Saffron sensed his hesitation and what he was reluctant to say. She squeezed his hand. "But he did come back. And nothing did happen." Saying the words helped reassure her as well as Alexander.

They began discussing Elizabeth's latest complaint about her boss since it was the furthest thing Saffron could think of from their misadventure.

"Elizabeth said she'd stop by after work, shall I bring her round?" Saffron added. She really wanted to ask whether Alexander was expecting any visitors. She didn't know anything about his family, if they were in town or if they'd been informed. She didn't like the idea of him sitting all alone until he was released.

As if he read her thoughts, he shook his head, looking uncomfortable. "I'd rather not have visitors." He glanced at her, his mouth tense. "Unpleasant memories, you understand."

Recalling the story of his injury, Saffron bit her lip. "Am I intruding, then?"

"Considering the unpleasant aftermath of the xolotl"—Alexander cocked an eyebrow—"I rather think we're beyond that, don't you?"

"Yes, vomiting side by side, even if the other was unconscious, certainly made close friends of us." Saffron rolled her eyes. "And now you're going off to parts unknown, likely to be surrounded by plants like xolotl. Have the doctors given you the all clear to travel?"

"If the university is able to recover or replace whatever money Blake and Berking stole and the trip moves forward, I'll be leaving with the rest of the team. Unless my recovery takes much longer than expected."

Saffron looked up to see him looking out the window somewhat despondently. "I'm sure you'll be back to normal in no time at all," she said brightly. His color was already returning, and she was certain he'd be allowed to try walking soon. "You were given a higher dose than I was, so it's natural that you've taken a bit longer to recover."

He shook his head as if to banish a thought. "It'll be even harder to leave now," he said, then added, "I'll have to clear it with Inspector Green. In case I'm needed for the trial."

She hadn't thought about the trial. She would likely have to testify, and the fuss that her family would raise would probably be just as distressing as actually giving her testimony. She sighed. It would have been less daunting if Alexander was there too, but she had to hope, for his sake, that he would be able to go on the expedition, as planned.

As if sensing her apprehension, Alexander's tone lightened. "Now that the investigation is over, what will you do? I'm off to get lost in a jungle; what shall you do to shock the university?"

Saffron stood, walking to the window. Her feet were completely steady, even if her feelings weren't. "I'm not sure.

Dr. Maxwell will be coming back soon, so I suppose I'll continue on with him. Or . . ."

"Or?" Alexander repeated.

"Or I could stow away on the ship to Brazil, as Elizabeth suggested," Saffron said, shooting a rueful smile over her shoulder.

He chuckled. "I wouldn't mind."

"I might see if I can find something more relevant to work on. The investigation was so urgent, you know, so pressing and important. Chlorophyll is important, but no one is waiting with bated breath to find out the exact chemical composition of the pigment of a leaf. I rather liked feeling like my work was important." Saffron hadn't put it to words yet, but she realized as she said it how true it was. She wasn't sure she could happily go back to how things were before, plodding through Maxwell's research. She sighed at the windowpane. "I'm sure I won't be able to carry out my study, considering Dr. Berking only agreed to it as some sort of inducement for betraying Dr. Maxwell."

"It could be approved by your new department head." Behind her, there was the shush of fabric and the creak of the bed. She turned to see Alexander was very nearly standing, a grimace on his face.

Worried he'd topple over, she started forward. "Are you sure you should—"

Alexander put a finger to his lips. "Don't—you'll send the nurses stampeding in." Slowly, he eased his weight onto his bare feet and smiled broadly when he managed to stand steadily.

"Well done," Saffron said, only slightly sarcastically.

They stood, looking at each other, smiling. Surely it was the heat from the sun coming in through the window that made Saffron feel so warm.

Alexander took a slow step forward, testing his balance, and Saffron's hand shot out to offer support. His took it, but not for support, she realized with a flush of pleasure.

The excitement faded when her thoughts returned to Berking. "Berking said that he used some of my father's work to create his poison," she said.

Alexander frowned. "He did?"

"Yes, after he hit you. He said he used my father's method to increase the concentration of toxins in his aconite. I . . . I saw one of my father's files in Berking's office when I was going through his things. Something about hybridization. I'm afraid"—she took a deep breath but found her lungs didn't want to fill completely—"I'm afraid he was telling the truth." She wasn't sure she wanted to know if that was her father's purpose. What did that mean about her father, if he had he worked to make dangerous plants *more* dangerous?

With steps becoming more confident, Alexander arrived beside her and leaned on the windowsill. "Afraid of what? Knowledge isn't innately bad. His intention could have been for medicines rather than poisons. If Berking did something nefarious with it, he's to blame , not your father." His fingers lifted her chin, silently encouraging her to meet his eyes. "Take it from someone who has experienced firsthand what knowledge in the wrong hands can do. Scientists spent long hours perfecting the weapons used in those trenches."

"Thank you," she whispered, not sure what else to say.

His thumb brushed her cheek softly, once, twice. Now Saffron found it hard to draw breath for quite another reason. Alexander's dark eyes were not enigmatic as they usually were, but their intent clear in how they dipped to her lips.

For a breath, they stood poised for more. Warm sun pressed at her back, and Saffron imagined that would be how his kiss would be, gentle and warming and lovely. Anticipating it, her eyes fluttered closed, and lifting her chin—

"Mr. Ashton! You're not meant to be up!" a nurse squawked from the door, oblivious that she'd ruined a perfectly tempting moment. She hurried over, fussing and clucking like a mother hen.

"I should return to my room," Saffron said quickly, face heating. "You need to rest." There was an understanding twinkle in Alexander's eyes that made her insides melt. Clearing her throat, she added, "I'll come back to see you later, shall I?"

Alexander nodded and she squeezed his hand once more before agreeing to be escorted back to her room.

The inspector himself came to see Saffron and Alexander two days later. Saffron had been released, but she had no plans to return home until that evening when Elizabeth left work and came to collect her. Inspector Green stood in the doorway of Alexander's room with his hat in his hands and something resembling a content expression on his otherwise bland face.

"Good morning, Inspector," Alexander called to him from over Saffron's shoulder. He sat in his bed, still in hospital pajamas. Saffron sat in a chair next to him, fully dressed with playing cards in hand.

"Good morning. May I come in?"

"Yes, of course. You've caught us in the middle of a hopeless game." Alexander threw his cards down.

He had been letting her win rather shamelessly. Saffron grinned and turned to face the inspector. "Why, Inspector, you actually look pleased."

"I am, Miss Everleigh," he replied, the hint of satisfaction becoming more evident. "Last night we caught Richard Blake. He was attempting to board a ship to—"

"America?" asked Saffron.

"France," Alexander countered.

"Morocco, actually," said the inspector.

Alexander smirked at Saffron.

"That doesn't count!" she protested. "Inspector?"

He considered them, then shrugged. "You wouldn't say Canada was England."

Alexander rolled his eyes and Saffron laughed. "Well then, you've caught him. Is he talking, like Dr. Berking?" she asked.

"He hasn't said a word. We did find something on him that might be of interest to you."

Saffron sat up in her chair straighter. "The poison? Are your people testing it?"

Inspector Green shook his head. "Not the poison, though he did have a vial on him when they caught up with him. Luckily it smashed before he could do anything with it. Not enough of a sample to test, unfortunately."

"You think he meant to—" Saffron broke off with a loud exhale. She really ought not to consider all the horrible things Blake might have done with that poison. "But what did Blake have with him, then?"

"The money," the inspector said, his eyes twinkling for once. "Nearly the entire amount the university had collected for the expedition."

Before Saffron could exclaim her delight and surprise, Alexander's disbelieving voice asked, "He had all of it with him?"

"Apparently that's what delayed him long enough for us to get a hold of him. He was arrested outside a bank," the inspector said.

Saffron was relieved that the money had been recovered, but too many questions preventing her from being content with that information. "I should like to have known what exactly their mysterious poison was, though. Have you found R. Glass?"

"Yes. Dr. Rupert Glass admitted to collaborating with Dr. Berking but staunchly stands by his claim that he was ignorant of the solution's purpose. He professes he had nothing left to hand over and had apparently already destroyed the research he'd accumulated when he grew suspicious after the poisoning."

Saffron withheld a snort. "I'm sure the *five hundred pounds* from Dr. Berking helped. Richard Blake isn't likely to talk, I think. He didn't even want to know what Alexander and I had figured out. He hardly showed any expression the entire time he had us. It was frightful how calm he was."

The inspector shrugged. "Well, some are like that." He looked at them carefully before adding in a low voice, "The barristers wouldn't like me telling you this, so you are not to repeat it. Berking confirmed that Mrs. Henry was the target, not Dr. Henry."

"But why?" Alexander asked.

Saffron had spent long hours in her hospital room considering just this point. "It was the College Committee meeting, wasn't it, Inspector?"

He nodded, and Saffron suppressed her urge to grin.

Alexander mirrored the inspector with his nod. "She wasn't going to the Committee about Dr. Henry's inappropriate relationship with Miss Ermine or his idea for a new branch in the history department. She was going because she found out about the embezzlement."

Saffron looked to him in surprise, and his expression turned smug.

"According to Mrs. Henry, she noticed irregularities in paperwork she saw on Mr. Blake's desk during a few of her office visits," said Inspector Green. Saffron thought "office visit" was a very tame way to explain a lovers' rendezvous. "She became suspicious and she arranged a meeting to report it."

"Richard Blake realized she'd discovered the embezzlement, and Berking agreed to create a poison to kill her?" Saffron asked. That seemed rather elaborate.

"Or did she discover his true identity and was going to expose him?" Alexander asked.

Saffron turned to him, mouth agape. "Blake's true identity?"

The inspector's mouth inclined into a half smile. "Apparently, Mr. Ashton has discovered it himself." Alexander shot Saffron a wink, leaving her shocked and not a little charmed. "It seems the man we know as Richard Blake is, in fact, James Harper. For the past decade, he's been running small confidence plays, often taking on the role of a philanthropist soliciting donations for scholarships. This is by far his grandest scheme yet."

"How did Berking know who Blake really was?" Saffron asked.

"They met at a house party in Lincolnshire, when Blake—Harper—was living under another name and went after the fortune of one of the guests. Berking later recognized him when he took up at the university. When the opportunity came to swindle the university out of thousands of pounds, they put a plan into motion. Dr. Berking had been experimenting with his new breed of aconite for some time. He seemed rather proud of his creation and eager to try it."

That explained part of it, but she still had unanswered questions. "Dr. Henry was supposed to take the fall for embezzlement, of course, but what about the poisoning? If they meant to have Dr. Henry arrested, they could have chosen a better method. We figured out it wasn't him right away!"

"Wrong method," Alexander and the inspector said simultaneously, and they eyed each other with cool surprise.

"Exactly! He'd probably strangle her or throw her down the stairs or—"

"Something else," Alexander said firmly. "Perhaps their aim was to muddle the field so much that the police would ignore them long enough for the expedition to leave. It would be perfect; they'd get out of the country on a believable pretext and slip away the moment we reached Brazil."

Saffron frowned. "If their goal was to run off with thousands of pounds, why wait for the expedition at all? Why didn't they just take the donations and run?"

No one seemed to have an answer to her question.

"I don't like to think what Mrs. Henry must have felt when she heard her lover tried to kill her," Saffron mused aloud.

The inspector frowned slightly. "Mr. Blake, or Mr. Harper, wasn't her lover, according to her testimony. She was attempting to discover what exactly Dr. Henry did to gain the funding from the Ermine family, and thought Blake would be a good source of information. She might have mentioned that Dr. Henry suspecting they had a relationship was a bonus."

Saffron blinked. She certainly hadn't considered that possibility.

Inspector Green tapped the top of his hat and moved toward the door.

"You know, Inspector," Saffron said, "the police poisons expert who came around, he knew nothing about poisons apart from arsenic and strychnine. I'm fairly certain I'd be a better expert than him."

The inspector smiled, a wry expression that crinkled his eyes. "Maybe you would, Miss Everleigh. I'm glad you've both recovered. Mr. Ashton, good luck on your expedition." He left.

Saffron grinned widely at Inspector Green's retreating form before turning to Alexander and laughing. "He *smiled*!"

CHAPTER 24

Stepping into the sapphire evening, Saffron and Alexander looked out over the dark lawn and the tall hedges beyond. The stone balcony was cool with crisp spring air. The invitation to the party given in honor of the departure of the expedition team at the Leisters had been received with incredulity among those involved in the poisoning investigation. Saffron had telephoned Elizabeth immediately, laughing into the telephone that she'd have to borrow another dress. Elizabeth had decided to find a set of common poison remedies for Saffron to carry in her handbag, lest another guest turn up poisoned. She'd gotten a dress, a mauve number glittering with beading, but was lacking in antidotes.

"It seems you've earned the undying support of Dr. Henry. He spoke rather warmly of you just now," Alexander said with a sideways look. "If I didn't know you'd convinced him to reform his meandering ways, I'd advise you to watch out for him, Everleigh."

"It is a pity that he is not quite so admiring as to offer me a place in the expedition, even if he did ensure my study was to go forward." Saffron smiled ruefully at him. "And I'm not concerned in the least. Dr. Henry is now a devoted husband. Didn't you see how attentive he's been to Mrs. Henry? She looks very well recovered for having been in a coma for ages."

"It wasn't such a long time, little more than a week. And yet you seemed to accomplish quite a bit." He bumped her shoulder gently, earning him a giggle. "You uncovered an embezzlement scheme, caught two would-be murderers, were poisoned twice, and still had time to do an experiment."

Saffron's eyes lingered on his smile. Alexander looked handsome as ever, fully recovered and back in his smart black dinner jacket, his hair smooth and eyes shining in the light from the windows. They had spent quite a lot of time together the past week, between completing Alexander's research and following through on the obligations they had to the police department. It was bittersweet, coming to know him better only to say goodbye.

"I do feel rather accomplished," she replied. "You've done mostly the same, except you only had to take wretched xolotl once."

"Once was more than enough. I expect if you ever had it again, it would barely affect you," Alexander said, then turned to her and added seriously, "Don't let's go testing that, please."

"Don't be ridiculous," she said primly. "I needn't try something three times."

They stood with their arms on the cool stone rail, listening to the steady buzz of conversation and the tinkling of glasses behind them.

"Are you excited to be moving forward with your own study?" Alexander asked, slanting her a grin.

"Absolutely!" Saffron let out a laugh. "I hope Berking somehow finds out that it was approved anyway." Alexander smirked, and she put a hand on his arm. "You'll have to be especially careful with my samples, you know."

"Why, because they're almost all poisonous?"

"No, because if you damage them, I'll be furious."

Alexander shook his head with a chuckle. "Come, Everleigh, let's take a turn in the garden, and you can show me how to collect a proper sample."

She glanced around to ensure no one would catch them sneaking off, then allowed herself a delighted smile. They walked to the end of the balcony and descended the stone steps to the garden.

Away from the chatter of the party, there was only the faint swishing of her dress, the crunch of the gravel path beneath their feet. The hedges were dark and winding, the sounds of the party and the chill breeze diminished by their density. It was reminiscent of Dr. Berking's garden, yet not at all the same. Nevertheless, Saffron's heart was beating fast.

"Miss Everleigh," Alexander said with a smirk in his voice, "what do you think of this specimen?" He gestured to a rose bush, evident even in the dark.

She gave him a look and bent over it slightly. "Why, Mr. Ashton, that would be a rose bush. Surely we're not here to steal roses. I'm not dressed to crawl around in the dirt again." She turned to make a face at him and found him very near her. Her heart leapt hopefully.

"No," he murmured, "that's not why we're here."

For a moment they looked into each other's eyes, then Alexander closed his and kissed her.

Her pulse danced where Alexander's hand cupped her jaw, lifting her face to his. They met with sweetness and the beginnings of heat. Alexander pulled away long before Saffron was satisfied.

"We should go back," came his quiet voice, a little rough.

Saffron, hands on his chest, didn't move. With a small smile of her own, she whispered, "Without the stolen roses?"

The watery light of early morning filtered through the high, glass-paned ceiling, catching the mites of dust and swirls of steam in the large open space of the train station. The expedition team was due to leave in an hour to make their way to the coast and the steamer waiting to take them to Brazil. Saffron and Alexander had agreed to meet early, to avoid the critical eyes of the crew.

Saffron couldn't think of anything to say apart from reminding Alexander to be careful, and she had already said it twice. Anything else and she might ruin their goodbye with tears.

"Well," he said at long last, "I suppose I'm off."

Saffron took his hand in hers and squeezed it. "I'll be looking out for updates. Beyond just the official ones through the university, I mean."

With a tilted smile, he nodded. "Don't expect them too often. Post is uncertain at best, you know. But rest assured, if I come across any *Rosa amazonica*, I'll be sure to let you know right away."

Heart swelling, Saffron stood on tiptoes to bring her lips to his.

"Saffron." Alexander frowned down at her, eyes dancing between her eyes. After a moment, his expression cleared. "Take care."

Saffron smiled up at him. "Don't worry about me, Ashton. As for you, don't go eating any strange-looking leaves."

Alexander took her hand and pressed his lips to it, and then he was gone.

The note wedged in Dr. Maxwell's door inspired much the same trepidation as a summons to the department head's office had previously inspired, though for a very different reason.

The powers that be at the university had made Dr. Aster the new head of botany, but he had not yet moved into Dr. Berking's former office. A summons from him meant one of two things: Saffron was about to receive a lot of extra work, or she was in trouble.

Wondering which she was in for, she skirted the boxes outside Aster's door that were stacked and neatly labeled for the move. She knocked once before being told to enter.

Dr. Aster sat before her amid empty bookshelves and a bare desk, his lined face blank as a sphinx's. In his brisk voice, he said, "Miss Everleigh, you are aware that Dr. Maxwell has extended his leave of absence from the department and applied for a sabbatical. As such, your position as his research assistant has been rendered unnecessary."

Saffron was speechless. She hadn't considered that with Maxwell gone she wouldn't have a job in the department. Scrambling, she began, "I could assist another professor, perhaps—"

"I understand that during your involvement in the investigation of Mrs. Henry's poisoning, you carried out a small experiment regarding the effects of extract of *Solandra xolotum*."

Her stomach dropped. Aster couldn't abide any disregard of rules. She was about to be sacked. There was no point trying to deny it. "Yes, sir, I did."

Aster frowned, and Saffron braced herself for her dismissal, but he said, "Take a seat," and she did. "Detective Inspector Green asked me to advise him on the feasibility of it being done with a reasonable assurance of accuracy. It was clearly not something one could publish," he said sternly, his tone smacking of disapproval, "but I assured him that your word as a scientist could be trusted, even if your loyalties lie with Dr. Maxwell."

Tongue-tied by this unexpected support, Saffron simply replied, "Thank you, sir."

Aster raised a faded eyebrow and continued as though she hadn't interrupted. "As it happens, with the various staffing changes, a research position has been made available."

"I didn't know that, sir," she said, a cautious hope blooming in her heart.

Aster steepled his fingers. "There is a good deal of time in the intervening months before you can complete the pigmentation project. An opportunity has come up recently that requires the same scientific curiosity and purpose, and occasional disregard for convention that you seem to excel in. We will consider it your application for your graduate studies."

Shock rendered her speechless, but before she was swept away by excitement, Saffron spoke the thought that had been on her mind for weeks. "Dr. Aster, before you say any more, I must ask you something. Dr. Berking said something during our . . . confrontation, about my father. And his work, his unpublished work."

Aster's gray eyes sharpened a degree. "I'm afraid your father's unpublished work is not up for discussion." Saffron mutely nodded, filing that away for later consideration. "However, there is room for discussion regarding the potential for research in the realm of phytotoxicity."

Saffron left the meeting sometime later, her mind whirling with possibilities. With more poisonous plants in her future, the next six months were going to be very interesting after all.

AUTHOR'S NOTE

As with all historical fiction, my intent was to be as accurate as possible—with one very big exception: *Solandra xolotum* doesn't exist. Shocking, I know. I delighted delving into research about plants and their study, but it was too tempting, too *fun*, to come up with my own big, bad, poisonous plant to terrorize Saffron. I will say that quite a bit of research went into the xolotl vine even if it wasn't real, as well as all the other plants in the book. I've been an avid plant enthusiast for years, cultivating my own jungle in my living room and bathroom. Now I have the added benefit of being able to identify poisonous plants as I walk about my local gardening center.

As for the expedition to the Amazon, the years following World War I were a time of huge scientific development. We all know about the Roaring Twenties and its party culture, but so much was happening in the world of science too. The first transatlantic flight was completed, insulin was discovered, fossilized dinosaur eggs were uncovered—and that's all before the events of *A Botanist's Guide* take place in spring of 1923.

Released from the threat of war, scientists and explorers traversed the dark corners of the world to see what they could find. Percy Fawcett, whom Saffron mentioned, would have been a headliner in the world of archaeology, zoology, and many other disciplines for his continued exploration of South America, though he later made headlines for disappearing into the wilds of Brazil in 1925. Also around this time were significant discoveries in Egypt, South Africa, and Ur (Iraq). You can understand why Dr. Henry was so keen for the university to develop an anthropology program; this was a time of huge discoveries and he wanted in on it! Anthropology itself was a burgeoning practice; it was not yet a distinct field of study in many places.

Much has been written about soldiers experiencing shell-shock, so I wanted to explore a lesser known avenue of symptoms and recovery. Alexander's recovery from the Great War is complex and isn't straightforward—few cases are—nor it is over. I will just say that many hours of research and consideration went into developing his symptoms and coping strategies, with many more to come.

I want to offer a special thanks to the University College London's Library Services for providing me with much-needed resources that helped me better understand the University College in 1923, particularly where things were. I did my best to make sense of the departments' locations, but as Saffron mentions, the University College was constantly adding new buildings to their campus and moving things around. I, myself, added a new building to the fictional version of the campus: the greenhouses. I found no evidence of a greenhouse on any campus map or directory, but I desperately wanted one! I hope you find the inaccuracy is worth it, as I do.

ACKNOWLEDGMENTS

This book would not exist without many people, but first and foremost is my husband. Erfawn never questioned for a minute—at least out loud—my sudden and somewhat irrational need to write a mystery novel, nor did he doubt my ability to actually write it, let alone get it published. Thank you for your unwavering support and your hours of listening to me babble about poisonous plants and helping me solve all the problems I got my characters into. Thank you for giving me the time I needed, as a new mother and a new writer, to make this happen. And thank you for inspiring my favorite fictional biologist.

My parents are the reasons the novel I had to write was a historical mystery. Years of Sherlock Holmes and Poirot sank into my brain and became a part of me that I treasure. Thank you both for the gift of your encouragement to pursue my love of writing and reading, and now for your insights into this book and others. I truly have the best family, full of supportive, loving people who didn't even blink when I told them I was writing a book about a crime-solving botanist. Thank you all for your enthusiastic support!

I have to hand it to my alpha readers and best friends, Erin, Audrey, and Arezou, for reading the first—incredibly bad—draft of this book. You all believed in Saffron when she was just a little baby detective, and me when I was just a little baby writer. Thank you for providing me a stepping-stone on the way to *A Botanist's Guide* becoming a real book.

I owe a debt of gratitude to Christi Barth, who transformed my manuscript. Christi, I don't know what made you choose to read my manuscript and take on the massive job of editing it, but I cannot thank you enough for your tough love and gems of wisdom about Saffron's life choices. You were absolutely right! Thank you for being such an unexpected but essential part of my journey.

Thank you to Aleah, Caity, Talieh, and many others for suggesting excellent changes that enriched this book. Special thanks to Jack, without whom Alexander's flirting game wouldn't be half so adorable.

My writing community has been wonderful since the moment I decided to make an Instagram account chronicling my writing experiences. I'm so lucky to have found so many amazing people who decided that my stories and my career are worth supporting. Thank you all! I'm so honored to be a part of this little corner of the internet with you.

Finally, thank you to my editor, Melissa Rechter, and the whole team at Crooked Lane Books for bringing *A Botanist's Guide* to life. Melissa, I cannot thank you enough for not only wanting my book but also for guiding it into its current state that I could not be more proud of. After long months of doubt, you brought me hope and joy. Thank you to Madeline, Rebecca, and all the amazing, patient people who contributed to getting Saffron's story out into the world in such style.